"You are n...

Quinn's words echoed in Dena's mind long after she'd returned to bed. Even in her half-asleep state she hadn't missed the gleam of interest in his eye, although she wasn't sure why it had been there. Not many men would find bed head and flannel pajamas a turn-on.

She could definitely see why some women found him attractive. With his physical attributes he could probably make any woman a little weak-kneed. Not that it mattered. If she was looking for romance—and she wasn't—it wouldn't be with him.

Someone like Quinn would be more work than the average guy. And she'd discovered a long time ago that that was what men were—work.

She closed her eyes and forced her thoughts to the advertising campaign she'd been assigned the day before. If she was going to lie awake in the middle of the night, she might as well think about something that would be of use to her. Quinn Sterling was not in her future. Soy nuts were. If she could think of a clever package for the honey-roasted product, she'd be one step closer to her goal.

As for the man who lived upstairs…it was unlikely she'd run into him again. She'd lived here for close to a month and had seen him only once. He was the kind of neighbor she wanted—out of sight and out of mind.

Dear Reader,

When I created the boardinghouse at 14 Valentine Place, I made a rule. No guys allowed. It was to be a residence of women, each with her own room, but with a shared kitchen where late-night conversations would always include food—preferably chocolate.

Leonie Donovan, the landlady I created in the first book of this series, agreed with me, which is why I put her in charge. When it came time to write the second book, however, I discovered that Leonie, like many fictional characters, has a mind of her own. In between stories she had gone ahead and remodeled the third floor of the boardinghouse, creating an apartment that—to my surprise—she leased to a man. I no longer had my house of women. A man had pushed his way in. I sensed trouble.

As it turns out, it was a good kind of trouble. You'll see what I mean as you read Quinn and Dena's story. If it weren't for Leonie renovating the third floor, they wouldn't have met.

If this is your first visit to 14 Valentine Place, I hope you'll come back again. For those of you who've read the first book in this series and have written to ask about future stories, I'm pleased to report that my next book will be Krystal's story.

I love hearing from readers. Feel free to write to me at Pamela Bauer, c/o MFW, P.O. Box 24107, Minneapolis, MN 55424, or you can visit me via the Internet at www.pamelabauer.com.

Sincerely,

Pamela Bauer

Books by Pamela Bauer

HARLEQUIN SUPERROMANCE

The Man Upstairs
Pamela Bauer

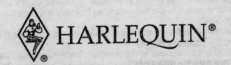

HARLEQUIN®

TORONTO • NEW YORK • LONDON
AMSTERDAM • PARIS • SYDNEY • HAMBURG
STOCKHOLM • ATHENS • TOKYO • MILAN • MADRID
PRAGUE • WARSAW • BUDAPEST • AUCKLAND

If you purchased this book without a cover you should be aware
that this book is stolen property. It was reported as "unsold and
destroyed" to the publisher, and neither the author nor the
publisher has received any payment for this "stripped book."

ISBN 0-373-71106-9

THE MAN UPSTAIRS

Copyright © 2003 by Pamela Muelhbauer.

All rights reserved. Except for use in any review, the reproduction or
utilization of this work in whole or in part in any form by any electronic,
mechanical or other means, now known or hereafter invented, including
xerography, photocopying and recording, or in any information storage
or retrieval system, is forbidden without the written permission of the
publisher, Harlequin Enterprises Limited, 225 Duncan Mill Road,
Don Mills, Ontario, Canada M3B 3K9.

All characters in this book have no existence outside the imagination of
the author and have no relation whatsoever to anyone bearing the same
name or names. They are not even distantly inspired by any individual
known or unknown to the author, and all incidents are pure invention.

This edition published by arrangement with Harlequin Books S.A.

® and TM are trademarks of the publisher. Trademarks indicated with
® are registered in the United States Patent and Trademark Office, the
Canadian Trade Marks Office and in other countries.

Visit us at www.eHarlequin.com

Printed in U.S.A.

In loving memory of a very dear aunt,
Mabel Hayes

PROLOGUE

WHILE THE BAND TOOK a break, a man in a tuxedo grabbed the microphone on the ballroom stage and asked, "Is everybody having fun?"

A roar from the guests indicated everyone, indeed, was having a good time.

Everyone except Dena Bailey, that is. Weddings were never fun for Dena. They were more like punishment. If the bride hadn't been her college roommate, she wouldn't even be at the wedding reception.

"Hey, we got a great crowd here tonight to help Maddie and Dylan celebrate their first day as Mr. and Mrs. Donovan," the best man continued. "At this time we need Maddie to come forward so we can find out which one of you single ladies is going to be the next one to take that walk down the aisle."

The announcement was Dena's cue to leave. Not even for Maddie would she try to catch the bridal bouquet. She grabbed her purse and headed for the exit.

The lighting in the hallway was bright compared to the dimness of the ballroom, causing Dena to squint as she made her escape. When she glanced across the corridor she saw a line of elegantly dressed women waiting to enter the ladies' room. She turned and walked in the opposite direction in search of another rest room.

A few minutes later, in a deserted corridor near the rear entrance, she found one. With relief she pushed open the door, the echo of her heels on the tiled floor the only sound as she stepped into the washroom.

She automatically glanced in the mirror hanging above the trio of sinks lining the wall. She looked tired, and for good reason. As usual, she'd been working too many hours.

Grateful for the absence of women's chatter, she crossed the washroom only to stop abruptly. Urinals lined one of the walls.

Dena stared at the porcelain fixtures in disbelief. Instinctively her eyes flew to the stalls. She bent slightly, hoping she wouldn't see any feet. There weren't any, and she let out a gasp of relief.

Wasting no time, she hurried back to the door, but before she could reach for the handle, it swung toward her, startling her as much as the sight of the urinals had. Standing in front of her was a man—a very attractive man in a dark suit—who took one look at her and grinned.

"A little crowded in the ladies', is it?" Amusement laced his words.

"I..." she began, then stopped herself. Any explanation would only prolong her embarrassment.

"Are you the only lady in here or do I need to give a holler?" he asked with a flirtatious gleam in his eye.

Dena shook her head. "It's just me."

He gave her a thorough appraisal. "Just you, huh?" The look on his face said he definitely appreciated what he saw. "Are you here for Maddie and Dylan's wedding?"

There was no point in denying it. "Yes, I'm a friend of Maddie's."

"Good. You can show me where the party is. I just got here." His grin was as bold as his body was big. He was definitely handsome, a small scar on his chin adding to the rugged good looks.

"The ballroom's just down the hall and to your left. I'm sure you'll be able to find it," she said stiffly.

"You're not going to wait for me?"

With a dull ache throbbing in her forehead, she really was in no mood for flirting. "I think you're a big enough boy to find your own way, don't you?"

He stepped to the side and, in a gallant gesture, held the door open for her, motioning with his other arm that she should pass. "See you at the dance."

She almost said, *Not if I have my way,* but held her tongue. As she walked by him, she couldn't help but notice how broad he was. Or how good he smelled. Like a campground early in the morning with the scent of pines lingering in the air. She wondered who he was, then realized it didn't matter. She'd already decided to leave the party. She'd done her duty.

As soon as she was back in the ballroom, she looked for Maddie.

"There you are," the bride said, extending her hands in a warm welcome that matched her smile. "I'm sorry we haven't had time to talk."

"It's all right," Dena assured her. "You have so many people here who want to see you. We can catch up another time. Everything's been just lovely. Thank you so much for inviting me."

"You're not leaving, are you?" Her face fell slightly.

"I really would like to stay, but I have an awful headache, and I have to get up early to catch my flight. You don't mind, do you?'' Dena gave her an apologetic look.

Maddie squeezed her hand. "Of course not. Did you have a good time?''

Dena Bailey looked at the beaming bride and knew what she had to say. "Yes. It's been fun seeing everyone again.'' Although "everyone" was actually a couple of women who'd lived on the same dorm floor as she and Maddie during their college years.

"It means so much to me that you came. I've missed you. I wish we could get together more often.''

It was exactly what Dena had been thinking all weekend, and she'd been waiting for the opportunity to tell Maddie her news. "We might just get to do that. I may be moving to St. Paul. I interviewed for a job while I was here.''

"You did! That's great...'' Her voice trailed off and her eyes held a look of disappointment. "Only I'm not going to be here. Dylan's taken an assignment in the south of France. Of course, we'll come home to visit.''

Dena could only smile weakly and wish them good luck.

"If you haven't found a place to live, you should talk to my mother-in-law,'' Maddie suggested. "She's looking for someone to rent my room. It would be perfect for you. It's on the bus line, close to Grand Avenue and all those wonderful little shops and restaurants. The rent is reasonable, too.''

"It's really kind of you to offer, but—'' Dena began.

"But nothing," Maddie finished for her, pulling her by the hand. "Come. We'll go talk to Leonie right now. Trust me. You're going to love 14 Valentine Place."

CHAPTER ONE

"ARE THOSE GORILLAS on your socks, Bailey?"

Dena had been sitting with her feet propped up on her desk, but she dropped them to the floor when she saw the art director in the doorway of her cubicle. With his slicked-back hair and his dark framed glasses, Greg Watkins reminded her of a smaller version of Clark Kent. She half expected that if he ripped open his shirt she'd see an *S* on his chest. Although he couldn't leap from tall buildings or bend steel with his bare hands, he did flaunt his power over her on occasion. She hoped this wasn't one of those times.

"The world's a jungle out there," she answered.

"Don't I know it," he said with a knowing lift of his brows.

"So what can I do for you?"

"You can tell me whether or not you're going to make a donation to the Aaron Jorgenson auction. He's the high school kid who was injured in the skiing accident. Kramer's taken a special interest in this event because the kid goes to his church." Greg had a habit of referring to people by their last names, even the creative director who was the head of the advertising agency.

"They're having a benefit dinner to raise money to help pay the medical bills, right?"

"You got it. I don't see your name on the list."
He waved a clipboard in midair.

"I don't think I'm going to be able to attend," she
said apologetically, then reached for her purse. "But
I'd be happy to make a cash donation."

"It would be better if you donated an item for the
auction...preferably something that will bring in big
bucks."

"Like what?"

He shrugged. "Anything. I'm donating a tour of
the Channel 8 studio and lunch with a news anchor.
You probably heard that my sister's their news-
caster?"

Dena nodded. "I suppose I could ask my brother
to help me out, but I don't think lunch with a me-
chanic would have quite the same appeal, do you?"
She gave him a wry smile.

"Probably not," he answered with his own understanding grin. "But there are any number of items
you could donate. Seriously, Bailey, this could be an
opportunity for you to catch Kramer's eye."

"You mean if I bring in something unique he'll
remember my name?"

"You keep doing work like that and he'll notice
you," he said, looking over her shoulder to the mock-
ups lining her shelves.

"I'm good at packages," she admitted in a tone
that was not the least bit pretentious, just honest.

"So I've noticed...as have a lot of other people.
So what do you say? Are you going to donate an
item?"

She hesitated a second, then said, "All right, put
me down. For what, I don't know, but I'll come up
with something."

He pulled a pen from behind his ear and wrote her name on the clipboard. "I'm sure you will. You're clever. If you weren't, you wouldn't be here."

She knew it was true. To land a job at an advertising agency like Delaney Design, one needed to be better than good. Getting hired had been a boost to her ego and an affirmation that she'd made the right decision in leaving her job in marketing to pursue a career in graphic design. Unfortunately, with the new job came the pressure to perform. Everyone at Delaney was talented. It wasn't enough to simply be good.

Greg Watkins straightened. "You'll need to let me know by next Friday what you're donating to the auction. The benefit is February 10. I have to tell you, Bailey, Kramer's going to be pleased to see your name on the list." He gave her a mock salute and slipped out of her cubicle.

Dena didn't want to simply please the creative director. She wanted to impress him, to prove to him that she belonged at the prestigious agency.

It wasn't anything new—proving herself. She'd been doing it most of her life and she'd do it now. She reached for the phone to call the one person who might be able to help her—her brother.

As CHILDREN, Dena and Ryan had been as close as any brother and sister, but when they were teenagers, their parents had divorced and the fragile bonds that had held their family together were broken. After graduation, Ryan Bailey saw no reason to stay in the small town in Iowa where they'd been raised. He moved away with his high school sweetheart, eager to make a new start in life.

Left alone with her father, Dena envied her brother

his freedom. No matter how hard she tried to get her father's attention, there was only one thing in life that mattered to him now that his wife was gone—his work. His idea of being a good parent was to send Dena to boarding school, where she felt just as isolated as she had living with her father. After graduation, she didn't return home. Like her brother, she left Iowa, but she made her exodus alone.

It was how she'd lived most of her life—alone. She may have had a mother for thirteen years, but she'd learned at an early age not to expect much from her. As a small child she'd never understood why her mother wasn't like other kids' mothers. She never played with her children and rarely laughed with them. It wasn't until Dena was thirteen that she understood the reason why. She hadn't wanted to be a mother in the first place.

It was a fact of life Dena couldn't change no matter how hard she tried. So she learned to take care of herself, to rely on her own tenacity and resourcefulness rather than depend on anyone else. She was self-sufficient and proud of it, only now that she'd moved to Minnesota, she was beginning to realize how lonely her life had been and how much she'd missed Ryan.

That's why she didn't hesitate to turn to him for advice about the auction donation. As usual, she'd worked late that evening and stopped at his house on her way home.

"Dena, it's good to see you," her sister-in-law, Lisa, said as she opened the door to her. "Come in. Ryan took Luke sledding at the park, but they should be home shortly. I was just about to make some hot chocolate...or would you rather have a cup of tea?"

"Hot chocolate sounds good." Dena removed her jacket and slung it over the back of one of the wooden kitchen chairs before taking a seat. "Where's Bethany and Jeremy?"

"Jeremy's at hockey practice and Bethany's at a birthday party for one of her friends from school. It's her first pajama party so I'm a little anxious about it," Lisa admitted as she poured milk into a pan on the stove. "I didn't want her to go. I think eight's a little young for slumber parties, don't you?"

Dena shrugged. "I honestly don't know. When it comes to raising kids, I don't have a clue." It was the truth. With no younger siblings and having spent a good portion of her teenage years at boarding school, she'd missed out on the typical baby-sitting experience. The only time she'd been around kids had been during the holidays that she'd spent with her brother and his family.

"Ryan and I have days when we feel the same way," Lisa said with a grin.

"You must be doing something right. You have good kids," she said sincerely.

Lisa sat down across from Dena. "You've only seen them on their best behavior. Just wait until you've been here awhile," she said with a crooked smile.

Dena glanced around the room—at the drawings on the refrigerator door, the toy trucks lined up next to the wall, the bulletin board covered with heart-shaped reminders of appointments and school activities. The picture on the shelf over the sink caught her eye. It was a photograph of her brother with his three children. Three-year-old Luke was on his shoulders, his pudgy arms wrapped around his father's neck. Bethany clung to one arm, twelve-year-old Jeremy was on the other.

"Ryan is so different from my father. He never played with us kids."

"He probably didn't have the time—he worked so many hours," Lisa said.

Dena nodded and didn't follow up on the comments, not wanting to discuss her father's shortcomings. Not that she would be telling her sister-in-law anything she wasn't aware of. Having known Ryan since they'd been in the seventh grade, Lisa was privy to all the family secrets. She'd been his steady girlfriend when Dena's mother had abandoned her family, leaving two teenaged kids in the care of a father whose response to losing his wife had been to bury himself even deeper in his work.

Even though she was the one to inadvertently mention her father, she was grateful when Lisa changed the subject. "So tell me how everything is with you. Are you happy with your new job?"

"So far, so good," she said with caution. "It's going to be a lot of pressure, but that's to be expected. It's the nature of the work. I'm going to have to put in some long hours, but it'll all be worth it."

"Ryan said you were stopping over because you need a donation for a charity auction?" Lisa remarked with a lift of one eyebrow.

"Yes." She started to explain, but before she could finish, the back door opened and in trudged her brother and nephew, both of them dusted with snow. As they exchanged greetings, Dena thought Ryan looked like a lumberjack, with his red plaid jacket, knit stocking hat and full beard. He pulled the hat from his head to reveal wavy blond hair the same shade as Dena's.

"Perfect timing," Lisa said, getting up from the table. "Dena just got here."

Ryan kicked off his boots, then took a seat at the table next to his sister. "So what kind of auction item are you looking for, again?"

"That's what I was hoping you could tell me," she answered. "You've lived in this area for quite some time. What type of item do people purchase at a charity auction?"

"It depends on the kind of crowd it is," her sister-in-law told her as she helped Luke out of his snowsuit. "When they had a silent auction at Bethany's school to raise money for the new gymnasium, the hot item was a basketball signed by one of the Timberwolves. I would think that memorabilia signed by professional athletes would always be popular."

"I suppose I could go to one of the sports stores and get an autographed baseball," Dena pondered aloud.

"If you do that it'll cost you a few bucks," her brother pointed out.

"Why don't you just ask that guy upstairs from you to donate something?" Lisa suggested. "Didn't you say he's a professional hockey player?"

"That's what I've been told, but I haven't even seen the man, let alone talked to him. If it wasn't for the fact that I heard some noise up there one night last week, I wouldn't even know anyone lives upstairs."

"You'd think you would have run into him by now."

"I'm relieved I haven't. I don't have time to get chummy with any of my neighbors."

"You don't have to get chummy with him," Lisa said. "Just ask him to autograph something and donate it to the auction. I bet people would pay good money for one of his hockey sticks."

"If he has a name people recognize."

"What is his name?" Ryan asked.

"Quinn Sterling," Dena replied.

Ryan's jaw dropped open. "He's the hockey player who lives on the third floor of your building? You didn't tell me he was in the NHL."

"I didn't know," she said in her own defense.

"Quinn Sterling," her brother repeated in amazement. "Who would have expected him to be living in a boardinghouse with a bunch of women."

"It isn't a bunch. There are only three of us and we each have our own apartment," Dena reminded him.

Ryan shrugged. "I guess the guy has to live somewhere...and it probably helps him keep a low profile."

"So what's he like? Is he nice?" Lisa asked, turning her attention to the stove.

Ryan chuckled sarcastically. "Defensemen usually aren't described as 'nice.'"

Dena wrinkled her face. "He isn't one of those guys who's always fighting, is he?"

"I'm sure he's spent his share of time in the penalty box. He has a reputation for being bad...which is one of the reasons the fans love him."

"Then he's popular?"

"In Minnesota he is. He's a good hockey player," her brother stated matter-of-factly. Luke was at his side, arms outstretched, waiting for his father to lift him onto his lap. Ryan scooped him up and propped him on one knee.

"Would you say he's like the Michael Jordan of hockey?" Dena wanted to know.

Ryan gave her an indulgent look. "Basketball and hockey are two different sports, and no one's like Michael Jordan. Quinn's made a name for himself, although I don't think he's ever made the All-Star team."

"But would a hockey stick signed by him bring in big bucks at a charity auction?"

"Probably anything signed by Quinn would do that." Lisa had set three mugs of hot chocolate and one small cup for Luke on the table. Ryan reached for the small cup and helped his son take a sip.

Dena thought again of how different he was from their father. So patient, so protective. So interested in his son.

"Quinn Sterling was born and raised in St. Paul," her brother continued. "That's one of the reasons he's so popular in this area. Hockey fans around here were very happy when the Cougars got him on a trade."

"Sounds like the right guy to ask for a donation, Dena," Lisa stated.

"Yes, but how am I ever going to get it?" Dena pondered aloud. "I can't just walk up the stairs, knock on his door and say, 'Hi, I'm your new neighbor, give me a stick.'"

"Why not?" Lisa asked, taking the chair next to Ryan's.

Dena's eyes met Ryan's and he chuckled. "Lisa would do it." His eyes were full of affection as he smiled at his wife.

It was obvious to Dena from the glances they exchanged they were just as much in love now as they'd been as teenagers. Ryan had proved his father wrong. How many times had he warned Ryan that if he were to marry Lisa, he'd end up in the same predicament his father was in? Dena was relieved to see her brother and his wife so happy.

She pushed a loose strand of hair back from her face and sighed. "I wish I didn't have to do this. This is so not me."

"Even if you work up the courage to ask for the stick, you might have a problem getting to the guy," Ryan warned her. "Professional athletes know how to avoid the public."

"She's not the public, she's his neighbor," Lisa pointed out.

"A neighbor he's never met," Dena reminded her sister-in-law.

"And I think he's one of the hockey players who keeps a low profile," Ryan added.

That didn't come as a surprise to Dena. She hadn't seen anyone going in or out of his place, but then she hadn't had any guests since she'd moved in, either. The day Leonie had shown her the vacant room on the second floor she'd explained the rules of the house. Guests were welcome as long as they didn't impose on anyone's privacy.

So far the only resident who took advantage of that rule was Krystal Graham, the hairstylist who occupied the other half of the second floor. She had a steady stream of visitors, and Dena could understand why. Krystal was a people person. From what her brother was saying, the man upstairs probably wasn't.

"You might want to think of another item for the

charity auction," Ryan said, reaching for a napkin to dab at hot chocolate that had dribbled down Luke's chin. "We don't know this guy. For all we know, his persona off ice could be the same as it is on ice."

"He's not going to be mean to his neighbor," Lisa insisted. "Stop trying to discourage her."

"You don't think I can get the stick, do you?" Dena said to her brother.

"It's going to be difficult," he warned her.

"Yeah, so what else is new?" she retorted.

"So you're going to go for it?" Lisa wanted to know.

"Yes. I want my donation to the auction to stand out from the others. I just have to figure out a way to get the stick."

"The Cougars have a game at the Excel Center tomorrow, which means Quinn Sterling is in town," Ryan announced.

"Now's your chance," Lisa encouraged her. "If you don't want to knock on his door, you could always bump into him on the stairs."

An equally unsettling thought for Dena, who knew that she was right. It was now or never. The auction was only a little over a week away. If she didn't get to him this weekend, there was a good chance he'd be on the road and she wouldn't have another opportunity.

"You're right. I'm going to do it. Wish me luck."

BEFORE DENA COULD DO SOMETHING so bold as to introduce herself to a professional hockey player and ask for an autographed stick, she needed to be prepared. That's why she made sure to leave her brother's house early enough so that she had time to stop at the library on her way home.

Later, armed with a stack of periodicals and a couple of videotapes, she climbed the stairs to the second floor at 14 Valentine Place. Once she was in her room, she slipped a tape cassette into the VCR and pressed Play.

As scenes of hockey players flashed across the screen, a voice announced the featured segments of the weekly sports program. If she watched the entire thirty minutes she could get an analysis of the games played the previous week, hear an interview with the head coach of the Minnesota Cougars hockey team and watch a demonstration of stickhandling at its best. Since she'd checked out the tape for one reason only—to see the player profile feature—she pressed the fast-forward button until she found that particular segment.

Images of bodies being pushed into the boards and sliding across the ice as skaters battled for the small black puck flashed on the screen. "Every team has one…a big, mean skater who patrols the blue line using his physical presence as a weapon," the narrator said as a player rammed another against the boards. "He's as tough as nails, adding muscle and strength to a defense that is out there for one purpose—to keep the puck away from the guys who want to stuff it in the net."

Dena grimaced as two men collided with a thud that could be heard above the noise of the crowd. "Around the league he's established a reputation for being a leader on and off the ice, and with good reason," the narrator continued. "With a solid work ethic and an attitude that conveys he's going to get the job done, he's what every head coach wants a defenseman to be—rough, tough and ready to do battle. This week we profile number thirty-two…''

The hockey player who'd been banging bodies into the boards stopped in the center of the rink, the camera catching the action of his blade on the ice at the same moment the narrator said, ''Quinn Sterling.'' It was then that Dena saw for the first time the face of the man who lived upstairs.

The first word that came to mind was *gladiator*. Maybe it was the helmet he wore. Or it could have been the rugged features that seemed to be all angles. Dena frowned as she realized that it was also a familiar face. Where would she have seen him before? Maybe as a professional athlete he'd done a commercial she'd seen. He certainly had the kind of look that could sell products.

As the profile continued, Dena listened to stats and figures that had little significance to someone who didn't follow hockey. Then the question was raised. ''Is Quinn Sterling one of the meanest guys on the ice?''

The camera moved to one of Quinn's teammates, who grinned and said, ''All hockey players have a mean streak. It's just that Quinn wears his on his jersey.''

The next shot was of Quinn. He stood with his helmet off, his dark hair damp from exertion, defending the accusation. ''It's my job to make sure my teammates are safe and protected on the ice. If that means I've got to get rough to do it, then I'm gonna do it. No one's going to run up on one of my guys.''

Footage of him getting rough followed. Dena winced as a sequence of collisions was shown, all of them resulting in bodies being knocked to the ice. When a brawl erupted, gloves dropped and fists were raised. Dena decided she'd seen enough and stopped the tape. She didn't need to watch grown men who were supposed to be professionals behave like little boys on the playground.

She looked at the stack of sports magazines and wondered if she should even bother to read any of the articles on Quinn Sterling. Curiosity had her flipping one open and reading a brief bio. He was born and raised in St. Paul and played his first hockey game at the age of five. He'd left college early to enter the NHL draft. Now he made his living fighting on the ice.

She heaved a long sigh and tossed the magazine aside. The task of having to ask him for the donation seemed to be an even more unpleasant one than it had earlier in the day. She wondered if it wouldn't be easier to simply go buy an autographed stick or jersey from a sports shop. Of course it would be easier, but it would also be costlier.

Lisa could be right. Quinn Sterling might be happy to donate the stick simply because she was his neighbor. She just had to work up her courage and ask him for it.

As she scooped up the periodicals scattered across the floor, she noticed one was a woman's magazine. Whoever had pulled the magazines for her from the library stacks must have accidentally included it. She looked again at her request slip and saw that it wasn't a mistake.

According to the guide to periodicals, Quinn Sterling was in the magazine. Dena flipped through the glossy pages until she came to the article called,

"Why We Love Those Bad Boys." It didn't take long to find his name in boldface type.

"What could be more tantalizing than a professional hockey player who plays rough?" the writer asked. "He's cold and cruel on the ice, but what we want to know is what he's like when he's not slamming bodies up against the boards. This thirty-one-year-old bachelor may look like every girl's dream with those baby-blue eyes, but don't expect him to behave like the boy next door. Taming this bad boy is definitely going to be a challenge. He's been quoted as saying that the woman hasn't been born yet who can tempt him to hang up his blades."

Dena rolled her eyes and groaned. "And this is the guy I have to ask for a donation for a charity event?" As she turned the page a photograph of Quinn Sterling stared back at her. Without his helmet he still looked rugged. And tough. And handsome.

He also looked familiar. Again she asked herself why. Her answer came as she noticed the small scar along his jaw—a scar that hadn't been noticeable on the videotape.

She *had* seen him before. The night of Maddie's wedding. In the men's rest room. Dressed in a suit, he'd looked very different from the man in the hockey uniform. He'd flirted with her, and she smiled as she remembered their encounter.

The question was, would he remember her? She doubted it, not with the number of women who probably came and went in his life. If she was lucky, she wouldn't even be a blip on his memory radar.

All weekend she watched for a sign that he was home, but not once did she see him or his silver SUV parked out back. His absence made her do something she hadn't done on previous Monday mornings. She went into the kitchen on the main floor.

"This is a nice surprise," Leonie Donovan greeted her. "I was beginning to think you didn't eat breakfast."

Dena didn't want to admit that she often skipped breakfast and simply said, "I usually grab something on the way to work."

Leonie nodded in understanding. "You put in long hours, don't you?" She didn't expect an answer to her question and continued, "Krystal's the same way. I haven't seen much of her lately, either."

"What about Mr. Sterling? Does he use the kitchen much?" she asked as she busied herself getting a cup of tea.

"Quinn? No." There was a hint of regret in her voice. "When I had the third floor remodeled, I put in an efficiency kitchen up there, but I doubt he does much cooking. He's seldom home."

Dena filled the kettle and set it on the stove. "I noticed. Actually, I've been trying to connect with him."

Leonie raised her eyebrows. "You have?"

She nodded. "I have a favor to ask him. Maybe you can tell me if you think he'd be interested in this." She sat down across from Leonie and told her about the charity event being held at the high school, including what items had already been donated to the auction. "I was hoping he'd be willing to autograph a stick or some other hockey memorabilia for the event."

"I don't see any reason why he wouldn't do it, especially since he went to the same high school as Aaron Jorgenson," she said over her cup of coffee.

"He did? I knew he was from St. Paul, but I didn't realize that."

She nodded, then set her cup back in its saucer. "His family used to live right around the corner. He was always over here with my boys, slapping pucks around on the small skating rink my husband would make in the backyard every winter."

Which would explain why he was at Dylan and Maddie's wedding, Dena concluded silently. "Did you ever think he'd get to the NHL?"

"I knew he loved the game," she admitted, then smiled. "Lots of young boys dream of becoming professional athletes. I think mine did at one time, too. It's nice to see that dream come true for Quinn. If anybody deserves it, he does. He's worked hard to get where he is." There was admiration and respect in her voice, which had Dena wondering if Leonie realized the kind of player Quinn was.

"You sound very fond of him," she commented.

Leonie smiled. "I am, and with good reason. He's a good guy. I'm going to have to introduce you two."

An alarm rang in Dena's head. One of her reservations about moving into 14 Valentine Place had concerned her landlady's occupation. Maddie had told her Leonie was a romance coach, but she had also assured her that her mother-in-law wasn't the kind to try to do any matchmaking with her tenants. Now Dena wasn't so sure Maddie had been right about that.

As if Leonie could read her mind, she said, "Don't look so frightened. I'm not going to throw you two together with a couple of candles and some Barry Manilow music. I just meant you should know each other because you're neighbors. I like to think that my tenants look out for one another.''

Dena gave her an apologetic smile. "I'm sorry. I shouldn't have jumped to that conclusion.''

"It's all right. I should have explained to you when you moved in just what it is a romance coach does. I help people put romance in their lives. Have you seen my column in the paper...*Dear Leonie?*''

Dena nodded.

"Then you know what kind of questions people bring to me about romance. I also teach a class on making relationships last. And I'm thinking about adding one on flirting.''

Dena thought, judging by the way Quinn Sterling had flirted with her, he'd be a good resource, but she didn't tell Leonie that.

"I also do one-on-one counseling. When it comes to romance, some people really don't have a clue, and sometimes all they need is a little push in the right direction. My goal has always been for people to discover the joy romance can bring. There's nothing more wonderful than the right somebody to love.''

Dena didn't want to tell her that so far that particular pleasure had evaded her. Not that she was looking for it. The romantic relationships she'd had thus far had suited her just fine. Not exactly romantic, but they hadn't left her brokenhearted, either.

"So you see, Dena, I'm really not a matchmaker,'' Leonie concluded.

She smiled in relief. "That's good to hear. I'm really not looking for the right somebody to love.''

She held up one hand. "I understand. I told you when you moved in that I regard all of my tenants as just that—tenants. Their personal lives are their own, as is mine. When we're in this house, we're simply friends. Fair enough?''

Dena nodded. She could see why Maddie had come to regard Leonie as a mother long before she'd married Dylan. Dena knew it would be tempting to let this woman mother her, especially since her own mother had never really filled that role.

''Now, back to Quinn. With all the Cougar road trips, it's no surprise the two of you haven't met,'' Leonie said thoughtfully.

''We both have busy schedules, I'm sure.''

Leonie nodded. ''And he keeps to himself. I know Krystal talks with him occasionally, but then Krystal can get anyone to talk. Quinn values his privacy. It's one of the reasons he lives here. With the success he's had, he could afford a fancy penthouse apartment anywhere, yet he chose to rent the third floor of my house.''

''This is a lovely place,'' Dena told her. ''It has a charm you don't find in newer housing.''

''Why, thank you, Dena. I'm glad you like it here.''

''I do.'' It was the truth. She'd had her reservations about sharing a bath and the kitchen with the other tenants, but she'd discovered that Maddie had been right. There was something about the big old Victorian house that made her feel comfortable.

''I figured if you were a good friend of Maddie's that you'd fit in with us,'' Leonie said with a twinkle in her eye.

Dena was beginning to think she would, too. At least with Krystal and Leonie. As for the man upstairs...she guessed it really didn't matter whether they liked each other. He was never around, and once she got the hockey stick she could forget about him, which reminded her she still had to get the auction item.

"If Dylan's a private person, I probably shouldn't bother him about the stick," Dena commented.

"I don't think he'll see it as a bother, but if you'd like, I could ask him for you."

Dena said a prayer of thanks right then and there. "You wouldn't mind?"

Leonie took a sip of her coffee, then said, "No, not at all. I'll see what I can do."

TRUE TO HER WORD, Leonie talked to Quinn. The very next day when Dena arrived home from work, she found a hockey stick propped against her door. Attached to it was a note that said, "Leonie told me about the auction for the Jorgensons. If there's anything else I can do, let me know." It was simply signed with a capital *Q*.

Leonie knew she needed to thank the man. Taking a deep breath, she took the stick and climbed the stairs to the third floor. To her relief, there was no answer to her knock on his door, and she went back to her apartment, where she studied the signature on the hockey stick.

The writing was bold and confident, the *Q* a big flamboyant circle compared to the rest of the letters, which weren't much more than a series of upward strokes and wavy humps. His entire name was underscored.

She propped the stick against the wall, then sat down at her desk. She pulled a note card from the drawer and began to write.

"Mr. Sterling, Thank you so much for the auction donation for the Aaron Jorgenson benefit. It was very kind of you and your generosity is appreciated. Sincerely, your neighbor, Dena Bailey.''

She went back upstairs and slipped the note beneath his door.

The next day, when she brought the stick with her to work, it raised more than a few eyebrows of admiration. As the auction drew nearer and other donations arrived, Dena was confident that hers would bring the highest bid. Unfortunately, she was disappointed. As much as the fans in St. Paul loved Quinn Sterling, they were willing to pay more for lunch with the lovely Channel 8 news anchor than for an authentic, autographed hockey stick by their hometown hero.

Dena had hoped that her donation to the auction would get the creative director's attention, but other than a personal thank-you note, it didn't. What it did do, however, was give her a small amount of fame. Male co-workers made a habit of stopping by her cubicle to inquire about her neighbor.

Her popularity, however, was short-lived, and within a few days, it was business as usual. She forgot about the man who lived upstairs from her, and she put all of her energy into her fast-approaching deadline.

CHAPTER TWO

IT HAD BEEN A GRUELING ROAD TRIP. Quinn was tired and his body ached. He'd been tripped, elbowed, punched and banged into the boards during the past three games, and he could feel it in his muscles and bones. In addition to a black eye, he had a bandage on his cheek and a contusion on his right quadriceps. Hazards of the trade, he told himself as he dragged his weary body up the stairs to his apartment.

Judging by the way his body felt, he would have thought there were only a couple of weeks of the regular season left, not two months. Maybe it was age catching up with him. He was, after all, on the wrong side of thirty—at least for a hockey player. But he wouldn't think about that now. He'd just had one of the best games of his career. There was no reason to think about that.

Aware that it was close to three in the morning, he moved as quietly as he could, not wanting to disturb the other residents of the house. He grimaced as the stairs creaked with his weight.

It was at times like this that he wondered if he'd made a mistake moving into 14 Valentine Place. Although it afforded him plenty of privacy, he'd been reluctant to accept Leonie Donovan's offer to rent the third floor of the house, because he worried that his irregular hours might disturb her other tenants.

She'd had no such reservations. Not that she would have expressed them if she had. Leonie had been like a second mother to him most of his life. As a teen he'd eaten just as many meals at her house as he had at his own. That's why, when he'd been traded to the Minnesota team, she'd been one of the first people he'd contacted.

"Shane is going to be so happy you're coming home," she'd gushed when he'd announced his return, hugging him as if he were one of her own children.

So far he'd only seen Shane once—the day he'd moved into the house. They'd been the best of buddies as kids, but now it was evident that their lives had gone in very different directions. Shane's life centered around his wife and son. Quinn's life was hockey. Not that Shane wasn't still interested in talking about the sport, but Quinn could see that the passion they'd once shared as kids was now a thing of the past.

He didn't understand it. Nothing had ever come close to replacing the love he had for the game of hockey. There was nothing like the sound of cold, hard steel cutting through ice, the clash of sticks sending the puck gliding across the rink, and the cheers of the crowd urging him on.

Now the sound he heard was a loud thud, thud, thud. A thick glass mug that had been tucked in the side pouch of his duffel bag tumbled onto the floor, falling down the stairs like an errant hockey puck. It was a souvenir molded into the shape of a western boot. The mug had been given to him by Smitty, the young goalie who'd bet him that he couldn't shut down the shooters on the opposing team. Quinn had won the bet and the goalie had refilled the heavy glass half a dozen times as they'd sat in the bar celebrating the team's victory.

That had been on day one of their road trip. Today was day five and Quinn still had the mug. It had been dropped numerous times and knocked off several hotel tables, but nothing had caused it to break. As solid as a rock was how Smitty had described it, which was why he'd insisted Quinn take it home with him. It was how the goalie viewed Quinn—able to take a heck of a beating and not break.

Now the glass boot was once again tumbling along the floor. Any hope that its clumping wouldn't awaken his neighbors vanished when a light appeared beneath a door. Quinn knew he'd disturbed someone on the second floor.

Within seconds a door opened. Staring at him with a startled look on her face was a woman. She wore a long-sleeved white T-shirt and a pair of red pajama bottoms that had tiny penguins all over them. Her blond hair hung in total disarray around her shoulders. Looking as if she'd just been awakened from a deep sleep, she stood in the doorway, her feet bare.

Leonie had told him a new tenant had moved into Maddie's old apartment. What his landlady hadn't told him about the woman was that she was a sight for sore eyes. Not that she was beautiful in a Hollywood sort of way, because she wasn't. What she had was a refreshingly natural look. His mother used to use the term ''plain pretty,'' and he'd never understood how someone could be plain and pretty, but now he knew what she meant.

''What are you doing?'' she asked in a voice still

husky with sleepiness, but also carrying a note of alarm.

"I'm sorry. I was on my way upstairs and I dropped something."

"What?"

"A mug. It's at the bottom of the stairs," Quinn answered, trying to figure out why it was that when she spoke he had the feeling they'd already met.

She eyed the duffel bag over his shoulder suspiciously, then she focused on his face and grimaced. "Ooh. Your eye!"

He knew his skin had darkened to a motley black and blue. "It looks worse than it feels." He moved closer to her. "I know we haven't met before, but you look familiar."

Self-consciously, she pushed her hair out of her eyes, then offered him her hand. "I'm Dena Bailey."

"Quinn Sterling." He took the soft hand in his. It was warm.

"Oh, of course." As if it suddenly registered who he was, she said, "Quinn Sterling, my neighbor." A tiny smile of embarrassment made her cheeks dimple. "You donated the hockey stick."

"I did."

"Thank you." She shuffled her feet either in nervousness or because the floor was cold.

"You're welcome," he said with a smile meant to put her at ease.

"That stick was a very popular item."

"I'm glad." He watched her, trying to gauge her reaction to learning his identity. He'd been a professional hockey player long enough to know that being Quinn Sterling could bring out the phoniness in a woman. So far, this woman didn't appear to have a fake bone in her body. "How long have you lived here?"

"Not quite a month. Why?"

"I'm surprised we haven't run into each other before now."

"I'm not here much," she told him, then quickly added, "because of my work—I'm a graphic designer."

Leonie may have told him that but he didn't remember. Come to think of it, he hadn't paid much attention when she'd talked about the new tenant and her request for an autographed hockey stick. Now he wished he had.

Dena stifled a yawn, then said, "I'm sorry. You're really going to have to excuse me. I have to be at work at seven tomorrow and it is late."

So much for his concern that she might be a groupie eager to get to know him. "I'm sorry I woke you."

"It's all right." She dismissed his apology with a flap of her hand, then started across the hall.

"Isn't your apartment behind you?"

She paused. "Yes, but the bathroom isn't," she answered. "Krystal and I share."

Bathroom. That was it. Now he knew where he'd seen her. The night of Maddie and Dylan's wedding, she was the woman he'd seen in the men's room at the hotel. "Were you at Dylan's wedding?"

Briefly her eyes widened, then she narrowed them again in a slumberous pose. "Yes, I was. Were you?"

"You don't remember seeing me there?"

She gave him a blank look. "Do you remember seeing me?"

"Oh, yeah," he drawled, unable to keep the smile

from spreading across his face. "You are not a
woman a man forgets, Dena Bailey."

He could see the compliment made her uncomfortable. She didn't say another word but padded across
the carpeted hallway into the washroom. He was
tempted to wait for her, but judging by the way she'd
looked at him, he didn't think she'd appreciate finding
him still there.

So instead he went downstairs, picked up the mug
and headed up to his own room, knowing there would
be more opportunities to talk to her. She did, after all,
live right below him. It was an intriguing thought.

YOU ARE NOT a woman a man forgets. Quinn Sterling's
words echoed in Dena's head long after she'd returned to bed. Had he spoken them because he meant
he wouldn't forget her being in the men's room at
Dylan and Maddie's wedding? Or had he been coming on to her?

She guessed it was a little of both. That sly grin
had said, "We share a secret and I wouldn't mind
making a few more discoveries about you." Even in
her half-asleep state she hadn't missed the gleam of
interest in his eyes, although she wasn't sure why
he'd be curious about her.

Not many men would find bed head and flannel
pajamas a turn-on. And she certainly had sent no
vibes his way. There was no reason to, especially not
after watching the videotape of him in action on the
ice.

Big and bad. How many times had she seen that
written about him? That black eye tonight certainly
made him look bad. For all she knew he could have
gotten it in a bar fight. And no one could say that it

was his hockey gear that made him look big. Even
out of uniform he was as wide as a football player
and taller than most men.

Yes, she could definitely see why some women
would find him attractive. With his physical attributes
he could probably make any woman a little weak-
kneed—especially one who'd been awakened from a
deep sleep in the middle of the night.

Not that it mattered. If she were looking for romance—and she wasn't—it wouldn't be with a professional athlete. She could only imagine what it
would be like to date someone who was constantly in
the public eye and the object of groupies.

No, someone like Quinn Sterling would be more
work than the average guy. And she'd discovered a
long time ago that that was what men were—work.
They demanded her attention and they wanted her
passion. All she wanted to be passionate about was
her job. It consumed her energy, her emotions, and
that's the way she wanted it, because the payoff was
an indescribable feeling of accomplishment. There
was no greater satisfaction than having something she
had created on display in the marketplace for the
world to see. Guys would come and go in her life,
but her designs had staying power.

She looked again at the clock. In less than three
hours she would have to get up and go into the office.
She needed to stop thinking about her encounter with
Quinn Sterling and go back to sleep, even if he was
one of the most attractive men who'd ever flirted with
her.

*The woman hasn't been born yet who can tempt
him to hang up his blades.* The quote from the
women's magazine echoed in her mind. As if she'd

try to get him to do anything. She bunched up her pillow and rolled over.

She closed her eyes and forced her thoughts to the advertising campaign she'd been assigned to only yesterday. If she was going to lie awake in the middle of the night, she might as well think about something that would be of use to her for her work. Quinn Sterling was not in her future. Soy nuts were. If she could think of a clever package for the honey-roasted product, she'd be one step closer to reaching her goal of making art director.

As for the man who lived upstairs…it was unlikely that she'd run into him again. She'd lived at 14 Valentine Place for close to a month and had only seen him once. He was the kind of neighbor she wanted— out of sight and out of mind.

WHEN DENA ARRIVED at work later that morning, Greg Watkins told her that Jack Kramer wanted to see her. Her heart beat faster in anticipation of the reason she'd been summoned to the creative director's office. Always the optimist, she expected it to be good news.

"Dena, come in and sit down," he said when he saw her, gesturing to the Scandinavian-style chair next to his desk. "I wanted to tell you how pleased I am with your work so far. You're doing a fine job here at Delaney."

She relaxed and smiled. "Thank you. That's good to hear."

"I think you're going to be a good fit for Delaney, and what I really like is that you're a team player. That's exactly what we need here. It's the reason the Aaron Jorgenson benefit was a success."

"I'm happy I was able to do my part."

"As were so many generous people," he said, obviously pleased. "That's why we've decided to do another fund-raiser. Has Greg told you about our next project?"

She shook her head and he continued. "We're going to put together a calendar featuring distinguished alumni from the state's high schools...a sort of look at the stars of Minnesota. Each month will feature a different celebrity." He went on to name several prominent public figures who'd already agreed to be featured on the calendar. Included were a senator, a comedienne and two film stars.

"It sounds like a wonderful idea for a fund-raiser," Dena said. "Calendars are always popular."

He nodded in agreement. "Delaney Design will be donating the graphic designs, and we have several vendors, including a printer, who have offered to donate their services and supplies at either a reduced fee or for no charge at all. That means we should be able to put the calendar together at a very low cost."

She nodded. "If there's anything I can do, please let me know. I'd be willing to volunteer my evenings."

He held up his hand. "No need for you to do that. I've already had a couple of designers offer to do the layout. But I do have another way you can help me."

Disappointment welled in her throat. So she hadn't been called into his office because of her performance on the job.

He leaned forward, his arms on his desk. "Here's the deal. We have most of the people we'll be featuring on the calendar, but everyone agrees that it's important to have the person who represents January be someone special. That's why we'd like to have

Quinn Sterling. Not only would he make a great winter picture with the hockey uniform and the skates and the whole bit, but he also attended the same high school as Aaron Jorgenson. He's the perfect choice for the first month on the calendar, don't you agree?'' He looked at her with a grin that said he was very pleased with himself.

By now the lump that had started to fall in Dena's stomach the minute she had heard Quinn Sterling's name had settled like a brick in a pond. ''You want me to ask Quinn Sterling if he'll pose for the calendar?''

''He is a friend of yours, isn't he?''

''I wouldn't exactly say he's my friend...'' She trailed off uneasily. ''We live in the same building, but to be honest, I hardly ever see him. Apparently, during the hockey season, players are on the road a lot. Is it even going to be possible to arrange a shoot with the kind of schedule he has?''

His smile faded. ''Are you saying you don't want to help with the project?'' The warmth that had oozed out of him only minutes ago was replaced by a coolness that caused Dena to shift uneasily. ''You don't have to be a part of this project. This isn't officially a Delaney Design endeavor. It's strictly volunteer.''

Her palms grew damp. She wanted to say, *I think I'll pass on this one,* but she didn't. She couldn't. Not when two other designers had already committed to the project.

''Oh, no, I want to help,'' she quickly reassured him. ''I'm just trying to put this together in my mind. One of the concerns I have would be the use of his photo. I assume the professional athletic leagues like the NHL have contracts with their players that might make it impossible for us to photograph him in his uniform and put it on a product we want to sell.'' It was her only hope and it was quickly dashed.

''Legal's already checked into it. All the appropriate forms that need to be signed are in here.'' He slid a manila folder across the desk in her direction. ''We've worked with athletic organizations before. In fact, one of our accounts is for the Cougar bobblehead dolls.''

''We're doing hockey player bobbleheads?''

''A limited number. That's why I'm not concerned about this calendar licensing. Basically all you need to do is get Quinn Sterling to agree to the photo shoot, and then you can consider your job done. Greg Watkins will take it from there. So what do you say? Can I count on you?''

As much as Dena wanted to say no, she answered, ''Yes, you can.''

His face softened into a grin. ''Thanks, Dena. This project is very important to me. I won't forget that you are one of the reasons it's going to be a success.''

She smiled weakly and mumbled an appropriate response, hoping she hadn't made a promise she couldn't deliver. She reached for the folder. ''What's the time frame on this?''

''We're hoping to get the calendar to the printer by the end of May, but we also know that scheduling the photo shoots is going to be tricky, especially when we're dealing with celebrities. It's all in there,'' he said, nodding to the folder in her hands.

She didn't open it, but said, ''So, then, you'd like me to talk to Quinn Sterling when?''

''As soon as possible. You should be able to reach

him at the Cougar main office if not at your apartment building.'' He picked up the newspaper that had been on the side of his desk and said, "According to the sports page, the Cougars are in town this week.''

Dena could have said, *Oh, Quinn Sterling's in town all right. He has a black eye and a dangerously attractive smile.* She simply nodded and said, "I'll do my best.''

THAT EVENING a letter from Maddie was waiting for her when she arrived home from work. As she read the newlywed's note about her honeymoon and subsequent move to France, Dena was filled with a longing for her college days when she and Maddie had been the best of friends.

They'd been as different as night and day—Maddie being a social butterfly and Dena a studious bookworm. Maddie wore her emotions on her sleeve, but Dena guarded hers carefully. She did such a thorough job of keeping them close that many people thought she lacked feelings. Maddie knew better. They'd stay up until the wee hours of the morning sharing confidences.

It was at college that Dena had discovered what it was like to have a best friend. Throughout adolescence there had been girls who were friendly to her, but none who'd ever truly understood her the way Maddie did. Now, as Dena sat in Maddie's old apartment, holding her words in her hand, she wished that her friend was beside her, giving her moral support. She'd always managed to make life a little easier for Dena, which was exactly what she needed when it came to her assignment involving Quinn Sterling.

But Maddie wasn't there, and this was one job
Dena was going to have to tackle by herself. She went
over to her desk and pulled out a sheet of stationery
to write another note. If he wasn't home when she
knocked on his door, she'd leave him a note.

"Could you please call me when you have a few
minutes? I'd like to talk to you. Your neighbor, Dena
Bailey." She spoke the words as she penned them.
Then she put her phone number at Delaney Design
under her name, thinking it was better to keep things
on a business level.

As much as she wanted to get things settled, she
was a bit relieved when he wasn't at home and she
could shove the note beneath his door. She was on
her way back down to her apartment when she saw
Krystal Graham coming up the stairs. They met at the
second-floor landing.

The redhead looked up toward the third floor and
asked, "Were you looking for Quinn?"

"Yes, but he's not in." Dena saw no point in pretending.

"Now, why am I not surprised?" Krystal drawled.
"I don't know why he just doesn't move a bed over
to the ice rink." She shoved one hand to her hip.
"You know, as cute as he is, sometimes I think it
would have been better if Leonie had rented that third
floor apartment to another woman."

It certainly would have eliminated the predicament
Dena found herself in at the moment. She wasn't sure
what kind of a response the younger woman expected
from her and was relieved when Krystal continued.

"Hey…have you eaten dinner?"

"Not yet, but—"

"Great. You can have some of my pizza. I haven't

eaten since noon today and I'm starving. If you haven't tried that little place around the corner, it's really good and they deliver.'' Before Dena could utter a single word of protest, the stylist had pulled her cell phone from her purse and speed-dialed the pizzeria. ''What do you like on yours?''

Dena wanted to say she didn't have time for pizza, that she'd brought work home and she needed to get it done, but the look on Krystal's face had her saying, ''Mushrooms and onions?''

''Great! Me, too,'' she said with a gamin grin. ''What about some Italian sausage?''

Dena nodded. ''And some green olives.''

''Green olives on half,'' she repeated into the phone. ''And extra cheese.'' When she'd finished placing the order, she snapped the phone shut and said, ''This is so cool! I was hoping I'd run into you so we could have some time for girl talk. I'm sure Maddie's told you that 14 Valentine Place is absolutely the best place for women our age to live?''

''She did brag about it a bit,'' Dena admitted.

''She must have told you about watching movies in Leonie's great room?''

Dena knew that the large living area off the kitchen was what everyone referred to as the house's great room. Leonie had told her that it was a communal area for the tenants to use. So far Dena hadn't taken her up on her invitation, preferring to watch television in her own apartment.

''One thing about Leonie is that she likes having people in the house,'' Krystal told her. ''That's why she converted this place into apartments. You don't need to worry that you're imposing on her privacy if you go downstairs. She loves having us girls around.''

"I'm afraid I work most evenings," Dena told her in an apologetic tone.

"Then I'm glad I caught you tonight. How about if I meet you in the kitchen in say…twenty minutes or so? I need to shower and change. I've been working in these clothes." She gestured to the short leather skirt and sweater sticking out from beneath her jacket.

"That's fine."

"Great. If you get down there before me, help yourself to any of the beverages in the fridge. There's beer and soda or bottled water…you're welcome to whatever you can find," she said over her shoulder as she headed toward her door.

Dena nodded and forced a weak smile, wondering if she'd made a mistake accepting Krystal's invitation. If she was going to keep her neighbors at arm's length, it probably wasn't wise to be sharing a pizza with one of them, especially one who was looking for "girl talk."

When Krystal came into the kitchen, she was wearing tight black pants and a yellow sweatshirt. She arrived at the same time as the delivery boy. Dena watched her talk to him as if he were a good friend instead of a complete stranger, envying the ease with which the younger woman carried on a conversation.

As soon as he'd gone, Krystal said, "Wasn't he just the cutest thing? A little too young for my taste, but cute." She set the pizza in the middle of the table, then grabbed a Corona from the refrigerator.

"I noticed you asked if he had an older brother," Dena remarked, taking the chair directly across from her.

"Of course. A girl has to explore every possibility," she said as she helped herself to a slice of pizza.

Judging by the number of different guys that Dena had seen outside Krystal's door, she assumed her housemate was definitely looking at her options.

"Have you heard from Maddie?" Krystal didn't wait for an answer but continued on. "I got a letter the other day. She said that she and Dylan had a fabulous time on their honeymoon, but I guess that should come as no surprise, right? What woman wouldn't be in seventh heaven with a guy like Dylan, right?"

"He seemed very nice," Dena said between bites of pizza.

Krystal sighed dreamily. "He is. The world could use a whole lot more of his kind."

"He has brothers, doesn't he?"

"Yeah, but Shane's married and Jason's only twenty."

"And the other one?"

"Oh…you mean Garret." She looked startled that she'd forgotten to mention him. "He's so quiet I sometimes forget that he's a Donovan."

"Isn't he a doctor?"

She nodded. "He's just finishing up his residency. He's a sweetie, but so different from Dylan. Dylan's big and brawny and an adventurer. He's lived all over the world."

"And Garret?" she prodded.

"He doesn't have Dylan's muscular build, but he's not bad looking. You just never know what he's thinking because he doesn't talk very much."

"He's probably a good listener. That's what you want in a doctor, isn't it?"

"Oh, definitely. And you're right. He is a very good listener." She uncapped the Corona and took a long sip. "He's over here a lot. He doesn't have a washer and dryer in his place so he uses the laundry room here."

"I haven't seen him around, but then I haven't met many people since I moved here," Dena told her.

"Then you should come with me on Saturday night. A bunch of us girls are going out. We can show you which places rock and which ones don't."

"Thanks, but I better say no."

Krystal shrugged. "Okay, but if you change your mind, let me know. You don't have a steady guy, do you?"

"No."

"Me, neither. What about an unsteady one?" she asked with a crooked grin.

Dena couldn't help but smile back. "No, not that kind, either."

"Would you like one...or maybe two?" Her eyes sparkled mischievously.

Dena chuckled. "Why? Do you have a couple to spare?"

Krystal grinned. "As a matter of fact, I do. And they're not bad guys to have around if you just want to have some fun." She took another sip of beer, then said, "I meet a lot of men through work."

"Leonie said you work at the day spa and salon over on Grand."

She nodded. "You have great hair. It's natural, isn't it?"

"Yes."

"I can tell. If you haven't found a stylist yet, you might want to check out the salon. I mean, don't feel like you have to come to me, but you can—if you want."

There was something especially charming about Krystal that made Dena feel as if she needed to watch out for her. Curious, she asked, "How old are you, Krystal?"

"Twenty-seven."

She was only a couple of years younger than Dena, yet Dena felt almost maternal toward her. It was an unfamiliar feeling and caught her off guard.

She almost said, *You don't act twenty-seven,* but stopped herself. "You don't look twenty-seven."

Krystal frowned. "Oh, shoot, not you, too. I'm always hearing that. Do you know how many times I've been ID'd to get served a glass of wine?" She didn't wait for an answer but changed the subject. "It's not always easy to meet people when you're new to the city, so I want you to feel free to call me anytime you're looking to go out and have some fun. And we don't have to go looking for guys."

"I'm really not looking for guys." She emphasized the word *not.*

"What about Quinn? You were coming down from his place earlier this evening," she reminded her, obviously wanting to know why.

"I need to talk to him," she said.

"Yeah, you and about ten thousand other women," Krystal said on a chuckle. "Take a number and get in line."

"This is for professional reasons, not personal," Dena was quick to point out.

"If you say so."

"It is," Dena insisted, not liking the dubious look on Krystal's face.

She held up her hands. "Hey—you don't need to explain to me. I've got eyes. I mean, even if he didn't have a gorgeous face, that body alone could make a girl shiver. Those wide, thick shoulders, those big strong hands, and just that rough, tough look he has about him..." She sighed and trailed off dreamily. "Well, you wouldn't be the first girl who wanted to get to know him better."

"I don't want to get to know him better," Dena said with a bit of impatience, although she knew it was probably a waste of time to try to convince Krystal she wasn't interested in Quinn. Women like Krystal didn't understand how any woman could look at him and not see a hottie.

"It's probably just as well," Krystal stated pragmatically. "I mean, being a hockey player and all, he probably has women chasing him all over town."

"Have you seen any?" As soon as Dena had uttered the words she knew it sounded as if she were interested in his love life. "I mean, women don't stalk him to this house, do they?"

She giggled. "No. I don't think hockey players are quite as popular as rock stars or Hollywood celebrities."

"Personally, I don't see the attraction."

Again curiosity flickered in Krystal's eyes. "I suppose you want to thank Quinn for donating that hockey stick to the benefit the other night." She explained, "I heard Leonie ask him for it."

Dena saw no reason not to let her assume it was her motivation for seeing him. "Yes, I do. It was very kind of him."

Just then Krystal's cell phone rang. She flipped open the cover, then quickly shut it again. "Telemarketer." She sighed. "I was hoping it was one of my guys."

One of my guys. "You're seeing more than one?"

She held up two fingers. "Or maybe I should say one and a half. There's this guy at my health club and then there's Roy…he sort of drifts in and out of my life, so he doesn't count as a full one, although if I could get him to be a full-timer, I'd end my days of juggling."

"Juggling?"

She laughed. "It's not what you think." She took another sip of beer. "Believe me, I'd rather have one serious relationship with one good guy, but until that happens, I'm doing what most men do—sampling what's out there."

Again her phone rang and again she opened and shut it with a sigh. "Not Roy."

The sound of feet on the stairs alerted Dena to the fact that Quinn had returned. Krystal knew it, too, and looked at Dena and said, "You might get your chance to talk to him, after all."

When more footsteps sounded a short while later, Dena knew Krystal was right. Within a few minutes, Quinn appeared in the doorway of the kitchen. "Anyone seen Leonie?"

"She's at her class, but you can come in and talk to us," Krystal said with the same flirtatious banter she'd used on the delivery boy. When he came closer, she said, "Ooh—what did you do to your eye?"

He smiled, as if proud of his wound. "I got popped a good one during a game."

"You are one mean dude, Quinn Sterling," she said with a teasing smile and a playful punch on his arm. The ease with which Krystal talked to him contradicted the impression she'd given that she'd hardly had a chance to get to know him. But then Dena realized that for people like Krystal, it only took a few minutes to become comfortable talking to someone. Quinn was no exception, even if he was a pro athlete.

Then, to Dena's horror, she pulled Quinn by the arm and urged him to take a seat at the table. "Here. Have some pizza. It's great for black eyes," she said with another grin. "And you can talk to Dena." Then she excused herself, saying, "I have to make a call. I'll see you later." Before Dena or Quinn could utter a word, she had flitted out of the room.

Dena looked at the man sitting across from her and wanted to get up and run after Krystal. He wore a pair of faded jeans and a dark blue sweater that clung to his broad, muscular chest.

Suddenly all the adjectives Krystal had used to describe him glared back at Dena. Wide, thick, strong, rough, tough. Her heartbeat quickened and she wished it wouldn't.

Quinn reached over to take a slice of the pizza. "Hi, Dena."

The smile that accompanied his greeting kept her reply simple. "Hi." He smelled good. Another reason for her pulse to behave erratically. "Your eye still does look pretty bad."

"It'll take a few days for the color to disappear," he said, his gaze never flinching from her face. "Leonie gave me some cream to put on it. Something with aloe in it, I think." He took a bite of the pizza, and said, "This is good."

She agreed.

Then he said, "I wasn't really looking for Leonie." He pulled her pink stationery from his pocket and waved it in the air.

To her chagrin, she could feel her face warm. "You were supposed to call me at work," she said primly.

"I'd rather talk to you here in person."

That sent another rush of heat through her.

"What is it you need to talk to me about? Do you want another stick?" He held her gaze.

"Actually, it's a little bit bigger favor than that," she confessed.

"Bigger, huh. A jersey?" The same teasing glint that had been in his eyes last night was there this evening, too. "Or do you need tickets?"

"No, no tickets. What I need is..." she began, wanting to steer the conversation from a flirtatious tone to a more businesslike one, but he wasn't about to let her.

He held up his hand. "No, don't tell me now. Have lunch with me tomorrow and we'll discuss it."

Lunch with him? Not a good idea, a little voice inside her head warned. "It would be easier if we could just discuss this now. I work downtown and—"

"That's all right. So do I."

The last thing she wanted was to be seen in a public place with a well-known hockey player. She could only imagine the attention he'd draw. He was so big...and so good-looking. "It's really hard for me to get away for more than a quick bite during the lunch hour."

"I have a reputation for being quick." Again his tone was provocative, and to her dismay, it sent a tiny shiver through her.

He was one good-looking man and he knew it. It annoyed her that she wasn't immune to his charm. She didn't want to be attracted to any man at this time in her life, and especially not a celebrity.

Then he said, "I prefer to discuss business over food, Ms. Bailey. This is about business, isn't it?"

She almost blushed. Almost. "Yes. Of course."

"Then should we meet tomorrow for lunch?" Those baby-blue eyes demanded an answer.

"All right. Lunch it is." When a gleam of satisfaction lit his eyes, she added, "My treat."

"It's a date," he said, rising to his feet.

Which was exactly what Dena didn't want it to be.

CHAPTER THREE

DENA DRESSED FOR WORK the next morning as she did most days—in comfortable jeans, a T-shirt and a jacket. As usual, she chose to make her fashion statement with her socks, selecting a pair that had the Paris skyline on them. She added her artist palette pin on the lapel of the blazer and felt ready to tackle the day...and Quinn Sterling.

They had agreed to meet at a coffee shop just around the corner from Delaney Design. It was also close to the Excel Center and a good place to have a professional lunch—for that was what it was going to be. It didn't matter what she'd seen in his eyes last night. Today was business.

It was a typical winter day in Minnesota, with a strong wind making the air feel a lot colder than the temperature indicated. Dena expected Quinn to be waiting inside the lobby of the building where the coffee shop was located. He wasn't. He stood outside in the cold, wearing a leather jacket, but no gloves and no hat—as if there wasn't a subzero windchill factor. He was tough. It seemed that adjective popped in her mind frequently when she was around him.

When he saw her he smiled and said, "Hi, neighbor." It was a sexy kind of grin that said he was happy to see her—and not because she lived downstairs from him.

"Hello." She tried to make her smile one of a business nature. Under her arm she carried a portfolio, which she switched to the other arm in order to shake his hand.

He held the door for her so she could enter first the office building, then the coffee shop. She felt his hand at her back as he ushered her toward the small sign that read: Please wait to be seated.

"It's cold out there." She felt the need to make small talk as they waited for the hostess to seat them.

"It's not bad for the middle of February," he commented, then turned his attention to the young woman who greeted him by name.

"Two?" the hostess asked, eyeing Dena curiously.

"You got it," he said with a broad smile, his hand still at Dena's back.

"Right this way." The young woman picked up two menus and motioned for them to follow her. Dena could feel eyes glancing in their direction as they walked the length of the coffee shop. When Quinn nodded and said hello to a couple of men seated at the counter, she knew it was because they'd recognized him as a hockey player.

He removed his jacket and she saw again just how massive he was. He looked too wide to be sitting on a bench seat made for one, and she thought he should have asked for a regular booth that seated four.

She looked around and wondered how many of the curious glances had come their way because he'd been recognized.

As if he knew what she was thinking, he said, "If heads turned when we came in, it's because I'm usually in here with a couple of banged-up hockey players, not a beautiful woman."

As much as she didn't want the compliment to affect her, she couldn't prevent the tiny rush of pleasure his words created. She gave him a look she'd perfected years ago—the one that said, *Give me a break. That line's as old as the hills,* and dismissed the comment with a question.

"Do you get recognized often?" she asked.

He shrugged. "It depends on where I am. If I'm at an ice arena, yes. If I'm at an art museum, no. Be honest. Until we met, would you have recognized me if you'd been sitting here in this coffee shop having lunch?"

"No. I've never seen a Minnesota Cougars game." As soon as she'd said the words, she wished she could retract them. It wasn't what she should have said, considering the favor she needed to ask. "But then I just moved here from Rhode Island," she explained.

Again that wonderful smile of his made an appearance as he said, "It's all right. You're not a hockey fan. You don't need to pretend that you are. Actually, I like the fact that you aren't."

"You do?"

He nodded. "It makes it easier."

She wanted to ask, *Easier for what?* but decided to let it go.

If she'd hoped that discussion of menu selections and the appearance of their server would put the tone of their conversation back on a less personal track, she was wrong. The first thing he asked her when they resumed talking was, "Why did you leave Maddie and Dylan's wedding early?"

"What makes you think I left early?"

"Because I searched the entire ballroom for you. If you had been there, I would have found you."

If she'd had any doubt as to his interest in her, it was certainly put to rest by the way he was looking at her. His words caught her by surprise and at the same time sent another tremor of excitement through her.

"I left early because I had to catch a plane the next morning. I was still living in Rhode Island at the time," she told him.

"That's a shame. That was one terrific wedding celebration. I'm only sorry that I came late to the party." She could hear the sincerity in his voice and see the regret in his eyes.

"It was a nice day for them," she said simply.

"Tell me what you were doing in Rhode Island," he urged, leaning forward so that he was closer to her.

"Working, which is what I'm supposed to be doing now." She reached for the portfolio that contained the legal documents he needed to sign.

"Oh, that's right. You want something from me." She thought she detected a hint of disappointment in his voice. "Not for myself. For Aaron Jorgenson."

"There's another charity event?"

"Not an event exactly, but it is a fund-raiser to help with his medical bills." She told him about the plans for the calendar featuring celebrity graduates of Minnesota high schools, ending with, "Each month will have a different celebrity in front of their alma maters."

He leaned back. "Ah, I get it. You want me to be one of the so-called Minnesota stars, right?"

She nodded. "Mr. January. You're perfect for the spot. Hockey is a winter sport, and you did go to the same high school as Aaron Jorgenson."

"What kind of a photo would this be?"

"Probably one of you in your uniform on the ice rink behind your old school but you can work out the details when you meet with the art director. And as for scheduling the photo shoot—it would be at your convenience, of course. Here." She pulled out the letter of introduction she'd been given and passed it to him. "This should answer any questions you have."

He gave it a quick glance, then set it down. "I'd have to have my agent look this over to make sure there's not a problem with my contract."

She nodded in understanding. "Of course. And if he says there are no problems?"

He shrugged. "Then I'll do it."

Relief washed over her. She couldn't believe it was so easy to get him to agree.

Then he said, "On one condition."

Apprehension crept through her. "And that is?"

"That you return the favor."

"And do what?" She chuckled. "I'm not a celebrity."

"You don't need to be a celebrity to do charity work," he reminded her.

"No, you're right." She took a drink of water to wet her dry mouth. "What is it you want me to do?"

"Help out one of the nonprofit organizations the Cougars sponsor," he told her.

She knew the local professional sports teams took active roles in the community because she'd seen them on the nightly news. "If you get me a list, I'd be happy to make a donation to one of them," she suggested.

"I'm not talking about giving cash, Dena. These

programs need volunteers who will give their time."
His eyes didn't waver from hers.

"All right. I'll volunteer my time. As I said, send
me a list and I'll be happy to help out."

"I trust you're a woman of your word?" he asked
with a lift of his water glass.

"Of course. You have a deal, Mr. Sterling." She
stretched out her hand and he took it in a grip that
said he didn't want to let it go again.

Fortunately their food arrived and he was forced to
drop her hand. Dena ate her soup and sandwich as
fast as possible, wanting to get back to her office. She
made the appropriate small talk but was grateful when
the waitress dropped the check on the table.

She snatched it up and glanced pointedly at her
watch. "I'm sorry, but I'm on a really tight schedule."

"No problem," he said, getting to his feet so he
could help her with her coat but she slipped it on
before he had a chance.

"If you'll just look at the information that's in that
envelope..." She trailed off, buttoning the front. "I
think it's all pretty self-explanatory."

"If I have any questions, I suppose I could always
tap three times on the floor," he said with a crooked
smile.

"It would probably be better for you to call Greg
Watkins. He's the person in charge of the project."

"I'd rather call you."

The look he gave her said it wasn't because he'd
have questions about the calendar. He was definitely
interested in her. She could see it in his eyes.

"I've got to get back to work," she said, tugging
on her gloves.

He escorted her out of the coffee shop, his hand at her back. When she walked beside him she felt small and fragile, a rare experience for someone as tall as she was. She discovered she rather liked the feeling and wished that it had been other circumstances that had brought them together. She imagined a guy like Quinn Sterling could make a woman feel special in a lot of ways.

As she said goodbye to him outside, she realized there was no place for those kind of thoughts in her mind. He was an assignment and one she'd completed. There would be no reason for her to have any contact with him again other than the occasional hello that neighbors give one another. She'd experienced the power of celebrity charisma and had come through without any scars. Now she could go back to the real world. Her work.

DENA THOUGHT that once she delivered the news that Quinn Sterling had agreed to be Mr. January, her part in the calendar project would be finished. She never expected Greg Watkins would ask her to go with him to the photo shoot.

"I hope this guy shows up," the art director said as they sat in the Delaney van with the engine running, waiting for Quinn to arrive. The camera crew had already set up their equipment on the skating rink. "If we have to reschedule, this snow and ice could be gone."

"He'll show up," Dena said as she stared out the window, hoping that she was right. The outdoor conditions were ideal, especially for the first week in March. She knew that an early spring could turn the solid ice into slush and force them indoors for the shoot. Besides, if Quinn didn't show up, she was going to feel responsible, which was ridiculous. All she'd done was get him to agree to do the calendar. She hadn't even recommended him for the job.

"Well, I hope he's on time. The professional athletes I've worked with have acted like the world should wait for them," Greg said with disdain.

Dena didn't comment but pushed back her cuff to see her watch. "He has seven more minutes to get here before you can call him late."

"This Sterling character must have had his picture taken often enough that this should be a piece of cake. I hope it goes *bing-bing* and we're done," he said, snapping his fingers. "I don't fancy having to stand out in the cold for hours on end."

"I thought that was why you brought me. So I could stand out in the cold," she quipped.

"I brought you because you were a part of the deal." He tapped his gloved fingers on the steering wheel. "Besides, if you want to be an art director someday, this is good practice."

She could have pointed out that she'd done her part of the deal—getting Quinn Sterling to agree to be in the calendar. Instead she focused on the fact that he'd brought her along because he wanted her to get experience. That meant he thought she had the potential to serve as one of the eight art directors at the agency, that she was talented enough to work at the same level as he.

"Yes, it is, and I thank you for such an opportunity," she said sincerely. She knew that he could have chosen any one of the graphic designers working under him to accompany him on the shoot, yet he'd chosen her.

"Don't thank me. I would have left you behind except Quinn Sterling said the only way he'd do the shoot was if you were there."

"You're kidding, right?" When he didn't answer, she said, "Oh my gosh, you're not." Disappointment replaced the thrill of pleasure his earlier words had produced.

"Do you have something going with this guy?" he asked, giving her a slanted glance.

"No!" she denied vigorously. "Good grief, he's my neighbor. That's all."

"I don't care what he is as long as he's on time." His attention was captured by the silver SUV approaching. "And it looks like he is."

Dena recognized the vehicle and knew it was Quinn.

"Okay, let's get this over with," Greg said when the SUV had parked on the other side of the photographer's van.

Dena pulled on her gloves and went out into the cold. They walked over to Quinn's SUV, where he stood with the back open.

Other than shaking his hand and saying hello, Dena remained quiet, content to let Greg do the talking. Determined to keep everything on a professional level, she followed the art director's instructions and paid close attention to the technical aspects as the photographer did his job.

To her surprise, Quinn treated her as impersonally as he did the others at the shoot. He said little, cooperating in a manner with which Dena knew Greg could find no fault. There were no flirtatious glances, no sexy smiles tossed her way. By the time it was over, she was wondering why he had even insisted that she be there and decided she'd misread his interest in her earlier.

When the last of the shots had been taken, he skated over to the wooden bench from where Dena had watched the shoot. He sat down beside her so he could slip a pair of skate guards over his blades.

"So how do you think it went?" he asked.

"Good. Richard Davis does beautiful work. I think you're going to be pleased with the results," she said, nodding toward the photographer. "Greg has already shown me the proofs for several of the calendar models, and they're incredible." It had started to snow, and huge white flakes fell around them. She caught some in her gloved hand and said, "Looks like we finished just in time."

When she glanced at him, he was staring at her. The look of interest was back on his face. There was no mistaking it and his words confirmed it. "I'm glad you came today."

"Greg told me you requested I be here."

"Yeah, I did," he said, taking off his gloves.

"Why?"

"Because I like being around you."

She thought the warmth of his words could have melted the snow settling on her coat. "I didn't think you even noticed I was here," she said softly.

He gazed into her eyes and said, "Believe me, I noticed."

"Dena!" Greg called out from a few feet away, causing her to look away from those penetrating eyes. "You can head back to the van if you want. I'm going to talk to Richard."

"I will. It's cold out here," she called back to him, then rose to her feet.

Quinn got up, too. "I have something for you. Come with me," he said, nodding toward the parking lot.

The cars were only a few steps from the ice rink. As soon as Quinn reached his, he stashed his sticks, gloves and helmet in the back, then went around to the side to open the passenger door. He reached into the glove compartment, pulled out a slip of paper and handed to her.

On it was a date and an address. "What's this?" she asked.

"Your end of our agreement," he answered.

"It's only a time and a place. What am I supposed to do with it?"

"Do you like to read?"

"I love to read."

"Good. That's an elementary school in St. Paul. The kids there love reading. The Cougars have set up a program that encourages them to read as many books as they can. Once a month we visit the school, read a few stories to them and then talk about books they've read—you know, what they liked and didn't like, that sort of thing."

"And where do I fit into this picture?"

"You're going to be a part of the program. They love having adults read to them."

"I'm sure they love having famous *hockey players* read to them," she corrected.

"Listen, some of these kids don't even have a clue what I do for a living," he pointed out, then added with a wry grin, "so you won't feel out of place."

Oh, yes, she would. Just being around him was enough to make her feel as if she were way out of her league.

"It's a great program and not a bad way to spend a morning," he went on. "And you're lucky because the next visit isn't until the twenty-fifth so you have a couple of weeks to prepare."

"Prepare?"

"To see me again," he said with a sexy grin.

Yes, it was getting to the point that she did need an advance warning as to when that grin was going to be flashed her way. She only wished she were immune to its power. It was sheer craziness to fall for that kind of charm, especially since he was a man whose life was in the public spotlight. She already had a list of bad choices she'd made when it came to men. There was no point in adding another name to it. And she wasn't naive enough to think that he was asking her to do the reading program because they were short on volunteers.

"I'd love to help the kids, but I really haven't been at my job long enough to be asking for time off," she suggested, knowing it would be wise to keep their relationship on a professional level.

"You want me to ask Greg for the green light on this one?" He nodded toward the art director, who was still on the ice.

She shook her head. "No, please don't. Maybe I could donate some books."

"I'm not asking for books, Dena. I'm asking for your time. We made a deal, remember?" There was a challenge in his eyes, and she had a feeling it had nothing to do with books and reading.

Just then her boss called out to her.

"Can I count on you to be there?" Quinn wanted to know.

She looked at the date and address of the school

one more time, then shoved the slip of paper into her coat pocket. "All right, I'll be there. I'd better go. We'll be in touch," she told him, then hurried back to the Delaney van.

ALTHOUGH DENA KNEW she could be quite happy without a man in her life, she had to admit there were times when having one around did come in handy. Bringing a new computer home was one of those times. At the electronics store, she'd had help loading the boxes into her car. Now, parked behind 14 Valentine Place, she knew it was going to be a challenge to get them into her second-floor apartment.

Her only option was to take them one at a time. She bent to get the largest box, wrapping her arms around its width. With a grunt she straightened, only to find Quinn at her side. He'd left his jacket indoors and had come outside wearing a gray University of Minnesota sweatshirt and a pair of jeans.

"Let me help you with that," he said, relieving her of the burden.

Grateful for the offer, she mumbled a thank-you, then bent to pick up a smaller carton.

"I can take another one," he said, nodding toward the remaining box in the car.

Of course he could. He was a big guy. She set a slightly smaller box on top of the one already in his hands, which left only a small bag of accessories for her to pick up. She reached for it, then closed the trunk.

He followed her up the stairs to the second floor where she unlocked the door and let him in. Most men would have been breathing heavily if they'd carried such a load. He looked as if he'd carried a loaf of bread.

"Any particular place I should set these?" he asked, making a quick survey of the room.

"The floor is fine," she said, gesturing with her arm.

"Anything else I can do for you?" His look intimated that his offer wasn't limited to hauling boxes up the stairs.

"No, that should do it. Thanks for your help," she said, noticing the way he took in the contents of her room.

"You're welcome. It's important for neighbors to help one another out, don't you think?"

"Yes," she agreed. "I'd offer you something to drink but I only have mineral water."

"Mineral water is fine," he told her, stepping farther into the room.

She had a small portable refrigerator in which she stored just enough things so that she didn't have to use the main kitchen on the first floor. She pulled a plastic bottle from it and handed it to him.

"Thanks." He unscrewed the cap and took a drink, then said, "This place sure has changed since the last time I was here. I suppose you know that before Leonie remodeled the house, this floor had boys' bedrooms on it."

"I did hear something about that," she said, aware of his scrutiny of her things.

"I can tell you one thing, it was never this neat."

Dena was glad she'd straightened the place before she'd left for the mall.

He moved over to her desk and leaned closer to

peer at the models on her shelf. "These are cool. Did
you do them?"

She nodded. "I'm working on packaging for soy
nuts."

He wrinkled his nose slightly. "Soy nuts?"

She reached for a small covered dish and removed
the lid. "Try some."

He held up his hand and shook his head. "No,
thanks. I tried soy milk once and that was enough of
an introduction to soy for me."

She shrugged. "These are actually pretty good.
They come in flavors like honey roasted, barbecue…"

Her words didn't convince him to give them a try.
"You do most of your work on a computer?"

Again she nodded. "Most of it."

"Is that why you bought the new system? So you
could bring work home?"

"Yes. Plus I also freelance. Brochures, business
cards…that sort of thing." When it became apparent
he wasn't in any hurry to leave, she said, "You probably have stuff you want to do. Please don't let me
keep you from it."

"Not tonight. It's why I was in Leonie's kitchen
when you pulled into the driveway." Again there was
no mistaking the interest in his eyes. She'd seen it the
afternoon they'd had lunch and again at the photo
shoot.

"Lucky for me. I'm not sure how I would have
gotten that box up those stairs without help." She
nodded toward the computer cartons.

"It wasn't luck. I was waiting for you to come
home. I'd already tried knocking on your door so I
went downstairs to see if Leonie knew where you

were.'' He moved closer to her and she caught the fresh scent of soap.

''Why were you looking for me?''

''To find out if you're having as much trouble trying not to think about me as I'm having trying not to think about you.'' His voice was seductively soft.

She wanted to roll her eyes and tell him she'd heard better lines from high school boys, but there was no sly twinkle in his eyes, no cocky tilt to his head. Just a sincerity that made her totally aware of him as a man.

If she had wanted to be coy, she could have tossed back her hair and asked why he imagined she'd been thinking about him at all. It was probably what a lot of women would have done. Not many women would pass up an opportunity to flirt with a guy like Quinn Sterling. And she could only imagine what hockey groupies would have done if they had been in her shoes.

Only Dena had never been any good at flirting. Nor was she of the groupie mentality. She didn't even like hockey. Yet if she were honest with herself, this man standing next to her had preoccupied her thoughts lately...and not only because of his connection with the charity projects.

She didn't want him to know that, however, and said, ''I'm sorry. I'm sure you get a lot of people asking you to give of your time for various charity functions. I promise I won't bug you anymore.''

''That's not what I meant and you know it.''

She tried to give him a blank stare of puzzlement, but there was no mistaking the look in his eye. He was attracted to her.

''Have you had dinner yet?'' he asked.

She was about to tell him she had, but then her stomach growled and he smiled and said, "You haven't. Good. I haven't, either. Come over to Dixie's with me. We'll have a little wine, eat some ribs and we can get to know each other a little better. If we're going to be neighbors asking each other for favors, we should at least do that, don't you think?"

She met his gaze boldly. "What I think is that you're not asking me because you want to be neighborly."

"And does that bother you?"

"Yes." She could see no point in lying.

"Why? Are you in a relationship with someone?"

"No, but we don't exactly have a lot in common."

"Now, that is something we don't really know yet, do we? If you come with me to Dixie's, we'll find out." The blue eyes held a hint of a challenge.

As much as she hated to admit it, she was tempted to say yes. It had been a long time since she'd found a man interesting. And it wasn't as if she would be expecting another dinner after this one. He probably had a long list of women he went out with.

"So what's it going to be, Dena? Yes or no?"

Not wanting him to see that she was attracted to him, she shrugged casually and said, "Yes."

He gave her a smile that said she'd made the right choice. "Great." He moved toward the open door. "Is seven okay?"

She nodded. "Seven's fine."

"Good. I'll see you then."

CHAPTER FOUR

QUINN STARED at the woman sitting across from him eating barbecued ribs. She was nothing at all like the women he usually dated. No painted fingernails. No fake eyelashes. No dark roots to her blond hair. As far as he could tell, she wasn't trying to fool him about anything. Actually, she looked as if she didn't care whether she impressed him or not.

He could see that Dena Bailey dressed to please herself and no one else. He guessed it was probably the artist in her that made her want to be different from the millions of women who pored over fashion magazines in search of the latest trends. She made a statement with what she wore.

This evening she had on a denim jacket that had all sorts of iron-on patches on it, including one that said, "What you see is what you get." So far he liked what he'd seen. He wasn't sure that it was a good thing, however. She was the kind of woman a man settled down with, and he wasn't looking for a serious relationship.

It wasn't that there weren't guys who were married and raising families while having a career in the NHL. The lifestyle of a professional hockey player made it difficult to be a husband and father, yet there were those who managed to make it work despite the amount of time they spent away from their families.

Quinn had been raised by parents who came home and ate dinner with their kids every night, and that was how he wanted his family life to be. Someday.

But not yet. As long as hockey was the most important thing in his life, there was no reason to think about settling down and starting a family. No reason to be interested in a woman like Dena. Yet he was.

When she licked a finger covered in barbecue sauce, he couldn't help but smile.

"What? Do I have sauce on my chin or something?" she asked, quickly dabbing at her face with her napkin.

"No, you're fine."

She eyed him suspiciously.

"I was just thinking that not many of the women I've dated in the past few years would have been comfortable eating barbecued ribs at Dixie's, that's all," he told her.

"And what kind of women have you been dating...as if I need to ask," she said, rolling her eyes.

"There haven't been any graphic designers in the group," he admitted.

"Well, that explains it. We designers are a messy finger bunch." To prove her point, she deliberately swiped at a rib and then made a creative swirl in her mashed potatoes. "There. Art." Again she licked her finger.

He found the action incredibly sensuous. "Are you trying to discourage me from being interested in you? Because if you are, it's not working."

She wiped her fingers on her napkin, then leaned both elbows on the table and met his gaze. "I'm still trying to figure out why you are interested. We really don't have much in common, Quinn."

"We both like barbecued ribs," he said smugly.

"And dark beer," she said, lifting her glass.

"We both put in a lot of time on the job." When she nodded, he added, "Our jobs are really pretty similar in nature."

That shifted her attention from her plate to his face. "You're kidding, right? You honestly think that playing hockey for a living and being a graphic designer are alike?"

"In certain aspects, yes."

"Such as?"

"They're jobs that you don't get unless you're blessed with a certain talent. In my case, an athletic ability that allows me to play hockey, and in yours, a gift of artistic creativity that allows you to design things."

She raised her brows in acknowledgment. "You have a point."

"And you told me you work best when you're under pressure. So do I."

"Okay, so we have a little in common. A little," she repeated, measuring just how little it was by holding her forefinger about an inch from her thumb. "I do work twelve months out of the year."

He grinned. "All right, I get a slightly longer break than the average person, but those eight months I'm working can be a grind. I spend half of my life on the road in more than twenty cities across the United States and Canada."

"So you consider playing hockey work, not a game?"

By the way one brow arched, he could see that she didn't. "It is work and it isn't," he contradicted himself. "It's a game and it's fun, but there's also a lot of hard work that goes into it...and I'm not just referring to the physical conditioning aspect.''

"So tell me what it's like," she encouraged him.

To his surprise, she listened with great interest as he explained aspects of professional hockey most people never questioned. Not once did he feel as if he were boring her, nor did she try to change the subject and talk about herself, as many of the women he'd dated had done. She didn't hang on his every word or bat her eyelashes at him in awe. She simply listened intently to what he was saying.

By the time they'd finished eating, he realized that he'd done most of the talking, which was exactly the opposite of what he had planned. He'd invited her to dinner because he'd wanted to find out more about her.

When their server asked if they wanted dessert, he was surprised when Dena ordered a slice of the chocolate cake and coffee. Not many of the women he dated finished their meals, let alone ate dessert.

"You like chocolate, too?" she asked when he requested the same thing.

"Yes. Another thing we can add to the list," he said with a grin.

"I think there's something else."

"And what's that?"

"We're both passionate about our work." She took a sip of the coffee the server had just poured, then looked at him over the rim and said, "We're also both in very competitive fields."

"That's true. People don't buy a ticket to see their favorite team lose." He opened a small container of cream and poured it into his coffee. "If you're going to play the game, you gotta compete. Fortunately, I've always loved a challenge.''

"Is that why you find me interesting?"

He liked her straightforwardness. He was used to women who pretended to enjoy his sport, even if they didn't know the first thing about hockey. Dena didn't even attempt to try to convince him that she found the game exciting.

"It is rather refreshing to meet someone who's not the least bit impressed that I'm a hockey player," he stated candidly. "In fact, I think for you, my job is actually a deterrent, isn't it?"

"I'm not going to get all gooey-eyed because you know how to swing that stick around on the ice," she said with a twinkle in her eye.

"You don't strike me as the type to get all gooey-eyed over any man," he observed on a thoughtful note.

"You're right, I'm not."

There was a warning in her tone. It said, *I may have agreed to come have dinner with you, but that doesn't mean I'm going to jump into bed with you because you're Quinn Sterling, Cougar defenseman.*

"Have you ever been married?" he found himself asking her.

She chuckled then. "No. Have you?"

He shook his head. "Not even close."

"Me, neither. The longest I've ever dated anyone is three months. I've discovered that not many men like to come in second to a woman's career."

It was as if she was telling him to be forewarned, not to expect anything from her, which was rather ironic, since he'd been dishing out that sentiment for most of his adult life. How many times had he told a woman that he wasn't ready to settle down because of his job? Could it be that he had finally met someone who thought like he did?

Curious, he asked, "So what exactly are your career goals?"

"I'd like to have my own agency someday, but first I need to move up the ranks at Delaney Design."

"Then there are opportunities for you there?"

She took another sip of her coffee. "Oh, yes, the next step is to make art director."

"You mean take Watkins's job?"

"Not necessarily his. There is more than one art director at an agency the size of Delaney Design."

The server brought the chocolate cake. Quinn enjoyed watching her savor each bite, encouraging her to talk about work as they ate.

When they had finally finished and he'd settled the check, he said, "I enjoyed this evening, Dena. It was fun discovering what we have in common."

When she stood, he helped her with her coat. As he did his hand brushed her hair. It was silky smooth and he wished it were hanging loose instead of tied back with a scarf.

"Thanks for telling me about hockey," she said as he steered her toward the exit. "I've never even been on a pair of skates so it's hard for me to understand why there's so much enthusiasm for the sport."

He shook his head. "I can't believe you don't skate. You said you grew up in Iowa. Winters there are about as long as Minnesota's are."

"Not quite, and not everyone who lives in a cold climate skates in the winter," she reminded him.

"Now, that is something I don't understand. When

we were kids my friends and I were outside on the ice whenever we had the chance.''

"Leonie said you skated at her house."

He nodded. "Either there or at the park. The city would flood two rinks—one for figure skating, the other for hockey."

"What about your parents? Didn't you have a rink in your backyard, too?"

He shook his head. "Couldn't. We lived on a hill. It was great for sledding, though."

"Didn't you ever skate indoors?" she asked as they stepped out into the cold.

"Not very often. Indoor ice time cost money. But I'd rather be outdoors, anyway. There's something exhilarating about skating outside on a crisp winter night."

"Are you sure exhilaration isn't a euphemism for frostbite?" she asked on a sardonic chuckle. "Winters are so cold in Minnesota."

"But you don't get cold if you're skating. That's the beauty of it."

"Then why do they have warming houses?"

He grinned. "All right. Maybe your toes get a little cold and then you go inside to hang out with your friends…grab some hot chocolate, eat some junk food from the vending machines. Be seen."

"Well, I'm sorry to say I missed that particular youth experience."

They had reached his SUV, and he opened the passenger door for her to climb inside. When he got in behind the wheel, he looked at her and said, "On our next date, I promise not to talk about hockey so much."

She tilted her head. "Was this a date?"

For an answer he leaned across the seat and placed a kiss on her lips. Her mouth was warm, soft and inviting, tempting him to give in to the desire building inside him. Surprised by the intensity of his longing, he pulled back. The look he saw in her eyes mirrored what he was feeling: she hadn't expected such a reaction to what should have been a simple kiss.

Only he was discovering there was nothing simple about Dena Bailey. He started the engine and drove home.

Neither one spoke until they were outside her door and she said, "Thanks for dinner."

"You're welcome." He should have said a polite good-night and left, but he couldn't resist taking her mouth one more time. Again desire shot through him as his lips seized hers. When her mouth opened slightly, every instinct inside him urged him to respond to the silent invitation.

But he didn't. He simply lifted his mouth from hers and said, "See you around, neighbor."

DENA HAD NEVER DATED ANYONE whose name appeared regularly in the newspaper. Although one dinner didn't exactly give her the right to say she was dating Quinn, it did cause her to look at the sports page to find the Cougars schedule for the upcoming week. She wanted to know when she could expect to see him again—if she was going to see him again. She wasn't naive enough to think that a couple of kisses and a "see you around, neighbor" meant he would ask her out on another date.

It was one of the reasons she hadn't told anyone about their dinner at Dixie's. She didn't want Lisa to get any ideas about a romance developing, and she seldom talked about her social life with her co-workers. She didn't need her personal relationships to be the topic of discussion over the company's water cooler.

As far as anyone at Delaney Design was concerned, her relationship with the hockey player was strictly business. That's why when a courier delivered an envelope from the Minnesota Cougars organization addressed to her, no one paid much attention. Even Dena thought the envelope contained documents pertaining to Quinn's photo shoot. She was surprised to find two tickets to a Cougars home game and a brief note saying they were compliments of Quinn Sterling.

She looked at the date and frowned. They were for the following Tuesday. On Wednesday she would be presenting her ideas for the soy nuts advertising campaign. That meant her Tuesday would be a crazy blur of working late into the evening to get ready. She couldn't possibly go to the game.

She picked up the phone to call Quinn, but then stopped before she punched a single number. It was a call she didn't want to make, a call she couldn't make, because she wanted to go to the game.

"Here, catch!"

She was distracted by the appearance of Greg Watkins in the doorway of her cubicle. He tossed a small cardboard box in her direction.

"What's this?" she asked as it landed in her hands.

"Your neighbor's bobblehead. Thought you might like one," he told her, then disappeared.

Dena tore open the packaging and pulled out the figurine wrapped in bubble wrap. It was a six-inch-high hockey player with the number thirty-two on his jersey. She smiled at the uncanny resemblance it bore to Quinn Sterling.

When she went home that evening she set it on the shelf above her desk. She was at her desk when there was a knock on her door. Hoping it might be Quinn, she was disappointed to see her brother outside her apartment.

"Don't look so happy to see me," he said with sarcasm.

She pulled him by the arm and urged him inside. "I am happy to see you. My mind was on something else, that's all."

He glanced over her shoulder to the computer station. "What? Work? You're not still at it, are you?"

"I'm doing a freelance project. Don't look at me like that."

"Like what?" he asked innocently.

"Like I'm doing something wrong."

He let that statement dangle and handed her three boxes. "Lisa sent me over with these."

"Ooh, the Girl Scout cookies!" She accepted them with enthusiasm.

"Bethany wanted to deliver them personally, but she's got a bad cold. Lisa's been sneezing, too, so I was elected to be the delivery boy. You got time for a cup of coffee?" He held up his other hand, which contained a Starbucks bag.

"Sure. Take off your coat and I'll crack open these cookies," she said, pulling the cellophane from one of the boxes.

He hung his red plaid jacket on one of the hooks near the door, then glanced at her computer monitor. "Do you work every night?"

"No, not every night," she said, again feeling on

the defensive. "The newsletter I'm doing now is a piece of cake compared to the project I'm working on at Delaney."

He studied her face. "You work too hard. You know that, don't you?"

She nodded. "I have to. I need to make up for lost time. Have you forgotten? I spent four years in marketing before I switched careers."

He chuckled. "You're only twenty-nine. You've plenty of time to make a name for yourself in the advertising world."

"I know," she said placatingly.

"So why burn the candle at both ends?"

"Because I want to." She reached for one of the coffees and sat down.

"Don't say that. You're starting to sound like Dad."

"I will never let myself become like Dad," she vowed, putting the emphasis on *never*. "I care about family, which is why I'm not going to even think about having one of my own until I've reached my career goals. As you said, I am only twenty-nine. Lots of women are starting families in their late thirties and even early forties." She took a sip of coffee, then said, "Now, let's talk about something other than work and eat some of these cookies."

He sat down beside her and plucked a chocolate-covered cookie from the carton. "I remember when you used to sell these things."

"Me, too. I had the nicest troop leader. It was Mrs. Bremer. Remember her? Tall lady with glasses... taught piano lessons." When he nodded she added, "She was an inspiration. I think I had more badges on my sash than any other Girl Scout in Iowa."

"Mom would groan every time you brought another one home," Ryan recalled with a nostalgic smile. "She hated having to sew."

"She didn't sew them on. Grandma did," Dena pointed out.

"Grandma did a lot of things for us," he said soberly. "She was more like our mother."

Dena nodded. "I still miss her."

"Yeah, I do, too." He paused, then said, "What about Mom? Do you miss her?"

Startled that he would even ask that question, she said, "What?"

"Do you miss her?" he repeated.

"No, why would I? She's been out of my life longer than she was ever in it. I can hardly remember what she looks like." It wasn't exactly the truth, but it was the way Dena wished it could be. She didn't want to remember a woman who'd turned her back on her children.

"She's never tried to get in touch with you?"

"No. Why? Have you talked to her?" Dena found herself holding her breath while she waited for his answer.

"Not recently."

"But you have talked to her since she left us, haven't you?"

He nodded, his eyes on the coffee in his hand.

"Why didn't you tell me?"

He shrugged. "I thought about it, but you were at boarding school and having enough problems...." He trailed off.

"Did she contact you, or did you look for her?"

"Lisa went on the Internet. Mom's in New York."

"I don't care where she is," Dena said sharply.

He nodded in understanding. "Anyway, we discovered nothing had changed."

"Did you think it would have?"

"It was right after Jeremy was born. Lisa thought she'd want to know that she was a grandmother."

"Ha!" It was not a happy sound. "She didn't even want to be a mother. Why would she want to be a grandmother?"

"Unfortunately, she didn't."

No matter how hard she tried, Dena couldn't prevent the sharp pain that cut through her chest. She swallowed with difficulty, then said, "How can she be so cold?"

Ryan reached over to squeeze her hand. "It's still painful for you, isn't it?"

"Isn't it for you?" She gazed into eyes full of compassion.

"No, it isn't," he said calmly, and she could see that he was telling the truth. "Maybe because I was almost eighteen when she walked out on us." He shrugged. "It all seems like such a long time ago. Besides, I have my own family now. And someday you will have one, too, and then it won't hurt so much."

Dena nodded, although she wasn't convinced that either statement was true. Judging by her experience with men, she sometimes wondered if she'd ever be a mother and wife. And even after sixteen years, the pain of her mother walking out on her still resonated in her heart.

She didn't want to talk about such things. "Maybe we should change the subject."

"Good idea. Before I forget, Lisa said I should mention our anniversary. It's the second weekend in May."

"Planning ahead, are we?" she asked with a quirky smile.

"Yes, as a matter of fact. I'd like to take her away for the weekend, but before I make reservations, I need to line up a sitter for the kids."

He looked at her, waiting for her response. After a couple of moments of dead air, she said, "You want me to stay with the kids?"

"Would you mind?"

"No, I'd love to do it, but..." She paused, wondering how to explain that she wasn't sure they'd want her to stay with them. "They don't know me very well."

"It's still two months away, and by then, you'll have been over enough that you'll probably be sick of them."

"The other problem is I'm not very good with kids. I mean, I haven't exactly had a lot of experience."

"Jeremy's twelve. He'll point you in the right direction if you have any problems." Ryan obviously thought that was the end of the discussion. He got up and walked over to her desk and picked up the bobblehead of Quinn Sterling. He tapped its head. "Where did you get this?"

"Delaney worked on the promotion. They're giving them away at a game next week."

"Jeremy would love one if you can get your hands on an extra. He's a big Cougar fan."

"He can get his own if he goes to the game with me next Tuesday. Think he'd like to take his aunt and be her guide to professional hockey?"

He chuckled. "Are you kidding! He's going to go nuts when he hears you're taking him to a Cougar game. But are you sure you want to go with a twelve-year-old boy?"

"You said he knows hockey like the back of his hand."

"He does, but I should warn you. A twelve-year-old boy at a hockey game can be…well, a little boisterous."

She held up both hands. "I'm warned."

"So how did you get the tickets?"

"Through work. I told you about that calendar we did with the Minnesota celebrities. Quinn Sterling is on it."

"So you've talked to him, then?"

"Yeah, why?" she asked nonchalantly.

He shrugged. "I was just wondering what he's really like."

"He's okay. He was polite," she said, avoiding his eyes. "I have proofs from the photo shoot we did with him." She found the glossies on her desk and handed them to her brother. "Here."

"I don't suppose you could get him to autograph one of these for Jeremy?" he asked as he flipped through the pictures.

She shrugged. "If I see him. He's not home much."

"That would be great." Ryan glanced at his watch. "I've gotta go. Have to pick up Jeremy from his game. He's going to be so excited when he hears what you have planned." He reached for his jacket.

"I'll call Lisa and let her know what time I'll be by to pick him up."

"Thanks, Dena. It's a nice thing you're doing for

Jeremy. I know you could have taken someone from Delaney."

"I'd rather take Jeremy because I know he'll enjoy the game."

"He sure will. The question is, will you?"

DENA DIDN'T FIND OUT the answer to that question because on Tuesday afternoon she got tied up in a meeting about the soy nuts campaign that lasted until well after the Excel Center had been emptied of its hockey fans. At the last minute she'd had to call Ryan to come get the tickets so that he could take Jeremy to see the Cougars play.

The following morning, when her brother phoned to tell her what a great game she'd missed, she felt twinges of regret. Not only because she'd wanted to see Quinn play, but because he'd sent her the tickets and she had had to give them away.

That night when she got home from work, she knocked on his door, hoping he'd be in so that she could thank him personally. She also wanted to explain why she hadn't been able to go to the game. However, he wasn't home and the rest of the week passed without her seeing him.

On Saturday morning she went down to the kitchen for breakfast, hoping she might run into him. The only person she saw was Leonie, who reminded Dena that she was hosting her annual Goodbye to Winter party that night. Dena was not fond of parties, and, after a hectic week at work, all she wanted to do was curl up with a good book in the privacy of her apartment.

And she would have done just that had Krystal not come to her door dressed in green velveteen pants, a glittering pin in the shape of a star on her hip and a sparkly gold camisole. "I came to get you for the party."

"I'm not going." She motioned toward her computer. "I have all this work…"

"You can't work on Saturday night."

"Who says?" Dena asked with a wry smile.

"Me." Krystal walked past her into the apartment. "Besides, Leonie is going to be so hurt if you don't at least put in an appearance."

Dena groaned. "Please tell me she won't care that I'm not there."

"What do you think? This is her one big bash of the year. And she's such a dear." If her intent was to make Dena feel guilty, she was succeeding. "Can't you come down for just a few minutes? You know, put in an appearance and then leave?"

Dena didn't want to. She wouldn't know anyone except Krystal and Leonie. *And Quinn,* a tiny voice reminded her. She eyed Krystal's clothing. "I'm not dressed for a party…not a fancy one, anyway."

"This isn't fancy," she said, flicking her wrist at her pants. "And you look great in what you're wearing."

Dena glanced in the full-length mirror. She had on a pair of jeans and a camel blazer. "I suppose I could add a scarf," she said, pulling open her closet to reveal an entire rack of silk scarves.

"These are great," Krystal said, running her fingers across the luxurious fabrics.

She chatted incessantly while Dena tried several scarves, discarding each one in indecision. "Are you sure this is dressy enough?" she asked, staring at her reflection in the mirror.

"If you want to change into something that makes you feel more comfortable, go ahead, but I think you look great," the stylist said, eyeing her critically.

That was the problem. Dena didn't have anything that could make her comfortable in a crowd of strangers.

Some of her angst must have shown on her face, for Krystal said, "You're not nervous about meeting Leonie's friends, are you? You shouldn't be. They're all really cool."

"Yeah, cool *strangers*," Dena pointed out, retying the knot on the scarf.

"If you're nervous, you should wear something blue. I read in Cosmo that it calms a person." Seeing Dena's dubious look, she quickly added, "It's true. The sight of blue triggers your brain's natural tranquilizers."

Dena whipped off the scarf around her neck and pulled another one from her closet. It was screen-printed with a replica of a painting by Monet, one of her favorite artists. She draped it around her shoulders.

"That looks great. You always manage to take ordinary clothes and make them unique with your accessories," Krystal complimented her. "It must be the artist in you."

"Thanks," Dena said as she ran a brush through her hair. She was about to pin it back with a leather slide when Krystal stopped her.

"No, don't do that. Just let it hang. With your natural wave, you have a Veronica Lake look."

"But it'll fall into my eyes," Dena protested as she set the brush down.

"So what? Guys love that."

"Guys?" She grimaced. "This party isn't some sort of matchmaking event for Leonie's clients, is it?"

Krystal laughed. "No, Leonie would never do that. She has a life outside of work, just like the rest of us. Besides, she's a romance coach, not a matchmaker. You'll have a good time. And I can promise you the food will be fabulous." She beckoned to her with her hand. "Now come. We're missing all the fun."

Dena took a deep breath as she descended the staircase to the first floor. When she saw how many people filled the house, she wanted to turn around and go right back up the stairs. She'd never been very good at walking into a room full of strangers and making small talk. Krystal, however, wasn't about to let her escape, keeping a firm grip on her arm.

She took her around, introducing her to an eclectic group of people. Some were neighbors, others were professional acquaintances of Leonie's, and others were family. Krystal seemed to know all of them, and Dena was grateful she had the effervescent stylist at her side.

Then everything changed. A tall, dark-haired man came toward them, a determined look in his eyes. When Krystal saw him, she muttered, "Omigosh, he's back!" Then she rushed into his arms, embracing him in a way that left no doubt in anyone's mind that he was more than a friend.

When they finally separated, Krystal looked back at Dena, then pulled the man by the hand toward her. "This is Roy."

Dena smiled and acknowledged the introduction, making the usual small talk. It didn't take long for her to see that the only reason Roy had come to the party was to be with Krystal. He couldn't take his eyes or his hands off her for even a minute. The way his arm snaked around her waist sent a message to Dena. He was ready to be her companion for the rest of the evening.

Dena wasn't about to stand in the way. She excused herself and headed for the hors d'oeuvres table. She was debating which ones she should try when she heard a voice say, "The shrimp pâté is really good."

Dena turned to see a slender man standing behind her.

He stuck out his hand and said, "Hi, you're Dena, right?" Seeing her puzzled look, he added, "I'm Garret Donovan, Leonie's son. We met at Maddie and Dylan's wedding."

Dena smiled. "Of course. How are you?"

"Considering the number of people in this room, I'm good," he said, returning her smile. "What about you?"

She glanced around. "For this size of a crowd, I'm doing okay, too."

"You probably don't know many people."

"Actually, I think Krystal has introduced me to almost everyone in the room."

"That sounds like Krystal," he said with a grin. "Where is she, by the way?"

Dena looked over to where Roy and Krystal stood entwined. "Over there."

Garret's glance followed hers. "Who's her Siamese twin? I didn't think she was bringing anybody to the party tonight."

"Oh, she didn't bring him. I don't think she even knew he was in town. She said his name is Roy."

"That's Roy?" He frowned.

From the look on his face, Dena could see that it

pained the young doctor to see Krystal with another man. Unless she was mistaken, he had it bad for the stylist and needed to be distracted.

"Were you about to get something to eat?" she asked, gesturing to the table of food.

He turned his attention back to the buffet. "The food is the only reason my mother was able to convince me to come to this thing."

"You don't like parties?"

"Oh, I like them all right—if they have two or fewer people," he quipped, reaching for a plate.

"I know exactly what you mean. Except I can handle up to four people at a time," she said with a wry grin.

He bent to say close to her ear, "Then would you mind telling me what we are doing here?"

"Pleasing your mother, maybe?"

He picked up a celery stick and waved it at her. "Good point." His eyes scanned the room. "Wait here a minute and I'll be right back." He handed her his plate. "Fill this up for me, will you?" Then he disappeared.

By the time she had sampled most of the hors d'oeuvres, he was back at her side and carrying two glasses of wine. "Here. Let's trade." He offered her one of the wineglasses in exchange for a plate of food. "Now, if you'll follow me, I'll show you where we can eat in peace."

She allowed him to lead her away from the crush of bodies and down the hallway to Leonie's office. He pushed open the door and gestured for her to enter. "I asked Mom if we could use this room."

"It's definitely quieter, isn't it," she said, sitting down in one of the leather wing chairs.

"I think it's probably the only room on the first floor that doesn't have people in it," he said as he took the chair next to hers so they were side by side. "Even Jason's room has bodies crammed into it."

"Jason's your younger brother, right?"

He nodded. "He's living in California right now, but Mom hasn't given up hope that he'll come back to Minnesota and return to school. She hasn't touched a thing in his room except to dust. He dropped out of college to go be with his girlfriend, who's pursuing her dream of becoming an actress."

"Ah. I see why she hasn't redecorated the room," she said with an understanding smile.

"That was a year ago," he pointed out.

"Then he must be doing all right."

"He's happy. That's what really matters."

"What about you? Are you happy being a doctor?"

"If you're asking me if I like my work, the answer is yes. The hours, however, are another thing. Residents get very little sleep, and my social life is practically nonexistent. I did finally manage to get a night off, and look at where I am—at a party." He chuckled in self-deprecation. "How smart is that?"

He wasn't expecting an answer and said, "So how do you like living at 14 Valentine Place?"

"So far I like it," she answered honestly. "This is a great house. Your mom has done a wonderful job of renovating it. And she's a good landlady, although I'm sure you've heard that before."

"Yes, I have. Has she told you the history of this place?" When Dena shook her head, he proceeded to tell her how his great-grandfather had the house built back in the early 1900s. All of it was interesting, but it was his tales about the escapades of him and his brothers when they were children that had her laughing out loud.

"Is this a private party or can anyone join in the fun?"

The sound of Quinn's voice had Garret's and Dena's heads turning. There, filling up the doorway, was the hockey player. He wore a forest-green sweater and a pair of casual slacks. The bruise around his eye had faded to a barely noticeable yellow.

"Quinn!" Garret jumped to his feet. "Come on in. You know Dena, don't you?"

"Yes," he said, pinning her with a gaze that said they shared a secret.

"I was just telling her some of the things my brothers and I did in this house when we were kids. You probably would remember a lot of them." Then he turned to Dena and said, "Quinn's from the neighborhood."

"So I've heard." Dena looked at Quinn as she spoke, giving him the same furtive look he'd given her.

"Shane and I are the ones who taught him to play hockey," Garret said with a wink.

"Yeah, and I inspired him to become a doctor," Quinn teased. "I usually ended up bleeding out on that backyard rink, and Garret was the one who always applied a pack of snow to stop it." There was a wistful twinkle in his eyes.

"Did you just get here?" Garret wanted to know.

Quinn nodded. "Your mom told me I'd find you in here."

"You know me and parties. Want to join us?" Garret shoved his plate to the other side of the desk. "Here. Take my chair. I'll use Mom's."

Quinn stepped into the room, carrying a bottle of Rolling Rock beer. As he took the chair next to Dena's, she caught the outdoorsy scent of his cologne.

He had barely sat down when Leonie stuck her head into the office. "Forgive me for interrupting, but I need to steal Garret for a couple of minutes."

Like a dutiful son, the young doctor jumped to his feet and followed Leonie back out into the crowd of partygoers, but not before giving Dena and Quinn orders to carry on without him.

When they were alone, Quinn said, "I like your hair."

Dena had to fight the urge to brush it away from her face. "It was Krystal's idea to leave it loose."

"Krystal knows her stuff." He took a long swig of the beer, then said, "You're missing out on the excitement being in here."

"I think I've had enough excitement for one night," she told him, setting her fork down on her plate. "And food."

"Good. I have, too." He stood and leaned over her chair. "Let's go someplace else."

"But I thought you just got here."

"I did."

"Then you can't leave!" she protested.

"Why not? I only came to see you." He took her plate from her and set it on the desk. "Come. I want to show you something."

"But what about Garret?"

"He's a big boy. He'll be fine."

"Maybe, but I still need to say goodbye to Leonie."

He shrugged. "Sure. You'll need to get your coat, too. And some gloves. And a hat."

"Where are you taking me?"

His grin was cagey. "You'll see."

CHAPTER FIVE

QUINN WAS WAITING for Dena on the second-floor landing when she came out of her apartment. He'd covered his forest-green sweater with a leather jacket and his head sported a stocking hat, cocked at an angle. His hands were bare, but she noticed a pair of gloves sticking out of his pockets.

"I'm glad you didn't change your hair," he said.

Again Dena was reminded of Krystal suggesting that guys found long hair sexy, and she was glad she'd taken her advice. She tugged on her tweed cap, saying, "Are you going to tell me where we're going?"

"I think I'll let it be a surprise." His arm brushed hers as they walked down the stairs side by side.

When they stepped outside, he automatically reached for her elbow to steady her on the slippery walk. They were halfway across the yard when he took her by the shoulders and turned her around. "Look."

She followed his gaze and saw a big round moon. "It's lovely."

"Yes, and it's perfect for what I have in mind."

She waited for him to kiss her, but he didn't. Instead, he led her over to the SUV, where he opened the door and made a gallant sweeping gesture indicating she should get in.

"So we get to travel for this surprise," she said, hoping he'd tell her where they were going. He didn't.

It turned out that they weren't going far. He'd only driven a few blocks when he turned into a parking lot. "This is it," he said, shutting off the engine.

Dena looked outside and saw playground equipment peeking out of the drifted snow. There was a small building in the distance, but no lights shone anywhere. Quinn hopped out of the car and came around to open her door for her.

"Come around to the back," he instructed her. "I have something for you."

What he had was a square box. Even in the dimness of the SUV's dome light she could see the package markings. Inside were women's figure skates.

"Go ahead. Open it," he urged as he handed it to her.

She pulled off the lid and saw a pair of skates. A peek inside the tongue told her they were the correct size. "How did you know what size I am?"

"You left your boots down by the door," he said with a crooked grin.

She lifted a skate from the box and held it up for inspection. It smelled of new leather and the blade sparkled in the moonlight. "They're lovely, but I don't know how to skate."

"I know. I'm going to teach you."

"That's very sweet of you to offer, but I think it's better if the only thing that's between my foot and the ground is the sole of my shoe," she said, stuffing the skate back in the box.

"I promise I won't let you fall."

"Don't make promises you can't keep," she

warned him. "You don't know how uncoordinated I am when it comes to sports."

"Figure skating isn't just a sport. It's an art...and I know you're very artistic." His tone was as sweet as honey. "And it would be a shame to waste a moon like that." He glanced skyward.

Dena had to admit it was a beautiful sight. The full moon cast a glow over the entire park, reflecting off the snow with a luminescence that most photographers could only dream to capture on film.

"Isn't this park closed after ten p.m.?"

"To most people, yes."

She raised one eyebrow. "So being a Cougar grants you special privileges with the parks department?"

He grinned. "No, having an uncle who's in the parks and rec department does, though." He held up a set of keys, dangling them in midair. "We have the warming house all to ourselves...if we want it. You can warm up those toes if you get cold."

Getting cold wasn't what worried her. It was making a fool of herself that had her feeling anxious.

"What do you say? Should I help you lace up your skates?" he asked.

He could be very persuasive when he chose to be. She looked at that handsome face pleading with her to give him a chance and found herself saying, "I think I can manage to get them on my feet, but I'm warning you. You better not laugh when I fall."

"You're not going to fall," he said with confidence as he reached behind her for his own skates.

Dena had her doubts as she laced up the figure skates. To her surprise, she had no problem when she stood. Although she was a little wobbly, with Quinn's arm to steady her she managed to walk over to the skating rink without feeling like a total klutz. Getting onto the ice, however, was another story.

Despite Quinn's promise that he wouldn't let her fall, she came very close to doing just that as her feet slid out from beneath her and she toppled backward. Technically, her body didn't hit the ice because Quinn grabbed her by her arms and kept her from going all the way down to the ground, but she knew that she had come dangerously close to being sprawled out in a very unladylike manner.

"Upsey daisy," he said, propping her back up as if she were a rag doll. "Here. You better stick close to me," he said, wrapping his arm around her tightly.

To her surprise, he didn't give up when at first she didn't succeed. "I think it's my ankles," she told him as she struggled to stay on the skates.

"Just relax. You're doing fine," he said, keeping his hold on her. "You just need to find your balance."

"That's what I've been trying to tell you. I don't have any unless the soles of my feet are flat on the ground."

He didn't pay any attention to her protests. Nor did he run out of patience as he instructed her in the basics of skating. Eventually she was able to glide around the ice without his assistance. He stood watching her in amazement, as if she'd just accomplished a walk on the moon.

"I knew you could do it!" His grin was wide, his stance proud.

"I can, can't I?" she said with an almost childlike jubilation.

Then he hooked his arm in hers and led her around

the rink. When they came to a stop, she stumbled but didn't fall, because he caught her against his chest.

"This is exactly what I had in mind," he told her, taking advantage of their closeness. She could feel his warm breath on her face, and it was all very romantic until she lost her balance.

In a moment of panic she grabbed onto his jacket and pulled him down with her. They went tumbling into the snowbank that rimmed the ice until he lay sprawled on top of her. Startled, she looked into his eyes and saw that he, too, had been caught off guard.

"I'm sorry," she said, her heart pounding in her chest.

"You apologize more than any woman I know," he told her. "This isn't such a bad place to be." His voice had turned husky, his eyes had darkened.

"Aren't you cold?"

"Uh-uh. Are you?"

"No." It was almost a whisper. "You make a good blanket."

Then his mouth was on hers. Unlike the other times he'd kissed her, this was no featherlight touch to tantalize her. It was a kiss full of promise as his mouth moved over hers in a sensuous exploration, giving her a taste of the desire that burned inside him.

It didn't matter that she was on a bed of snow or that the air temperature was below freezing. Warmth spread through her as the kiss deepened, tempting her to forget that they were on the cold ground in a public place. Quinn didn't forget, however.

"As much as I'm enjoying this, I can think of a better place to be doing this," he said as he reluctantly lifted himself from her with an ease she envied. As she struggled to her feet, her ankles wobbled.

"I think we should go sit in the warming house for a bit," she suggested.

He kept his arm around her, as if protecting her from the elements. "That's probably enough skating for one night. I want you to be able to walk tomorrow," he said with a grin.

Dena really didn't want to think about tomorrow, which was why she was pleased when he said, "How about if we go get something hot to drink?"

"Something warm would be nice," she agreed. "But before we go I want to see you skate."

"You've been watching me ever since we got here," he answered.

"No, I've been watching you teach me. Show me how you would skate if you were with a bunch of your hockey buddies."

He did as she requested, skating with a speed and finesse to which television didn't do justice. When he was done, he stopped right in front of her, a spray of ice flying into the air.

"Satisfied?" he asked with a grin.

She applauded but her mittens muffled the sound. "That was amazing. I didn't realize you could skate that fast."

"You would if you had used the tickets I sent you." There was a hint of a reprimand in his words, and she felt contrite. She should have mentioned the tickets when she'd first seen him.

"I'm sorry. I had planned to go to the game, but I ended up having to stay late at work that night, so I gave the tickets to my brother and my nephew."

"So that's who the bearded guy was," he said, a grin spreading across his face. "I should have noticed the family resemblance."

"You didn't think Ryan was a boyfriend, did you?" When he didn't deny it, she said, "I told you I'm not seeing anyone right now."

"Yeah, I know, and I'm really glad, because I'm not seeing anybody right now, either. Well, anyone but you," he amended.

Dena wanted to believe that what he said was true.

WHEN QUINN PULLED INTO the alley behind 14 Valentine Place, Dena assumed he planned for the two of them to return to Leonie's party. Judging by the number of cars lining the street, it was still going strong.

When she would have walked around to the front of the house, he stopped her. "Let's use the back entrance."

"I thought you wanted to go back to the party."

"What gave you that idea?"

"You said we were going to get something warm to drink."

"We are, but on the third floor, not the first," he said with a sexy grin.

So he was inviting her up to his place. Excitement stirred inside her.

At the foot of the stairs he paused. "If you'd rather go back to the party, we can do that."

In other words, if she wasn't ready to take their relationship to the next level, he understood. "No, I'd rather go to your place," she told him.

When they reached the third floor, he unlocked the door and pulled her inside. "Welcome to my world, Dena."

Unlike the apartments on the second floor, Quinn's had its own bath and a small efficiency-size kitchen.

There were actually four rooms, although the wall separating the living room from the kitchen was four feet high. He helped her out of her coat, hanging it next to his on a hook near the entry.

"This is nice," she said, looking around the apartment. "I didn't realize there was so much room up here."

"More than enough for me." He stepped into the small kitchen area. "You like hot chocolate?"

It wasn't what she'd expected him to offer her, thinking more along the lines of brandy or a coffee with Irish Creme. "That sounds good."

"Make yourself at home." He gestured for her to move into the living area, where one whole wall was an entertainment center that housed a projection TV as well as several other pieces of electronic equipment. Resting on the coffee table in front of the leather couch were five remote controls. The only other piece of furniture to sit on was a big leather chair in the shape of a baseball mitt.

She looked around, expecting to see trophies or awards representing his accomplishments as a hockey player. There weren't any and she couldn't resist asking,

"How come you don't have any trophies?"

"I've got a couple in my bedroom, but most of my awards are at my mom's. I thought when my dad retired and they moved into their condo that she'd finally get rid of the stuff that had been in my old room, but she didn't. Instead, she's got this shrine… or at least it feels like a shrine. You know, the pictures, the trophies…all that stuff," he told her from across the counter separating them.

"I'm sure she's proud of your accomplishments.

Are these pictures of your family?'' she asked, noticing a row of frames on one of the shelves of the
bookcase.

"Yeah, those are the Sterlings. Do you see the family resemblance?''

"Yes, most definitely.'' She studied the photos.
"You have three sisters?''

"Yup. Another reason why I spent so much time
at the Donovans'. It was like hormone city at my
house.''

When he finally joined her, she had taken a seat
on the leather sofa. He handed her a mug, then sat
down next to her. "Cheers.''

She echoed his sentiments, raised her mug to his,
then took a sip. The hot chocolate was topped with
whipped cream and laced with alcohol. "Mmm. This
is good. What is it?''

"It's called a Peppermint Patty. I'm surprised you
haven't had one by now. They're everywhere in the
Twin Cities during the winter.'' He reached for one
of the remotes on the glass-topped coffee table and
pressed a button. As soon as the music began she
recognized the voice. It was Chris Isaak.

"I have this CD,'' she said as the sensual love song
drifted around them. "Actually, I have all of his
CDs.''

"Me, too.'' His eyes gleamed with satisfaction.
"So have you warmed up yet?''

"Quite nicely, thank you.'' She took another sip of
the hot chocolate. "This helps.''

"Your cheeks are still red.''

"So are yours,'' she said over the rim of her mug.

"We were outside a long time. Some women I

know would have whined about being in the cold for that length of time.''

"What can I say? I'm a Midwestern girl at heart. All those years in Iowa must have made me hardy."

"You were a good sport."

"It was fun. I enjoyed it." She wondered how many other women he'd taken skating in the moonlight. "Thank you for the skates."

"Every Midwestern girl should have a pair," he said with a grin.

"Even uncoordinated ones?"

"You're a very graceful woman, Dena. Just because you're not athletic doesn't mean you're uncoordinated," he said with a sincerity that, combined with the alcohol, made her feel all warm inside. "Every time I'm with you I discover something else I like about you."

"And what was tonight's discovery? That I've got good antifreeze in my veins and can skate on the frozen tundra?"

"No, that you like being kissed in a snowbank." The look in his eyes reminded her that he had liked it just as much as she had.

She smiled lazily. "I have to admit, that was a first for me. Even though I grew up in Iowa, I never made out on the ground in the snow."

"So I introduced you to two things tonight," he said, a touch of male pride in his voice.

"Actually, three," she said with a lift of her mug. She took another sip of the Peppermint Patty and licked her lips. "Is there a number four?"

His answer was to set both of their mugs on the coffee table, then take her in his arms. The look in his eyes sent a shiver of awareness rippling through her. She knew what that look meant and wasn't surprised when his mouth covered hers in a passionate kiss that had both of them breathing heavily by the time it was over.

He pressed his forehead to hers, his breath warm on her face. "You taste so damn good."

"It's the peppermint and chocolate," she told him in a shaky voice.

"No, it's you," he said, trailing kisses across her cheek and down her throat before coming back to capture her mouth once more.

It had been a long time since Dena had been kissed so intimately by a man. Too long, she realized as she trembled with an unexpected yearning that should have warned her to pull back from his embrace.

But she didn't. She couldn't. Because she loved the way she felt in his arms. He was all strength and hardness, yet incredibly tender with his touch. As their hands made their way inside each other's clothes, she knew they were heading toward dangerous ground, yet an empty place inside her wouldn't allow her to consider stopping.

When he pulled his mouth from hers, he said in a husky voice, "Ever since I first saw you standing outside your door in those penguin pajamas, I've wanted you, Dena."

"I know," she whispered against his lips.

"I'm not a patient man," he said in between kisses.

"You were when you were helping me skate."

"This isn't skating." He stopped kissing her and gazed into her eyes.

"No, it's not. And I don't need anyone to keep me from getting hurt." Her voice was thick with emotion. "I can take care of myself."

"Are you sure?"

He was giving her a chance to change her mind. She'd known from the start that his interest in her was a physical one. She just hadn't expected that tonight would be the night he would want to show her. She'd always believed that becoming intimate with someone was a decision made after careful consideration.

It was the way she'd done everything. With careful consideration. *Think, Dena!* Her father had said the words often enough that now she said them to herself on a regular basis.

Well, tonight she didn't want to think. She simply wanted to go with her feelings and follow her instincts, which at this very moment were telling her that she should be with Quinn. So she looked him straight in the eyes and said, "Yes, I'm sure."

He smiled then, that lazy, sexy grin that was even more potent when his eyes were dark with desire. Then he scooped her up into his arms and carried her into the bedroom.

WHEN DENA AWOKE it was still dark. She was in an unfamiliar bed with a man who had become very familiar to her. At the memory, a rush of heat spread through her. For one brief moment she was tempted to snuggle close to him, to close her eyes and go back to sleep. But then her common sense overruled her emotions.

She shouldn't have listened to Quinn when he'd suggested she go to sleep in his arms. Spending the night had its drawbacks. She didn't have a change of clothes or a toothbrush, and then there was the whole morning-after awkwardness. Although there really

was no reason she should feel uncomfortable around
Quinn in the light of day.

On the contrary. After what had happened between
them last night, there was no reason to feel any un-
easiness with him. And she didn't. Only that was the
problem. It felt perfectly normal to be with him. It
was almost as if she belonged with him—and that was
what frightened her.

She hadn't been prepared for the intense feelings
he would stir inside her. But then, her behavior, when
it came to him, was not what she'd expected of herself. She hoped she hadn't made a mistake becoming
intimate with him.

She waited for her eyes to adjust to the darkness,
then quietly slid off the king-size bed, moving as
carefully as she could so as not to disturb the sleeping
man beside her.

She bent to pick up her clothes from the floor and
found only a pair of jeans. Her body warmed at the
memory of how Quinn had peeled the straight-legged
denims from her body, tossing them across the room
with the same reckless abandon he'd shown the rest
of her clothing. She got down on her hands and knees
and crawled across the carpet in search of her blouse
and other garments, then headed for the bathroom,
waiting to turn on the light until she'd closed the
door.

She looked in the mirror and grimaced. Her hair
looked as if a bird had been trying to nest in it. She
remembered how Quinn's fingers had played with it,
grasping it in longing as they'd reached the heights
of passion together. She shivered and quickly pulled
on her clothes, trying not to notice her reflection. She

didn't want to see lips swollen from intimate caresses or eyes still smoldering with passion.

She splashed cold water on her face, then looked again at her reflection. Nothing had changed. Staring back at her was a face that indicated she'd been made love to in a most thorough and intimate fashion. She couldn't prevent the tiny smile that tipped the corner of her mouth.

It had been very special for her, but what about for him? He'd used all sorts of superlatives while they'd been making love, and afterward he'd kissed her tenderly and made sure she knew he'd been satisfied. But she wondered if it truly was anything out of the ordinary for him. Maybe in the life of a hockey player, a night of passion such as the one they'd shared was as routine as a dinner date.

Which was precisely why she needed to leave. It was the uncertainty of not knowing just what their lovemaking had meant to him. And the fear of discovering that maybe it hadn't been as special for Quinn as it had been for her.

So she left the bathroom as quietly as she'd entered, padded across the bedroom carpet and into the living area, feeling her way in the dark apartment until she found the door. With the same caution, she tapped the floor until she found her shoes, then her jacket.

Carefully she turned the handle, pulled open the door and crept out into the hallway. Down the stairs she went, praying she wouldn't run into Krystal on the second-floor landing. What she didn't need was to be caught sneaking home from Quinn's in the middle of the night.

As soon as she was inside her apartment, she went

straight for the bed. Because it was almost morning, she didn't bother changing into her pajamas, but simply flopped down onto her mattress, pulling the comforter over her. As she closed her eyes and tried to get back to sleep, she was very much aware of the man she'd left sleeping upstairs, and wished she was still lying next to him.

THE NEXT TIME DENA AWOKE it was to the sound of someone pounding on her door. Her first thought was that it was Quinn. She pushed aside the comforter and got up off the bed. With a quick peek in the mirror, she ran a brush through her tangled hair and went to see who it was. To her disappointment, it wasn't Quinn, but Krystal.

"Were you sleeping? I'm sorry," her neighbor said, eyeing her wrinkled clothes curiously.

Dena knew Krystal had noticed that she still had on the same outfit she'd worn to the party last night.

"No, it's all right. Come on in." She motioned for her to step inside.

"I can't. I'm on my way out, but I need to ask a favor."

"Sure. What is it?"

Krystal stared at her, distracted. Then she asked, "Were you out all night with Garret?"

"No, I was not out all night with Garret," she replied a bit impatiently.

Her face brightened. "No, of course you weren't."

"Is that what you wanted to ask me?"

"No! A friend of mine offered to pick up a chair I bought at the furniture outlet. If you're going to be home today, I was wondering if you would let him in? I'd ask Leonie, but she's going to be gone all day."

"Sure, it's not a problem." Dena held out her hand and Krystal dropped the key into her palm. "Is there any particular place you want him to put it?"

"He knows where it goes." Which told Dena that the guy had already been in Krystal's room.

"What's this man's name?"

"Oh, it's Danny. He's about medium build, blond. Cute."

"Krystal, I'd be surprised if one of your guy friends did not fit that description," she said dryly.

She giggled. "What can I say? I have a thing for cute guys."

"I noticed."

"So what did you think of Roy?" she asked, curiosity sparking in her eyes.

"He's hot—although you don't need me to tell you that, do you?"

She sighed. "No, but I wish he was more dependable. We've dated on and off for five years, but it's been more off than on."

"I take it that after last night it's on again?"

"He'd like it to be. If he had said that a year ago, I would have been over the moon, but now…I'm not sure." She sighed. "It would be much easier if he wasn't so darn cute."

To Dena he didn't look as irresistible, but she didn't say that.

"You didn't mind that he and I hooked up last night, did you?" Krystal asked.

"No, not at all," she answered honestly.

"Good, because I wasn't planning to abandon you, but when I saw you go off with Garret I figured you wouldn't mind if I left with Roy.'' She eyed Dena curiously. ''By the way, where did the two of you go?''

''Just into Leonie's office. We were looking for a quiet place. He doesn't like parties any more than I do,'' Dena replied.

''I know. And what did you think of Leonie's son the doctor?''

''I liked him. He's a very interesting guy. We had a good conversation.''

''He talked?'' She looked surprised.

Dena chuckled. ''Wasn't he supposed to?''

''Of course, but usually he's pretty quiet...at least he doesn't say much around me.''

Dena shrugged. ''He wasn't shy with me last night. He's got a great sense of humor...as you probably already know.''

''Garret?'' She wrinkled her nose. ''Are we talking about the same guy?''

Dena smiled. ''As I said, I enjoyed talking to him. I'm surprised he's still single.''

''I think at one time he almost got engaged to another med student, but it didn't work out,'' Krystal said thoughtfully.

The sound of footsteps had both women turning their heads in the direction of the staircase. Dena's heartbeat accelerated as Quinn appeared. When he reached the landing, she could see that he carried her figure skates, hat and mitts.

''You forgot these,'' he said to Dena, shoving them in her direction.

''Oh—thanks.'' She could see Krystal was dying to ask why Quinn had these things, but at that moment her cell phone rang.

"Oh, shoot, that's me." She stepped to the opposite side of the landing, leaving Quinn at Dena's door.

"Feeling all right?" he asked with a twinkle in his eyes that told her they shared a secret.

"I'm feeling great," she answered with a flirtatious glimmer in her own eyes. "How about you?"

"I'm great, too."

"Good."

He studied her face, as if waiting for her to mention last night. She wasn't about to, not with Krystal standing less than six feet away. "I'm going to be gone for a few days and I didn't want to leave those in the back of the SUV in case you needed them," he said with a nod toward the skates.

"Yeah, I never know when the urge to skate is going to hit me," she responded with a sly grin.

He glanced toward Krystal, then leaned closer and said in a low, husky voice, "I enjoyed last night."

"So did I."

That brought a gleam of satisfaction to his eyes. He looked as if he was going to kiss her, but he simply smiled and said, "I'd better go. I'll see you on Friday."

When she gave him a puzzled look, he added, "It's payback time…or have you forgotten?"

Payback? For what? Last night? she wondered, then felt like a total fool when he said, "Northside Elementary."

The reading program. Her end of their bargain to do volunteer work. She *had* forgotten, but she didn't tell him that. "Of course. I'll be there."

"I can give you a ride to the school if you like," he suggested.

She shook her head. "Thanks, but I'll meet you

there since I'll be coming from work. I'm sure I can catch a bus."

"You don't drive to work?" he asked.

"Not with the cost of parking downtown. I don't mind the bus."

He didn't look convinced, but simply said, "Then I'll see you Friday."

She nodded and watched him walk away. He waved to Krystal, who was still on the phone. Dena was about to go back inside when the stylist snapped her cell phone shut with a roll of her eyes.

"That was Danny. Now he says he can't deliver the chair for me today." She sighed in exasperation. "Men." She eyed the box in Dena's hands. "What's with the skates? They look brand-new."

"They are. I only have them because of all this stuff that's been going on with Quinn." It wasn't exactly a lie, but it certainly was intended to be misinterpreted. "You know about the calendar he's going to be on, don't you? We had a photo shoot at the ice rink right behind the high school."

"Yeah, Leonie told me." She eyed her suspiciously.

"Have you seen her this morning?" Dena asked, wanting to steer the conversation away from Quinn.

"Yeah, I went down for breakfast and she was having her coffee. She was pleased with how everything went last night. I told her I thought it was a great party, although I didn't get to stay till the end. Roy wanted to go back to his place so we could talk."

"And did you?"

She nodded. "He told me his reserve unit got called up for duty. He's in the National Guard. That's one of the reasons why we've been so on again, off again.''

''He's gone a lot?''

''Yeah, and he never wants any strings when he is gone. Usually he serves in the States, but this time he's going overseas. It's one of those assignments where they don't tell you where they're sending you, for security reasons. He's not overly concerned, because he said it's not uncommon to be called for a peacekeeping mission and end up in a place where all you do is sit and do paperwork.''

''When does he leave?'' Dena asked.

''Next week. That's why I have to give him my decision tonight as to whether or not we get back together.''

''Together as in you don't see other guys?''

She nodded. ''Yup.'' She chuckled. ''Isn't it ironic? When I wanted him to be my one and only, he wanted to play the field. Now I'm having fun playing the field and he wants me to be his one and only.'' She checked her watch. ''Oh, shoot, I've gotta go or I'm going to be late. We'll have more girl talk later. See ya,'' she said with a wave and was gone.

Girl talk. Dena guessed that was what had transpired while Krystal had stood in her doorway, but as genuine and as nice as her neighbor was, Dena didn't feel comfortable confiding in her. Maybe in time she'd get to know Krystal better and their friendship would deepen.

Or maybe it wouldn't, she realized as she closed the door. She'd never found it easy to develop that kind of relationship with another woman. That's why her friendship with Maddie had been so important to

her. Again she found herself wishing that her college
roommate was still in St. Paul.

But Maddie wasn't there. She'd just have to go it
alone. It's what she'd done since she was thirteen.
Taken care of herself, keeping her feelings tucked
neatly away. There would be no girl talk when it
came to her relationship with Quinn. She'd have to
figure it out on her own.

DENA HAD NO PROBLEM getting time off to do the
volunteer program the Cougars sponsored at the elementary school. If anyone suspected she was partic-
ipating because of her connection to Quinn, they
didn't say it.

Since the night of Leonie's party, she hadn't seen
or heard from him. Not that she'd expected him to
call while he was on a road trip with the team. Actually, she was glad that he hadn't, because even with
him being out of town she'd spent far too much time
thinking about him.

Now the thought of seeing him again had her feeling like a teenager with a crush on a jock. And as
soon as she stepped out onto the sidewalk in front of
the Delaney offices, her heart did a flip-flop. He was
waiting for her, his backside leaning against the front
fender of his SUV, the engine running.

''What are you doing here?'' she demanded, hoping no one from the office was looking out the window.

He swept his hands out in front of the vehicle as
if he were a car salesman. ''Wouldn't you rather ride
in this than on some smelly old bus…a bus, I might
add, that won't take you directly to Northside Elementary?''

After only a slight hesitation, she walked over to the SUV. "Yes, I would."

As usual, he held the door open for her.

When she slid into the passenger seat, it was warm inside. "This is much nicer than the bus. Thank you."

"You're welcome." He skillfully maneuvered out into the heavy city traffic. When they stopped because of congestion on the downtown streets, he did a U-turn into an alley and drove in the opposite direction of the freeway.

They drove through the warehouse district until they reached an abandoned service station. When he pulled into its parking lot, she asked, "Why are we here?"

"So I can do this," he said, then leaned over and kissed her thoroughly. "I wasn't sure you'd appreciate me doing that in front of your place of work."

"You're right, I wouldn't—but I like it here." She pulled him back to her and they continued to kiss until they were both trembling.

"I missed you," he told her, nuzzling her neck.

"I missed you, too." She reached inside his jacket. "Mmm. I love how hard your chest is."

He groaned. "This is not the time to be telling me that. We have to get to the school." He reluctantly pushed her hand away, then drove back out onto the street. "Are you all set to read to the kids?"

"No, I think you know what I'm all set for," she teased, then immediately appeared contrite. "I shouldn't have said that."

He glanced sideways at her. "Yes, you should. I love to know that you want me."

She did, but she also knew that they couldn't walk into the school looking like a couple of lovebirds.

"Tell me about this program. How did you get involved?"

"My mom teaches second grade at Northside."

She was going to meet his mother? Dena shifted a bit uneasily. "So your mom will be there today?"

"Normally she would be, but she's having some dental work done so she's off today."

Dena breathed a sigh of relief, then sat quietly while he explained about the school's reading program. Finally he looked at her and asked, "You're not nervous about reading to the kids, are you?"

"No." It was the truth. If she was nervous it was because she was being seen in public with a professional hockey player. She wasn't quite sure what to expect, and whether Quinn would treat her like a girlfriend or simply another one of the volunteers.

When they arrived at the school, the first thing Dena noticed when she walked into the gymnasium was the huge banner hanging on the wall: Quinn's Kids.

She looked at him. "You didn't say it was *your* program."

His grin was almost a shy one. "It's not totally my program. The Cougar organization has donated books, and other players come to read to the kids."

But it was obvious by the way the school children greeted him that he was the one they waited to hear. Dena might have suspected that his enthusiasm wasn't genuine if there had been reporters or television cameras present. But there were no media representatives, just a gymnasium full of kids who wanted to tell Quinn about the books they'd read in the past month.

Dena enjoyed reading aloud to them and seeing

firsthand the impact reading was having in their lives.
She also noticed how much Quinn enjoyed his role
as mentor.

The man who slammed bodies into the boards and
brawled with other hockey players on the ice was
nowhere to be found that morning. This Quinn was
funny and kind and sensitive to what the kids said to
him, listening intently and responding with a concern
Dena hadn't expected.

"You're awfully quiet," he commented as he
drove her back to work.

Yes, she had been. It was because she was thinking
about what she had seen at the school. Quinn had just
spent the morning with hundreds of children, allowing
them to sit on his lap, tug on his sleeve, follow him
around, and not once had he looked bored or impa-
tient to leave. It was not what she had expected and
certainly didn't fit the stereotypical image of a professional athlete.

"I was just thinking about what a contradiction you
are. On the ice you're knocking people down and
banging them into the boards, but at the school you're
like a big teddy bear."

"I have to be mean on the job. Fans like the rough-
and-tough stuff."

"What about you? Do you like it?"

He shrugged. "It's part of the game."

They rode in silence for a few minutes, then she
said, "I think it's great that you have Quinn's Kids."

"You'll have to credit my mom for that one. I wish
she had been there. I wanted her to meet you."

Dena had never been very good at meeting mothers. She hadn't had to be since her relationships nor-

mally didn't last long enough to get to the "I want you to meet Mom" stage.

This one wasn't at that stage, either. At least it wasn't from her point of view. She was relieved to see her office building looming ahead.

When Quinn pulled over to the curb, she would have jumped out, but his hand snaked across the seat and grabbed hers. "Thanks for coming with me today."

"You don't need to thank me. It was part of the bargain, remember?" Her one hand remained beneath his, the other was on the door handle, ready to give her the opportunity to bolt.

"Okay, so we're even up on that score. How about dinner tonight?"

She grimaced. "I'd like to but I can't. One of the women at work is getting married and they're having a wedding shower this evening."

"I've got a game tomorrow and one on Monday, but Sunday's open."

"Sunday would be good," she acknowledged, very much aware of the hand that held hers.

"Okay. Sunday it is." He leaned toward her and lightly brushed her lips with his. She could see that he had meant for it to be a quick, brief peck, but once the contact was made, nature intervened. The kiss deepened, her lips moving beneath his provocatively.

A horn honking reminded them that they were in a no-parking zone. She pulled away from him. "You'd better go or you're going to get a ticket."

"It would be worth it if it meant I could get you to kiss me like that again." The sexy grin was back on his face.

She couldn't resist smiling. She felt the same way.

When he kissed her she wanted to say to hell with everything.

It was not a good sign. She needed to keep her head on straight if she was going to keep seeing him. She needed to keep their relationship in perspective. However, as she walked into the building she couldn't resist the urge to look back. He was still sitting at the curb watching her. And she liked it.

CHAPTER SIX

ON SUNDAY Quinn took Dena to an obscure little restaurant on the East Side where he knew it was unlikely anyone would care that he was a Cougar. The food was good, the atmosphere quiet, and no one paid much attention to anything except their dinner companions. They had a small table for two tucked away in a corner, and an old wine bottle with a candle dripping wax provided just the right amount of light.

She looked beautiful sitting across from him, and totally at ease. At times he felt as if he needed to say something clever to prove to her that he wasn't just an average guy, but then he remembered that she wanted him to be a regular guy.

It was a new experience for him. He was used to women treating him like a celebrity. Oftentimes his occupation was the only reason a woman wanted to be with him.

For ten years it hadn't mattered to him. He wasn't sure it did now. What he did know was that being a Cougar wasn't what had attracted Dena to him, and he liked that. There were actually a lot of things he liked about her. There was a genuineness about her he hadn't found in many women. She was comfortable with who she was and not afraid to speak her mind.

He couldn't remember when he'd enjoyed a dinner

date more, and later, as they climbed the steps of 14 Valentine Place, he felt the familiar stirrings of desire. He wanted to be with her.

As they approached the second-floor landing, she pulled her keys from her pocket. "Thank you for dinner. I had a really nice time."

"Would you like to come upstairs for a nightcap? A glass of wine, some hot chocolate…" He trailed off with a smile.

"Mmm. That sounds wonderful, but I know what happened the last time we had hot chocolate, and I have to work in the morning." They'd reached the landing and stood outside her door.

"I promise I won't keep you up late," he said with a seductive grin.

A faint smile flickered across her face. "Do I look like I just stepped off the bus from Gullible Town?"

He could hardly believe he was having to coax a woman to come up to his room. "It's true. I won't. I have a game tomorrow. Haven't you heard that athletes skip sex before games?" She gave him a dubious look and he added, "I need all my energy for the ice."

"You expect me to believe that?"

"You don't?"

She chuckled. "No."

"We could talk over coffee," he suggested.

"Talk?" She raised that one eyebrow again in a manner that was becoming very familiar to him.

"Yes, talk. I like being with you," he stated candidly.

When she didn't say anything, he added, "This is the part where you say you like being with me, too."

"I do like being with you, but I'm not sure that's a good thing."

It would have been much easier on his ego if a coy smile had accompanied those words. At least then he would have thought she was simply playing hard-to-get. But he knew her well enough to realize she wasn't flirting with him or trying to play some kind of game. She was just stating the truth.

"It *is* a good thing. Just let me prove it to you," he said, brushing his fingers across her cheek.

"I want to, but…"

"If you'd rather not come upstairs, we can go downstairs to the kitchen. Something's happening between us, Dena. You feel it. I know you do. We need to talk about where we go from here."

She hesitated and he thought she might say they weren't going anywhere. Then she stuck her key in the lock and said, "If we're going to talk we should probably do it somewhere where we won't be interrupted."

The tone of her voice made it sound as if he were an IRS agent asking her to explain last year's return. Maybe he'd misread the signs. He followed her inside and sat down next to her on the love seat, determined that, until she made it clear what she wanted from their relationship, he wouldn't touch her.

It was difficult not to take her in his arms and kiss her until she was wanting him as much as he was longing to be with her. One of the buttons on her shirt had come undone and he could see glimpses of a lacy bra. When she kicked off her shoes and tucked her feet beneath her, she was the picture of allure, yet she was unaware how enticing she looked.

"What do you want to talk about?" she asked,

pushing the long blond hair behind her shoulder. It was an innocent but sensuous move.

"Why did you sneak out on me the other night?" It was a question that had been bothering him ever since he'd awakened and found her gone.

"I didn't exactly sneak away."

"You left before morning."

She shrugged. "I didn't feel as if I knew you well enough to spend the night."

He wondered if she saw the irony in that statement. She knew him well enough to have sex with him but not well enough to sleep beside him.

"You didn't expect me to stay all night, did you?" she asked.

No, he hadn't, yet that hadn't stopped him from being disappointed when he woke up and found she was gone. "I didn't expect you to, but it could have been an interesting morning if you had," he said with a sly smile. When she looked away, he wondered if she regretted what had happened. "You're right. We don't really know each other very well. Maybe we rushed into sleeping together."

She looked at him then and said, "Maybe we did, but it felt right to me."

It was exactly what he wanted to hear. He reached for her left hand. "It felt right to me, too, and not just because it was great sex." He was pleased when she didn't correct him. "You're so different from any of the women I've known."

"I'm sure I am," she said with a lift of her brows.

"Different in a good way...a very good way," he assured her.

She looked down at their hands, where his thumb was moving slowly back and forth across her skin.

"You want me because I'm not like most of the women you meet. I don't throw myself at you."

"I don't want you to."

"So what do you want from me?"

Again he felt as if he were exploring new territory. Women usually made demands of him. Now he was the one having to say he didn't want her going out with other guys, that he wanted her to date only him.

"I want you to think of me as the guy in your life. The only guy."

She looked up him then. "Are you saying you want to be my boyfriend?"

"Isn't that what usually happens when two people who are dating want to see more of each other? They become boyfriend and girlfriend? I know we're not exactly high school kids, but I think the general idea applies to people our age, too," he said with a grin.

"Well, yes, but..."

He wasn't expecting a *but*. "I've been told I make a pretty decent boyfriend," he said with a false modesty, hoping to erase that look of seriousness on her face.

She smiled weakly. "I'm sure you do, but I don't make a very good girlfriend."

"I don't believe that," he said, not wanting to believe that she could be giving him the brush-off. "Tell me why you think that it's true."

"My work takes up almost every waking moment of my life," she answered. "My job is the most important thing to me."

"You think hockey isn't to me? You already know we have that in common," he reminded her.

"I'm not looking for a serious relationship."

If any other woman had said that to him, he

wouldn't have believed her, but with Dena he knew it was true. "Neither am I."

She smiled then. "I didn't think you were, but I thought I should make it perfectly clear where I stand on the issue. Commitment...marriage...children... that's all way far ahead in the future...if it's even in the future," she said in a warning tone.

"Why do you think I'm still single? Half of my working life I spend on the road. It's a lifestyle that's not easy for me, let alone a wife and kids. I know the day's going to come when I'll no longer be able to have that lifestyle. Then it'll be time to start thinking about whether or not I want a wife and kids. Until then, I don't want to think about it."

She was silent, and he said, "It seems to me that we're a perfect fit. We both want the same things. No promises, no expectations, no worrying about the future."

"But you're a hockey player," she said weakly.

He threw up his hands. "Okay, so I have one small flaw." He grinned then and said, "If you're worried about the attention I get from the public, you don't need to be. I've learned how to keep a very low profile."

He leaned closer to her so he could put his arm around her. "It'll work for us, Dena. I know it will, and it'll be great. I like you, and I want to be with you."

"I want to be with you, too." The provocative look in her eyes had him pulling her onto his lap.

"Then you agree we belong together...for now, anyway?"

"Yes."

It was exactly what he wanted to hear. He bent to kiss her, his hands finding the soft curves of her body. She felt good in his arms, and before long the rest of the buttons had come undone on her shirt.

As he bent his head to her breast she stopped him. "What about your game tomorrow?"

"It's not until seven at night. I'll have plenty of time tomorrow to regain the energy I'm going to lose tonight."

DENA HAD NEVER HAD a boyfriend quite like Quinn. He was different from any man she had dated and not simply because he was a professional athlete. When they were together he showered with her attention, and when they were apart he made sure she knew he was thinking about her, leaving her messages on her cell phone if she missed his call. Never had she been treated with such chivalry. It was not what she would have expected from a man who had a reputation for knocking men down on the ice.

They were together as often as their work allowed. They went to a play at the Guthrie Theater, a monster truck show at the Target Center, saw an exhibition of Norman Rockwell's work at the Minneapolis Institute of Arts, and watched videos on his big-screen TV.

Dena suspected part of the reason they had so much fun was because they'd set the ground rules for their relationship. It took the pressure off both of them. She had no delusions that he would last longer than any of her other boyfriends, and there was none of the usual second-guessing about where their relationship was heading.

They'd tried to avoid the public eye as much as possible, preferring to keep their relationship private.

Dena knew that Quinn liked the fact that she had little interest in the world of professional hockey. It meant that when he was with her he could simply be Quinn Sterling, the guy upstairs.

That was why she was a bit surprised when he asked her to go with him to a party given by one of the executives of the Cougars organization. Dena wanted to say no, but she could tell by the look on Quinn's face that the party was important to him.

As she rummaged through her closet searching for something suitable to wear, she wondered if she hadn't made a mistake. She didn't like parties, and this one would be full of strangers who were all part of a world foreign to her.

She didn't even know how to define suitable attire when it applied to a party of professional athletes. It didn't help that it was April and not really winter, yet not really spring. She pulled out a red silk blouse and held it up to her chest, grimacing at the small spot on the collar. She went across the hall to the bathroom. She was dabbing at the spot with a damp cloth when Krystal showed up.

"Hey, Dena. Want to go with me to see a movie tonight?"

"Thanks for the offer, but I already have plans for this evening," she told her, her attention on the fabric.

"With Quinn?"

Dena didn't know why she should be surprised that her neighbor would know that she was seeing Quinn. They all lived in the same house.

"Yes, with Quinn." She hoped her tone would discourage Krystal from probing any further. It didn't.

"Omigosh. You're dating a Cougar!" she said in

awe. "Do you realize what it means to date a professional athlete?"

"He's just a guy, Krystal."

"Maybe, but you better be careful. I know Quinn is a cool guy and he seems to be pretty nice, but most professional jocks are catch and release."

Dena looked up from the blouse. "They're what?"

"Catch and release. You know, once a guy catches a girl, he releases her," she explained. "Some guys aren't looking to keep any girl."

Dena said, "Maybe I'm the one who'll catch and release."

Krystal flapped her hand at her. "Yeah, right. As if any woman in her right mind would dump Quinn Sterling."

Dena didn't want to be discussing Quinn with Krystal. She turned her attention back to the blouse. "I don't think I'm going to get this stain out."

"Can't you wear something else?"

"I don't have anything else that I feel comfortable wearing," she said, tossing the damp cloth aside in disgust.

"That's because red is a power color." She lifted a sleeve and held it next to Dena's cheek. "You're lucky…it's not an easy color for blondes to wear, yet it's good on you."

"It would be if it didn't have a spot on it." She held the blouse up to the light and frowned. "Silk really should be dry-cleaned. I think I may have made it worse."

"I have some of those dry-cleaning sheets, if you want to try one," she offered. "You just pop it in the dryer with your blouse."

Dena eyed the garment. "This is probably all wrong for the party, anyway."

"What kind of party is it?"

"I don't know. All Quinn said was that it was in North Oaks."

Krystal whistled softly through her teeth. "Okay, you're talking bucks now. Is this a party for hockey players?"

Dena was reluctant to tell her very much and simply said, "Quinn said they were friends of his. To me they'll simply be a roomful of strangers."

"Strangers with money if they live in North Oaks," she stated with a knowing lift of her brows. "I bet it's going to be one posh party."

Dena's shoulders sagged. "Another reason for me not to go. I probably should have told him no."

Krystal sighed. "At least you have a date. Ever since Roy left, my life has been so boring."

"You're not seeing anyone else?"

"How can I? Roy is off serving our country. He wanted me to be here waiting for him while he does his duty. This is not a time to be juggling."

Dena hid her smile. Ever since Roy had waltzed back into Krystal's life and asked her to be his one and only, she had changed her attitude about dating.

"Has he been sent overseas?"

She nodded. "But where, I don't know. All the mail comes through the military post office so it's impossible to tell where he's stationed. Not that he writes often, because he doesn't." She stifled a yawn. "Maybe it's a good thing you have plans. I'm tired. I should probably curl up in my bed with the remote. You have a good time tonight, okay?"

"Yeah, thanks." Dena didn't think it was likely

that she'd enjoy herself. Posh settings were not her scene, nor were parties with hockey players, and she almost canceled at the last minute.

But then Quinn was at her door looking ever so handsome in a suit and tie. She was glad the silk blouse had a spot on it because it had forced her to look at another option in her closet—a fringed suede skirt that she topped with a matching vest. The look on Quinn's face told her it was a good choice.

As they drove to the party her father's training paid off. He'd always taught her, "Never let them see you sweat." In most situations in life she'd been able to follow that advice. Tonight was no exception. And she was glad.

When Krystal had said the St. Paul suburb was posh, she hadn't been wrong. A gated drive prevented unwanted guests from making an appearance. One look at the cars parked outside the house told Dena the people who lived inside were definitely in a different income bracket than she was.

She imagined it wasn't much different than many of the executive homes in the area. Its size alone was impressive. Once inside, Dena saw the reason. It had an indoor gym that included a small pool, whirlpool, weight room and steam room. Although it was home to a middle-aged couple with no children, the house had eight bedrooms, a kitchen that Dena was certain only caterers had ever used, a video arcade, an in-home theater, and a billiard room.

Determined not to let Quinn see how unsure of herself she was, she held her head high and placed a gracious smile on her face as she was introduced to hockey players, their wives and girlfriends. She knew her presence raised more than one eyebrow, and she wondered what kind of date Quinn usually brought to Cougar parties. Not that it mattered. She was the one he had chosen to bring tonight, and she knew most women would have loved to have been in her shoes.

Only she wasn't most women. As friendly as everyone was, she couldn't help but feel out of place. Being at the party reminded her of what different worlds she and Quinn lived in.

On the way home she knew he was going to ask the inevitable question. They hadn't been in the SUV but a few minutes when he said, "Did you have a good time?"

She told him the truth. "It was interesting."

"Is that a polite way of saying you were bored stiff?"

She chuckled. "It would be impossible to be bored at a party like that. I may have been a little outside of my comfort zone, but it was actually quite fascinating to see how hockey players party."

"Like most other people do, I would imagine. They eat, they drink, they laugh."

"Most people don't have that kind of venue for their house parties," she reminded him. "That house was incredible. I've always heard about people who have pools in their homes, but I'd never actually seen one before tonight."

"Some people believe a man's home should be his castle."

"And is that what you think?"

He glanced sideways at her. "Sure. It's just that some of us don't need as fancy a castle as others." He reached across the seat and took her hand. "I'm glad you were with me tonight. I usually don't bring a date to team parties."

That surprised her. "Why not?"

He shrugged. "I haven't wanted to until tonight. I told you. You're different from the women I usually date."

She reached across the seat and kissed him on the cheek. "You are so sweet."

"Sweet on you." He tossed another sideways glance her way. "And just as soon as this season's over, I'm going to show you. Are you as tired of winter as I am?"

"Winter ended last month. Remember Leonie's party? April is a spring month." It was said with tongue-in-cheek.

"Spring as in the lakes are still frozen," he stated dryly. "In one week hockey will be over, and once things quiet down, I'm going to take you someplace warm and sunny where we can lie on a white sand beach and sip those little drinks with the umbrellas in them. How does that sound?"

"It sounds wonderful, but I'm afraid I haven't been at my job long enough to have earned any vacation time."

"Then we'll have to make it a weekend. How about Cancun?"

Images of white sand beaches and blue skies came to mind. "I've never been to Mexico," she said dreamily.

"There are any number of resorts we could go to. All of them are beautiful. It's the perfect getaway at this time of year when you're waiting for the weather to warm up but it stays cold. And I can promise you I make a good tour guide."

She imagined him in a pair of sandals and cutoff

denims, his muscular chest bare. "When were you thinking about going?"

"I leave tomorrow for our final road trip and the last games of the season. Because we didn't make the playoffs, all that's left to do when I get back is to clean out my locker and say goodbye to my teammates. Then it's off to Mexico, so you'd better find that bikini you say you haven't unpacked," he said with a wink.

She didn't want to tell him that she hadn't been in a swimsuit since she'd been required to take swimming in gym class. "I should warn you, I swim about as well as I ice skate."

"Half those bikinis on those resort beaches never see a drop of ocean water," he said with a grin. "Besides, we're not going there to swim. I can think of plenty of other ways to keep you entertained."

She didn't doubt for a minute he would.

DENA PREFERRED not to celebrate her birthday. The last time she'd actually had a cake had been when she'd turned twenty. That was because Maddie had baked one for her.

And she especially wanted to skip her thirtieth birthday. Lisa, however, was not about to let the day pass. She insisted Dena come over for dinner after work.

To Dena's relief, her sister-in-law hadn't invited anyone else to join the party. She'd made a chocolate cake, which her niece had decorated with yellow candy letters that spelled out Happy Birthday Auntie Dena. There was a beautiful pink azalea in the center of the table—a gift from her brother and Lisa—and several small, odd-shaped packages next to her plate from the children.

"I bet you can't guess what's inside this one," Bethany said in a teasing voice as she fiddled with the purple ribbon on one of the packages.

"No, I most certainly cannot," Dena replied.

"You get to sit here because you're the birthday girl," the eight-year-old girl said, pulling back the chair that was normally her brother's place at the table. "And you get to wear this," She gave her a paper crown.

"Bethany, she doesn't want to wear some dumb paper crown," Jeremy chided.

"Yes, she does," Bethany insisted, then turned to Dena and asked, "Don't you?"

"Maybe I should wear it when we have the cake," Dena suggested.

"Don't you like it? I made it for you." The tiny face looked crestfallen.

"It's beautiful. Of course I like it." She set it on her head, although she couldn't get it to stay, as it flopped first to one side, then the other before falling off.

"I'll get some bobby pins," Bethany declared before scooting away.

Luke began banging his spoon on his plate. "I'm hun…greee," he drawled in a whining tone.

"See what you're missing being single, Dena?" Ryan said as he stilled Luke's tiny hands.

"How come you're not married?" Jeremy asked, which brought a gasp from his mother's mouth and a reprimand.

Bethany had returned and said, "Because she

hasn't met her Prince Charming. Talk about dumb questions.''

''All right, all of you. Cut the noise or you're going to make Auntie Dena wish she'd celebrated her birthday alone,'' Ryan admonished in a stern voice.

''She wouldn't want to do that, not when she sees this,'' Lisa said, carrying a large platter into the dining room. ''My famous spaghetti and meatballs, a recipe so secret that not even Ryan knows the ingredients.''

Dena knew her sister-in-law had fussed over the meal and smiled gratefully as she set the platter on the table. Like other times she'd dined at the Bailey home, she was a bit overwhelmed by the constant commotion a family of five created. Halfway through the meal Luke's fork went flying, landing on Dena's lap. She looked down to see a blob of red sauce on her white blouse.

''Oh, Dena, I am so sorry,'' Lisa said, jumping to her feet.

''It's all right. This is washable.'' Dena dabbed at the spot with her napkin.

''You should put cold water on it right now. Otherwise, the stain may set,'' Lisa suggested.

''You're probably right,'' Dena said, getting up from the table. ''If you'll excuse me, I'll do it now.''

To her relief, the spot was easily removed by dabbing at it with a cloth soaked in cold water. After only a few minutes, Dena returned to the dining room, the only sign of the mishap a wet spot on her blouse.

Before she even sat down, Bethany said, ''Auntie Dena, you had a phone call.''

It was then she noticed her cell phone had been pulled out of her purse and was next to her plate.

"Your phone was ringing in your purse and Bethany didn't want you to miss a call so she answered it for you," Lisa explained.

"It was Quinn Sterling," Bethany blurted out, which explained the reason for the interest on the other faces at the table. Then the little girl added, "I told him you were in the bathroom."

Lisa grimaced. "I'm sorry, Dena. We've told the kids that when they answer the phone they should simply say that the person can't come to the phone."

"He wanted to know where she was," Bethany insisted.

"I wish I would have answered it," Jeremy said. "I would have thanked him for the picture he autographed for me. How did you say you got it?" he asked his aunt.

Lisa answered for her. "We told you. Dena works at the advertising agency that is doing the calendar of Minnesota celebrities."

"Did he leave a message?" she asked, trying to sound nonchalant.

"He just said to tell you he called," Bethany reported.

That started a barrage of questions from Jeremy, who wanted to know everything and anything about the Minnesota Cougar hockey player. Fortunately, Ryan intervened, reminding his son that this was a day to celebrate Dena's birthday, not discuss Cougar hockey. Dena hoped it would be the last she'd hear of it.

Later, however, when Lisa and Dena were alone in the kitchen, her sister-in-law came right out and asked her about Quinn. "There's something's going on between you and that hockey player, isn't there?"

"What makes you think that?"

"You mean, besides the way your eyes sparkled when Bethany said he'd called?"

Dena knew there was no point in lying. "We've become friends."

"Friends? What's that supposed to mean?"

"We enjoy each other's company. Look, Lisa, don't go reading anything into this. We live in the same building, we've had a few good times together…that's it."

"I thought maybe because he called on your birthday…"

"He doesn't even know it's my birthday," she said. "That's how *not* close we are."

"You don't want to talk about this, do you?"

She shook her head. "Do you mind?"

Lisa gave her shoulder a quick squeeze. "Of course not. I never want to pry into your personal life." Despite her words, there was a coolness in her tone.

"You weren't prying, but the truth is I don't know what's going to happen between me and Quinn. Yeah, we've gone out, and yes, I like him, but you know me and my track record with men."

"It's too new for you to be discussing it, isn't it?" she said with an understanding smile.

Dena nodded and, before she could say another word, Jeremy burst through the swinging door. "Dad wants to know what's keeping you. We're ready to light the candles."

"We'll be right there," his mother answered.

Just as quickly the door swung the other way and Jeremy was gone. Dena was about to follow him when Lisa pulled on her arm.

"Just promise me one thing. That you'll go slowly

with this guy. He is, after all, a professional hockey player. They collect women like they collect notches on their hockey sticks.''

Dena knew the words were spoken out of concern, but she really didn't feel the need for a warning from anyone when it came to Quinn. Calmly she said, ''Believe me, Lisa, I know what I'm doing. I'm not involved the way you think I am.''

''Famous last words,'' Lisa mumbled under her breath before she left the kitchen.

DENA HONESTLY DIDN'T BELIEVE she was involved with Quinn. They were having a little thing on a day-to-day basis. She was doing something few women had the opportunity to do—date a professional athlete. Sure, it was a heady experience. What woman wouldn't have her head turned a wee bit?

Hers was definitely turned, but fortunately it was only her head that was involved and not her heart. But then she got home and found the flowers. A dozen long-stemmed red roses in a beautiful cut-glass vase. The envelope perched between the stems was unopened. Dena slid her nail beneath the flap and pulled out the card.

Sorry I couldn't be there on your birthday. We'll have our own private celebration in Mexico. Quinn.

Dena fingered the velvety petals. Red roses. A symbol of love…at least for some. But she and Quinn weren't in love. They were in a convenient form of dating. That was all. By next year's birthday the petals would be pressed between two pages of a book, and he would more than likely be nothing but a memory to her.

She set the vase of roses on her nightstand next to

the bobblehead Quinn. She closed her eyes and inhaled the flowers' fragrance. She wouldn't think about what might happen next year. If her history with men was anything to go by, she still had more than sixty days before the coach turned back into a pumpkin.

DENA HAD WATCHED all three of the televised hockey games Quinn played on his road trip, wincing every time the puck came near him, for she knew it meant there was a good chance he'd be knocked down…or worse. To her relief, he didn't get into a single fight during the Cougars' final victory. When he was interviewed by the media immediately following the game, Dena's heart did a little thump at the sight of his damp hair and rosy cheeks. She found herself longing to see him again and looked forward to his coming home.

Only he didn't come home. Dena knew that the Cougars had returned from their final road trip. It had been reported in the paper and on the television news, yet she'd heard nothing from Quinn except a voice mail message he'd left saying that something had come up and he had to make an unscheduled trip to South Carolina.

Dena couldn't help but be curious as to what it was that had caused him to delay his return. Doubts began to creep into her mind as to whether or not he'd already tired of her and had moved on to his next conquest. When several days passed without word from him, it became more difficult not to think that he was having second thoughts about their relationship. He had been, after all, the one who couldn't wait to fly to Mexico as soon as the season was over.

It turned out she wasn't the only one having trouble with her love life. When she bumped into Krystal on the second-floor landing, she saw the younger woman had been crying, her eyes puffy and her face splotchy.

"Are you all right?" Dena asked.

She nodded, then pulled a tissue from her pocket and blew her nose. "I don't know why I'm crying. I'm really more angry than I am sad."

"Why? What happened?"

She sniffled, then said, "I just found out that Roy is two-timing me. He's been writing to another one of his old girlfriends, Jasmine Calloway. Apparently he pulled the same number on her that he did on me. Told her he realized he'd made a mistake breaking up with her and that he'd changed…that going off on the military assignment had made him realize how much he wanted to settle down with one woman."

"I'm sorry," Dena said sincerely, aware that she could very well be in the same boat. Maybe Quinn had another woman in another city.

"I feel like such a fool," Krystal said on a hiccup, dabbing at her eyes with another tissue.

Dena didn't know what to say. How could she give advice to Krystal when it was possible that she was in the very same predicament?

Krystal didn't wait for her to come up with a suitable response or a sympathetic phrase of understanding. She straightened her back, took a deep breath and said, "I'm not going to let that doofus mess up my life."

"You shouldn't," Dena agreed.

"You know what today is?" she asked the rhetorical question. "It's my independence day," she said with her chin held high. "And I'm going to celebrate. Want to come along?"

"Where?"

She shrugged. "Wherever the mood takes us. There's no shortage of places where a girl can go to have fun." When Dena didn't answer right away, she asked, "Or do you have plans with Quinn tonight?"

"I'm not sure…" she began. Seeing the curious look on her neighbor's face, she said, "We were supposed to get together when he came back from his final road trip, but so far I haven't heard from him."

"You're not worried, are you? I mean, Quinn's not the kind of guy to just dump a girl. He's no Roy, Dena."

She was tempted to ask what made her so sure, when not so long ago she'd called him a catch and release. It was possible that Dena had been released and didn't even know it.

She found herself speculating about his social life before they had started dating. Maybe he'd had a different woman in each city where the team played.

"So do you want to go out with me?" Krystal interrupted her musings.

Dena really didn't, but neither did she want to sit home waiting to see if Quinn would call. Because she knew the imagination could be a terrible thing, she said, "Sure, I'll go with you. Sounds like fun."

CHAPTER SEVEN

ON SUNDAY MORNING when Dena went down for breakfast, she found the kitchen empty. She wasn't surprised that Krystal hadn't come down. As she filled a kettle with water, she smiled as she remembered how Krystal seemed to have an endless supply of energy, dancing until the nightclubs closed their doors.

"I need a jolt of caffeine."

Dena turned at the sound of her landlady's voice. "I'm having tea if you want some."

"I need something stronger," Leonie said as she set the thick Sunday paper down on the table. "I was out late last night."

"I hope you had fun."

"Oh, I did. It was the wedding of one of my clients." She yawned as she reached for the coffee-maker.

"Must have been a satisfied client if it ended in marriage."

"What can I say? Sometimes they actually listen," she said with a wink. She pressed a hand to her lower back and grimaced. "I don't think I should have tried the limbo, though. Or maybe it was that tango I did with the best man."

Dena smiled as she imagined Leonie dancing.

"I wonder where Krystal is this morning. She's

usually the first one down,'' Leonie remarked as she measured coffee grounds into the basket.

''She may have danced one too many last night, too,'' Dena answered. ''We had a girls' night out.''

''Did you go to First Avenue? I know that's one of her favorite places.''

''No, she wanted me to sample the suburban nightlife. I think since I'm from Iowa she figured I'd be more comfortable on a dance floor hooked onto a bowling alley,'' she said dryly.

Leonie chuckled. ''And were you?''

''Yes.'' It was said on a note of disbelief. ''The music was good and the dance floor was huge. It rocked.''

''If there's a good time to be had, Krystal will find it,'' Leonie said affectionately.

''Don't remind me,'' the hairdresser said, coming into the room with a hand on her forehead. On her feet were a pair of slippers in the shape of bunnies and a pink robe covered her pajamas. She glanced at Dena and said, ''We should have come home when the bars closed.''

''You didn't?'' Leonie asked.

Dena looked at her landlady. ''We were celebrating Krystal's independence day.''

''Another one?'' Leonie looked at Krystal, who nodded solemnly. ''Oh, my. I thought maybe the third time was the charm.''

''Well, I can guarantee you there won't be a fourth time,'' Krystal assured her.

''Do you want to talk about it?'' Leonie asked.

Krystal padded over to the table and sank onto a chair. ''I'm all talked out when it comes to Roy. If I didn't exorcise him last night, nothing's going to do the trick.''

"She met quite a few candidates to be his replacement,'' Dena stated. The kettle whistled and she got up to turn it off.

"I'm not sure I want a replacement,'' Krystal said on a sigh.

Leonie patted her hand. "You'll feel better with time. A broken heart isn't mended in one night.''

Krystal pushed her hair off her forehead, balancing her head on her palm. "I should have never let him back into my life, Leonie. You knew he was wrong for me, didn't you?''

"I'd rather see you with someone who recognizes what a treasure you are,'' she said in a maternal tone.

"I should have come to you for advice. Then maybe…'' She brushed the air with her fingers. "It doesn't matter. What's done is done. In the future, I won't make the same mistake.''

"I believe you won't,'' Leonie said with conviction.

Dena brought the teapot over to the table and asked Krystal, "Would you like me to make you some toast?''

Krystal groaned. "Oh, please. Don't mention food.'' She grimaced and asked, "Why did you let me eat all those greasy wings? They gave me a terrible headache.''

"Are you sure it was the food and not those shots you were doing with a certain Tom Cruise look-alike?'' Dena asked.

Krystal smiled wistfully. "He was cute, wasn't he?''

When the phone rang, Leonie excused herself.

Krystal groaned, then dropped her head onto the table. "I feel awful."

"You should take some aspirin. It'll take care of your head if not your stomach. Want me to get you some?" Dena offered.

She lifted her head slightly. "Would you?"

"Sure." Dena went upstairs to her apartment to get the pain reliever for her hungover friend. When she got there, she automatically checked her phone for messages. There was one, which she immediately played back, hoping it was from Quinn.

At the sound of his voice, she sighed. She longed to see him and feel his arms around her. He apologized for not calling, told her that he missed her, then went on to explain that the reason he was in South Carolina was because two good friends—his college roommate and his wife—had been killed in a plane crash. He was with their family members and would be home as soon as he took care of some legal matters. Again he said that he missed her and wished he could be with her.

Dena was swamped with guilt. She'd been worrying that he was off with some hockey groupie having wild sex, when the truth was he'd been grieving over the loss of his friends. She was sitting on her bed thinking about him when Krystal walked in.

"I decided to go back to bed, so you can forget about the aspirin," she said, leaning against the doorjamb.

"I'm sorry I didn't come back down right away. I was listening to a message from Quinn."

"Didn't I tell you he'd call? He's a good guy." When Dena didn't speak, she added, "It was good news, wasn't it?"

"Yes and no." She told Krystal the reason Quinn hadn't returned.

"Oh my God, that's horrible," she said in disbelief. "He's probably staying in South Carolina to attend the funeral."

She nodded. "I think it's tomorrow…and he said something about there being some legal matters he needed to take care of."

"Did he say when he'd be home?"

She shook her head.

"Does Leonie know about this?"

"He said he was going to call her, but I think I'll go down and talk with her."

"If there's anything I can do to help, let me know," Krystal offered before shuffling back to bed.

Dena wondered if there was anything anyone could do to help Quinn cope with such a loss. She wanted to believe that he would return home and they would pick up where they'd left off before he'd gone away for that final road trip. But she wasn't sure that would happen. Only time would tell. And that was what worried her. Time had not always been on her side when it came to men.

IT WAS FOUR DAYS LATER that Dena arrived home from work and saw Quinn's SUV in the driveway. The thought of being with him again had her heart racing. She hurried up the stairs to her apartment, wanting to freshen up before she saw him. She was just about to put her key in the lock when Krystal came bouncing up the stairs from the kitchen.

"Quinn's back," she announced.

"I know. I saw his car out back."

"He's not alone."

Dena frowned. "What do you mean?"

She eyed her curiously. "I guess he didn't tell you, then."

"Tell me what?" Dena's heart began to bang against her chest. "What should he have told me?"

"Those friends of his who died? They had two kids. They're seven and twelve."

"And they're here?" She wondered if they were the "small legal matter" he needed to clear up.

"Just for a couple of days," Krystal told her. "I'll let Quinn tell you about it. You're going to come downstairs, aren't you?"

Dena had hoped that the first time she saw Quinn again it would be in private, not in Leonie's kitchen with four other people present. But she didn't want to wait to see him alone so she said, "I need to change first."

"That's all right. I came up to get some shampoo samples for Sara—she's the twelve-year-old. You can imagine how difficult it must be for those poor kids to think straight about anything. It'll just take me a minute to grab the shampoo. You want me to wait for you?"

"If you don't mind?" For some reason, the thought of having Krystal at her side when she walked into the kitchen was an appealing one.

"I don't mind. You scoot." She shooed her with her hands. "Make yourself pretty for Quinn."

"I didn't say I needed to make myself pretty," Dena protested.

"You didn't have to. I see the look that comes into your eyes whenever someone mentions his name." She grinned cheekily.

Dena didn't say a word but went in to change

clothes. When she emerged a short time later she wore a fresh coat of lipstick and her hair hung loose around her shoulders.

Krystal pointed to her head and smiled. "You're a quick learner."

Dena followed her down the stairs and into the kitchen where Quinn sat at the table, a dark-haired girl to his left and a blond boy on his right. When he saw Dena, he got to his feet. At first she thought he was going to come over and pull her into his arms. He had the same look in his eyes that he'd had on other occasions when he'd done exactly that. But he didn't even take her hand. He simply said hello and pulled out a chair so she could join them.

He introduced her to the children, who greeted her with a politeness that was very different from the boisterous welcome she usually got from her niece and nephews. There was no mistaking the sadness on their faces, and Dena searched for the right words to express her sympathy, wondering what could she possibly say that could make them feel better.

"I'm sorry about your parents," she finally said.

The boy, Kevin, began to sob. The girl only sat staring straight ahead, as if she didn't dare acknowledge the words of sympathy. Dena felt awful, wishing she hadn't said anything.

Quinn wrapped an arm around the boy and pulled him closer. Dena met his eyes with a helplessness. "I'm sorry."

Leonie, who was getting beverages from the refrigerator, came over to place a hand of understanding on Dena's shoulder. "I just made some lemonade for Sara and Kevin. Would you like some?"

What Dena wanted was to run back upstairs to her

room. She felt out of place, a sentiment that Krystal obviously didn't share. She gave Sara the shampoo and was carrying on a conversation with her as if they were old friends. The eyes that had looked at Dena with indifference softened when they were turned on the stylist.

"How old are you, Kevin?" Dena asked the boy when he'd swiped away his tears and straightened in his chair.

"Seven," he said on a hiccup.

Being that Bethany was eight and in the second grade, she said, "You must be in the first grade."

"Second," he corrected her.

"My niece is in the second grade. Is this your first time in Minnesota?" she asked.

He nodded and added, "I don't like it here. It's cold and brown."

"That's because it's early in the spring," Quinn interjected. "In a couple of weeks the grass will have greened up and the leaves will be on the trees."

"We're not going to be here in a couple of weeks," Sara said sullenly, folding her arms across her chest.

"While you are here you'll want to wear jackets," Leonie said in a comforting tone, taking a seat at the table. "It's easy to catch a chill this time of year."

"I could take them shopping," Krystal offered, and for the first time, Dena noticed a spark of interest on Sara's face.

"Thanks, Krystal, but I'll need to pick up a few things so I might as well take them," Quinn told her.

"Okay, but if you change your mind and decide you want help, let me know. I'm not working tomorrow."

Talk turned to the practical as they discussed sleeping arrangements and meal times. When Leonie suggested that Sara use Jason's room, the twelve-year-old simply shrugged and said in a monotone voice, "I don't care. I'm not going to be here that long."

Dena didn't miss the look that passed between Leonie and Quinn.

"Leonie, didn't you say that you have a roll-away we could borrow?" he asked.

"Yes. I keep it for a spare bed when company comes," she answered. "You're welcome to use it upstairs."

"I think I will. This way Sara can use it in the living room and Kevin can bunk in with me. My bed sleeps two easily."

Dena knew only too well how big his bed was and hoped her face wouldn't give her away. She took a drink of her lemonade and avoided looking in Quinn's direction.

"Why doesn't Sara stay with me?" Krystal suggested. "It would be more fun for her to be in a girl's room than with the guys. She can sleep on my futon."

Dena didn't think Sara looked any more eager to sleep on Krystal's futon than she did in Leonie's spare bedroom or on the roll-away in Quinn's living room. Actually, the girl looked as if she wished she could disappear. Dena knew the feeling well and empathized with her.

Sara shrugged and said moodily, "It doesn't matter."

It was clear from her tone that she didn't want to stay any longer than was necessary. "I think it would be best if the kids were with me," Quinn spoke up. "Leonie, why don't you show me where that roll-away is and I'll carry it upstairs?"

As he rose to his feet, Kevin, too, got up. It was obvious he wasn't going to let Quinn go anywhere without him. Sara, on the other hand, didn't move a muscle but sat slumped in the chair, her arms folded across her chest.

"This has to be really hard for you," Krystal said when the others had gone. "We moved a lot when we were kids, and I always hated it when I had to sleep in a strange place."

"We're not moving," the girl said with a hint of defiance.

Krystal wasn't about to give up. She reached for the young girl's arm. "I like your bracelet. Does it have special meaning?"

Dena noticed the leather twined around her wrist.

Sara's face softened a bit. "It's a friendship bracelet."

"What's your friend's name?"

"Alicia."

"Is she a school friend or someone from your neighborhood?"

"Both. She lives on the same street. I could have stayed with her instead of coming here, but Quinn wouldn't let me." Her statement revealed the reason for her sullen behavior. She hadn't wanted to leave her friends to go stay with a stranger.

"He's a good guy, Sara. He'll do whatever he can to get things straightened out. You'll see," Krystal said with confidence.

Sara wasn't convinced. She returned to her pose, which Dena thought was more of a slouching pout than a stab at defiance.

Krystal managed to get the girl talking about her favorite rock groups and what kind of TV programs

and movies she liked to watch. Dena contributed little, again envying Krystal her ability to always put
people at ease. By the time Quinn returned, Sara's
posture was not quite so slouched and she looked a
little less sullen.

"Sara, Kevin and I are going upstairs now. Do you
want to come along or would you rather stay down
here?" he asked. "Leonie said you can watch TV in
the great room if you like."

"I'll go upstairs," she answered, shoving away
from the table.

"Take Kevin and I'll be right there," Quinn said,
giving the boy a gentle nudge toward his sister. "I
need to talk to Dena for a few minutes."

"Maybe they want to pick out a couple of movies
to watch," Leonie suggested.

"I'll help them," Krystal said, jumping to her feet.

"Do you want to do that, Kevin?" Quinn asked
the boy, since Sara was not inclined to give him an
answer.

The seven-year-old turned woeful eyes on his temporary guardian. "Will you come with me?"

Quinn placed a hand on his shoulder. "I'll tell you
what. You go with Krystal and I'll be there in just a
few minutes, okay?"

With her usual warmth, Krystal drew the little boy
close to her, then motioned for Sara. "Wait until you
see all the movies Leonie has. I'm sure we can find
one you'll want to see."

Dena thought the girl might refuse to go, but then
she got to her feet, the same look on her face.

"I'm going to get you some clean linens for that

bed,'' Leonie said, then followed the others out of the room, leaving Quinn and Dena alone.

He wasted no time pulling her into his arms. He didn't kiss her, but simply held her close. "This wasn't how I expected my homecoming to be... standing in Leonie's kitchen, stealing a quick hug," he murmured close to her ear.

She loved the feel of his solid torso, the strength of his arms. "I'm so sorry about your friends." She looked into his eyes, and instead of seeing the usual flicker of desire, she saw pain. "Is there anything I can do?" she asked, knowing that there really wasn't a single thing she could do or say that would erase that sadness.

He released her and ran a hand over his hair. "It's been a nightmare. Thirty-two is too young to die, Dena," he stated quietly.

"Yes, it is," she agreed.

"They hardly ever went anywhere without the kids. Apparently he had to go to Florida on business and decided to take Patsy with him. They would have taken the kids except they were in school."

"You said it was a plane crash."

He nodded. "They were killed instantly. It's hard enough for me to cope with their deaths—I can only imagine what it must be like for those two." He nodded toward the doorway.

"Is there family somewhere who can help them?"

"There are a couple of elderly aunts on Patsy's side and a few distant cousins. Doug has a sister, but she just had some kind of surgery and couldn't even come to South Carolina for the funeral. Doug and Patsy named me as guardian in their will, I guess because I'm Sara's godfather.''

She squeezed his hand. ''They trusted you.''

The look on his face said he didn't understand why. ''I didn't want to take them out of school and bring them back here, yet what choice did I have?''

''You did the right thing,'' she said, rubbing his arm consolingly.

''They're so frightened,'' he said, shaking his head.

''Anyone would be, in their shoes. Everything will be okay.'' She tried to comfort him.

''It will be once I get those two settled. Doug and his sister were never close, but she's willing to take the kids as long as she can find someone to help out until she's back on her feet.'' He studied her face, then traced her cheek with his fingers. ''It must have been a shock for you to walk in here and see the kids.''

''Krystal told me about them before I came downstairs,'' she confessed.

''They might cramp our style for a few days,'' he warned.

''There'll be other days for us to be together.''

The sound of voices in the hallway alerted them to the children's return. Quinn reluctantly moved away from her. ''We'll talk later. I need to get the kids to bed.''

She nodded, then watched him walk away with Sara and Kevin, wishing she didn't have the feeling that their relationship was about to be tested in a way they'd never expected.

IT WASN'T THE HOMECOMING Quinn had planned. Instead of having Dena's soft, curvy body next to his in bed, he was lying beside a seven-year-old boy wearing flannel Spiderman pajamas. Quinn glanced at the young boy as he slept. It was the only time during the past week or so that he'd seen any peace on that innocent face.

He preferred the sleeping Kevin to the awake one. Asleep he didn't look so much like his father, and Quinn didn't have to look into eyes full of sadness. Nor did he have to notice how Kevin glanced sideways at him in the very same way Doug had slanted him looks. Kevin was every bit Doug's son, from the blond hair and blue eyes to the small dimple in his chin.

Pain rifled through Quinn at the memory of his friend. They'd been the best of buddies during their college days. Teammates. Roommates.

Memories haunted Quinn as he lay awake. The three of them sitting around Patsy's tiny table in her efficiency apartment while she tutored them in English lit. The party they'd attended when the hockey team had clinched a spot in the Frozen Four tournament. The hurry-up wedding at the justice of the peace with Patsy crying and Doug looking more nervous than Quinn had ever seen him.

They'd been such close friends during those college days. Once Quinn turned pro, everything had changed. He never sensed that it had bothered Doug that he'd jumped to the NHL, but he wasn't so sure about Patsy. She'd never treated Quinn the same after he'd announced his decision to enter the draft. And once he'd actually quit college, they'd gradually drifted apart.

It shouldn't have surprised him. Doug and Patsy were parents, trying to balance college life with marriage, while Quinn was fighting for survival in the NHL as a rookie. While they struggled with diapers and day care, he fought for a starting position on his new team, determined to have a spectacular debut in the professional world of hockey.

From that point on, their lives went in very different directions. Doug and Patsy finished college, then moved to South Carolina, where he took a job managing a restaurant. Quinn bounced from team to team, never settling in one place long enough to call it home. When they did manage to find time to see each other, things were never quite the same. Those college days were gone, although never forgotten by Doug and Quinn.

When Quinn did finally fall asleep, it was only to be troubled by dreams of the past. The next morning he felt as if he hadn't slept at all. Quietly he slipped out of bed, not wanting to disturb Kevin.

He stepped out of his bedroom and was immediately reminded that he wasn't alone. Sara lay on the roll-away, curled into a ball, her face turned into the pillow. Quinn tiptoed past, reaching for his cell phone from the kitchen counter, then went into the bathroom and closed the door.

He needed to check with Doug's attorney and see if any progress had been made in finding the necessary help for Doug's sister. He punched in the numbers. As he waited for someone to answer, he glanced in the mirror and grimaced. Between the bags under his eyes and the dark stubble on his chin, he didn't have a look that would inspire confidence in any kid.

He'd shave as soon as he finished talking to the lawyer. At least that was the plan until he heard a fist pounding on the door.

"Quinn, I gotta go to the bathroom…bad," Kevin mumbled in a small voice.

He opened the door and motioned for the kid to enter while he slipped quietly back into his bedroom. A secretary at the law firm informed him that Doug's attorney wouldn't be available until after four. Quinn asked several questions, but she was unable to give him any answers. He decided he might as well leave a message and hung up.

As he ended the call, he turned to see Kevin standing in the doorway. "Hey, buddy. You still tired? Want to climb back into bed?"

He shook his head. "I want to go home." His lower lip trembled and he began to cry.

Quinn lifted him up into his arms and sat down with him on the bed. "I'm sorry, Kevin, but you can't go home just yet."

"When will we be able to go?" he asked on a sob.

"I'm not sure. Look." He reached for the remote at the foot of the bed. "Why don't you watch TV for a few minutes while I make another phone call and try to get an answer for you?"

The cartoon characters that popped onto the TV screen were enough of a distraction for the boy that Quinn was able to leave the room. He was about to go back into the bathroom to call Doug's sister when he noticed the door was shut. A glance at the roll-away told him Sara had beat him to it.

With one eye on the bathroom door, he stood in the far corner of the living room, dialing the number the attorney had given him.

When a woman's voice answered with, "Roberta Grant," he said, "This is Quinn Sterling."

"How are the children?"

The voice sounded frail and weak. Quinn replied, "They're okay. Unsettled, but okay."

"It must be so difficult for them. It just breaks my heart to think of them without Doug and Patsy." He heard a sniffle, then she said, "I wish they were here with me right now so I could comfort them."

"It will be good for them to be with you—with family. Were you able to make arrangements to get someone to assist you with their care?"

"I wish I could say yes, but you see I had a bit of setback yesterday and I found out I need another surgery on my back. I'm not going to be able to take Kevin and Sara until it heals."

Quinn felt as if someone had just knocked the air out of him.

When he didn't say anything, she said, "Between my hospital stay and my rehabilitation, I won't be in any condition to take care of two children. You do understand, don't you?"

He wanted to say no, he didn't understand at all. What was he supposed to do with two frightened, lonesome kids who didn't want to be around him? He was a temporary guardian who knew nothing about the needs of a seven- and a twelve-year-old.

"Quinn?"

He sighed. "I'm still here." He raked a hand over his head. "When do you think you will be able to take the kids?"

"The doctor said I'm going to be off my feet for six to eight weeks. I'm sorry. I know this complicates things for you, and it breaks my heart not to be able to help my niece and nephew right now."

Six to eight weeks. It was already the end of April. That meant he'd have the children until the middle of June, maybe even the end of June.

"You want me to keep them." It was a statement, not a question, and one that gave him great concern. It wasn't that he didn't have experience with children. He had six nieces and nephews. Just because he was single didn't mean he didn't like children. Actually, he thought they were fun. Fun when they belonged to someone else. When they were his responsibility 24/7, that was another thing.

"Obviously my brother and sister-in-law had great confidence in you. Otherwise they wouldn't have designated you as the guardian of their children," she pointed out.

And he *had* been designated as their guardian. He remembered shortly after Sara's birth when Doug had asked him if he would object to being named in the will. Quinn had chided him for even bringing up the subject, joking about how they'd made a pact in college that one day they'd be the oldest hockey players on the ice on alumni night. They'd show the world that they could still lace up their skates when they were ninety.

Doug had said he hadn't forgotten their agreement and that there was no way in hell he wouldn't be passing him the puck at the alumni game when they were both one hundred. Naming him as guardian was simply a precaution he had to take as a parent. He'd said it was better to have a legal guardian named and not ever have to use one, than to need one and not have one.

"If keeping the children with you is an imposition, I'm sure if you spoke to Doug's attorney he could make arrangements with an agency that provides professional child-care services until I'm back on my feet."

Quinn felt a body at his side and looked down to see that Kevin had quietly come up to him and was once more his shadow, as he had been ever since he'd set eyes on him. The boy whispered, "Can I watch TV out here?"

Quinn handed him the remote and motioned for him to sit on the sofa. The bathroom door opened and out came Sara.

Quinn turned his attention back to the phone. "Roberta, let me think about this."

"Is that my aunt?" Sara demanded, her face lighting up at the discovery. "I want to talk to her." She practically pulled the phone from his hands.

Their conversation was brief. Quinn watched her animated features go from anticipation to rejection, as Roberta Grant told her the same thing she'd told him. After only a few minutes, Sara handed the phone back to Quinn. "She wants to talk to you."

Quinn ended the conversation, telling her he'd be

in touch. As soon as he'd hung up, Sara said, "She doesn't want us, either."

She dropped down onto the sofa, folding her arms across her chest.

"That's not what she said, Sara," Quinn corrected her. "She's going to be in the hospital."

"Whatever," she said disinterestedly.

"Where are we going to live if Auntie Bobbie doesn't want us?" Kevin asked, his face pale.

Quinn looked at the woeful face staring up at him. Kevin reminded him of a lost puppy, so desperate for someone to want him in his home.

"With me," Quinn answered. "You're both going to stay with me until your aunt recovers."

CHAPTER EIGHT

DENA HOPED she'd see Quinn on Friday, but he didn't call. She assumed he was preoccupied with his temporary wards, so she accepted an invitation from one of the graphic designers to join a small group of Delaney employees for drinks after work. Normally Dena wasn't a happy-hour person, but she saw it as an opportunity to get to know her co-workers better. She also thought it was probably a good idea to give Quinn some space to deal with his new responsibilities. That's why, when happy hour ended and she still hadn't heard from him, she stayed to have dinner, as well.

She was glad she had when she returned home and saw there wasn't a message on her home phone, either. As she got ready for bed, she wondered how he was coping with the kids and decided that she'd go down for breakfast the following morning to find out.

However, the only people at the large round oak table were Leonie and Krystal. Leonie sat with the newspaper and Krystal had the yellow pages of the phone book opened in front of her.

"I thought you'd be at work," Dena said to Krystal as she helped herself to a cup of coffee.

"I don't have to go in until noon," she replied.

Dena glanced at the open book and saw that she was looking at formal wear. "Are you looking for a tuxedo?'' she asked, as Krystal's finger moved down a list of numbers.

"Not for me. For Garret,'' she replied. "There's this big gala ball at the hospital next month, and he barely has time to eat, let alone call around to find a tux to wear, so I told him I'd take care of it for him.''

Dena wondered why Leonie didn't do it, but then Krystal added, "Actually, it's better if I pick it out. That way I can make sure it goes with what I'm wearing.''

"You're going with him?'' Dena asked.

"I wish I were going,'' Leonie remarked. "They're going to have a terrific orchestra,'' she said over her coffee cup.

"So why aren't you?'' Dena asked.

It was Krystal who answered. "Because he can't be with his mother when he sees a certain lady doctor. You see, when Garret was in med school he had a very intense relationship with a girl in his class.''

"They were going to get married, only she decided she was too good for him,'' Leonie interjected in a sour tone Dena had never heard her use before.

"Yeah, she moved on to bigger fish. She married some hotshot doctor,'' Krystal continued. "Now she's going to be at this big gala event Garret has to attend, and of course, when he sees her for the first time in three years he doesn't want to be alone.''

"So you're going with him as his date?'' Dena asked.

"I sure am, and I'm going to show that hoity-toity lady doctor that if she thinks Garret's been pining over her, she's sadly mistaken. Hey, I can hold my own when it comes to looking good,'' she said without any pretentiousness.

Leonie patted her hand. "It's really sweet of you to do this for Garret."

Krystal shrugged away the compliment. "It'll be fun. And I'm not just doing it for him. I've always wanted to go to one of those big society galas. You know how I love to dress up…and Shannon's going to do my hair."

"Sounds like punishment to me," Dena quipped good-naturedly.

Krystal simply wrinkled her nose, then turned her attention back to the phone book.

"Dena, I'm glad you came down this morning because I have something to ask you," Leonie said.

"Sure. What is it?"

"It's about Sara and Kevin. Quinn asked me if it would be all right if they stay with him until the end of June. I told him as far as I'm concerned, it's not a problem, but I do have leases with my tenants that say this is a residence for adults only. So if it's a problem having the children here, I want you to tell me. This is your residence, too, and I respect your rights."

The end of June? Dena frowned. She'd understood the children were only going to be with him for a few days.

When she didn't respond right away, Leonie asked, "Does it bother you that there are children in the house?"

"No," Dena answered honestly.

"You're sure? Up to this point Sara and Kevin have been rather quiet, but it could get noisy around the place at times, and I know you do a lot of work at home," Leonie warned.

"No, it's all right. I can work at the office if necessary," she replied.

"I don't think Quinn will allow things to get out of hand, do you?" Krystal said on a chuckle.

Dena shook her head. "He's been a very considerate neighbor so far."

Krystal grinned slyly. "Very considerate."

If Leonie saw the look that passed between the two women, she didn't comment. "I know he wants to do right by those kids."

"We all do," Krystal added. "They're going through a really bad time right now. I only wish there was something we could do to help. Leonie, you will let us know if there is anything, won't you?"

"Of course I will. Right now I think the three of them just need some time to get used to each other. Quinn's become a father overnight. That's quite an adjustment for any man."

"Thank goodness all of this happened after his hockey season was over. At least now he has the time to spend with them," Krystal commented. "What's he going to do about school? Will he enroll them here or will they make up what they missed once they're with their aunt?"

"He doesn't want them to get behind, so he's going Monday to enroll Kevin at the local elementary and Sara at the junior high."

Krystal sighed. "Poor Sara—to be twelve and have to change schools is hard. Junior high is awkward enough without having to leave and start over in another place." She shuddered in horror. "She's going to be a handful for Quinn."

"I'm sure he'll get a lot of support from his family.

There are enough of them in the area that he can turn to for help,'' Leonie said.

Dena knew his family lived nearby, yet he hadn't told her much about them other than the fact that his mother was a teacher. She hadn't met his parents or his sisters. Why would she? They'd agreed their relationship would have no strings.

Leonie folded her newspaper and rose to her feet. ''I have work to do. I want to thank you both for your understanding. Quinn and those kids have been through a lot the past couple of weeks. I don't think he needs the added stress of trying to find a more suitable place for them to live...not when it's only for a couple of months.''

''We feel the same, don't we, Dena?'' Krystal looked at her expectantly.

''Yes,'' Dena replied.

Leonie smiled gratefully and wished them both a good day, then left, leaving Krystal and Dena alone at the table.

''You don't have a problem with the kids being here, do you?'' Krystal asked, her brow creasing slightly in suspicion.

''No. I already told Leonie I didn't.''

''I know what you said to Leonie, but I also saw the way you squirmed when she brought up the subject. You looked so uneasy.''

Yes, she had been uneasy, but only because Quinn hadn't told her about the kids staying on with him. He could have called her and discussed it with her before he went to Leonie, but then why would he? Their relationship was one of convenience...at least that's how it was beginning to feel to her. She didn't want to admit any of that to Krystal, however.

"Yes, I was a bit apprehensive. We were talking about children who'd lost their parents in a very sudden, tragic way, and now they're having to deal with some big changes in their lives. It's very sad."

"And you're sure that's all it was?"

"Yes. What else would it be?"

She shrugged. "I don't know. It's just that you were so quiet the other night when we were all in the kitchen...and then today...well, I thought maybe you didn't like kids or something."

"I like kids," she insisted. "Please don't go jumping to any wrong conclusions about me," she said, annoyed that her voice had an edge to it, but the subject of children *was* an uncomfortable one and not because she didn't like them. She simply felt inadequate around them. "Of course I was quiet Thursday night in the kitchen. Those kids didn't know me, and when I tried to tell Kevin that I was sorry about his parents, you saw how he burst into tears. It was awkward."

"I'm sorry. I didn't mean to upset you," Krystal apologized. "I just think you and Quinn make a really cute couple, and I'd hate to see you break up over the kids."

Dena didn't want to discuss her relationship with Quinn. "I really don't want to be talking about this. Could we please not discuss my personal life?"

She hadn't meant for the words to come out so sharply. From the look on Krystal's face, she could see that she was hurt.

Her voice quivered as she said, "I'm sorry, Dena. I didn't mean to stick my nose in where it doesn't belong."

Remorse had Dena wishing she hadn't been so

abrupt with her. She wished it wasn't so difficult for her to talk about her feelings, that she could enjoy girl talk the way other women did, but she simply didn't know how.

What she did know was that she hadn't meant to hurt Krystal, who'd been nothing but friendly toward her. She needed to make amends and said in a gentle voice, "Let's just forget it, okay?"

"No, we're not going to forget it. I do this all the time. Because I blurt out everything in my personal life, I expect that others want to do the same thing. I respect your privacy, Dena, I really do."

There was such youthful sincerity in her eyes that Dena reached across the table and patted her hand. "I know you do, and I didn't mean to snap at you, but the truth is my personal life is pretty boring."

"You're dating a professional hockey player and you call that boring?"

Dena tried to hide her smile, but couldn't. "All right, it's not boring. Actually, it's rather exciting, but honestly, there really isn't anything special going on between me and Quinn," she stated evenly.

"Would you like there to be?" Before Dena could reply, Krystal threw up her hands and said, "See? There I go again. You don't have to answer that."

Dena didn't answer because she wasn't sure just what it was she wanted from Quinn. She'd thought they could date, enjoy each other's company and not get emotionally entangled. She still wanted to believe that.

"It isn't that I don't want to tell you about me and Quinn, it's just that I'm not comfortable talking about my love life," she explained. "I never have been. It's just the way I am."

Krystal leaned back and sighed. "And I talk about mine far too often. Do you think maybe we if hang out together more often you could get me to stop revealing so much of myself to strangers, and I could get you to open up a bit to your friends?"

Dena smiled. "Maybe. Or maybe we should just accept that we are who we are."

A smile slowly spread across her face. "Okay, no more talk of Quinn. I need you to repeat Roy's name."

"Why?"

"Because I want to hear it over and over so that the next time I hear it in public I won't lose it."

"Did you lose it recently?" Dena wanted to know.

She nodded. "At the salon. Of course it didn't help that I was already having a bad day. It started when I dropped a bowl of color on the floor. After that it was all downhill. I had one crabby client after another so that by the time someone asked me about Roy..." Her voice wavered and she said, "See. I still get choked up just thinking about it."

"The spilled dye or the whining customers?"

That brought a weak smile to her face. "It would be so much easier if I could just forget that guy existed."

"Hey, I thought our independence day celebration erased his existence."

"You're right, it did," she stated with a stronger conviction than Dena knew she was feeling. "I'd better make some phone calls or else Garret won't have a tux for the ball."

Just then her cell phone rang. She flipped up the top and said, "Omigosh! It's Ben. I haven't heard from him in ages."

"Ben?" Dena shot her an inquisitive look.

"I dated him last year. He's a rerun," she said, then added, "I'd better see what he wants." And just as quickly as her gloominess had come over her, it was gone. She hurried out of the room. Dena heard her say, "Hey, I'm so glad you called. I've missed you."

"WHEN LIFE HANDS YOU LEMONS, make lemonade." Quinn wondered how many times he'd heard his mother utter those particular words of encouragement. The only problem was, when he got lemons he wanted to reach for the tequila and salt.

Only he couldn't. He had the responsibility of two children. One was asleep in his bed, the other sat in front of MTV watching music videos and clutching a tattered stuffed bear called Dooda. Not how he'd hoped to spend his Saturday night. Still, he had no choice but to keep them with him until their aunt could take over. Now the question he faced was, what was he going to do with them for the next two months?

It was a huge responsibility, and one he didn't take lightly. Leonie had told him that Sara was probably old enough to stay alone and even baby-sit her younger brother, but to Quinn she seemed very fragile and young. Yet when he mentioned the possibility of getting a nanny, the twelve-year-old had become even more hostile than she already was. She'd assured him she'd been baby-sitting for the past year and that she didn't need anyone treating her like a little kid.

Perched on the roll-away in her T-shirt and jeans, clutching a stuffed animal, she looked very much like a little kid to Quinn. He wished there was some way he could reach out to her, but so far he hadn't had any luck. He would try again.

"Kevin's asleep already," he said as he sat down on the sofa. "How about you and I play a game?" he suggested. "I've got Scrabble, Monopoly, Risk..." He rattled off a list on his fingers.

"No, thank you," she said politely.

"What about some cards?" He tried to think of all the things he and his sisters had played when they were kids.

"I'd rather watch TV."

"We could rent a movie from pay-per-view. Should I check and see what's available?"

"I already looked. There isn't anything I want to see," she said sullenly.

Quinn thought for a moment. "What about Sony PlayStation?"

"I hate video games."

Frustration welled in him. It had been this way since the day he'd gone to South Carolina. He could do no right. Every suggestion he made she shot down, and he wondered if all girls her age were this difficult.

"You don't have to baby-sit me. I told you, I can take care of myself."

"I'm not asking because I think you need supervision. I thought it might be fun to play a game or watch a movie together."

She shot him a look that said he had to be kidding.

He was losing his patience. He folded his arms across his chest. "And what do you think I should do for entertainment this evening?"

"You could go downstairs and see your girlfriend."

So much for keeping his relationship with Dena

private. Knowing there was no point in denying his feelings for her, he simply said, "We didn't make plans for tonight." It wasn't exactly the truth. If everything had gone as planned, he and Dena would have been in Mexico.

"So can't you just drop in on her?"

"I could, but..." He was hesitant to say that he didn't feel like leaving Sara alone.

As if she could read his thoughts, she said, "Nothing's going to happen to me if you're not in the same room with me."

He wanted to believe she was right, because he needed to see Dena. He'd thought about her all day, wondering if she'd heard that the kids would be staying until the end of June. He'd wanted to tell her himself, but Kevin had blurted out the news to Leonie when they'd gone down for breakfast yesterday, and from the discussion he'd had with Leonie, he knew that she planned to talk to Dena. "I'll leave you Dena's number in case you need anything."

She shrugged. "Whatever. It's not like I can't walk down a flight of stairs and knock on a door."

"You sure you don't mind if I leave for a little while?" he asked as he scribbled Dena's number on the notepad next to the phone.

"I don't mind," she said on a note of boredom.

"You'll be all right?"

"I'll be all right," she repeated on the same note.

"Call me if there's a problem," he said as he slipped out the door. He practically flew down the flight of stairs to the second-floor landing.

As he knocked on Dena's door he realized that he hadn't given a thought as to whether or not she'd be home. To his relief, she was. She answered the door wearing gray sweatpants and a navy-blue tank top. Her hair had been tied up in a ponytail, but most of it had come undone and hung provocatively around her neck.

"Quinn! I wasn't expecting you," she said, her voice sounding breathless.

"Can I come in?"

She opened the door wider and gestured for him to enter. "I'm in kind of a mess. You'll have to step around it."

As soon as he entered her apartment he saw to what she referred. Rolled out on the floor was a bolt of pink-and-white polka-dot cloth with paper shapes pinned to it.

"What are you making?" he asked.

"A dress. I wasn't expecting company." She moved some of the fabric so he could step into the small area she used as a sitting room.

"Is it for you?"

"Yes."

"Do you make all of your clothes?"

"Some of them."

It was a first for him. Most of the women he'd dated wore designer originals, and they were definitely not the designers. "I'm impressed."

She chuckled. "Why? It's not that difficult."

"Are you kidding? I took Living Skills when I was in the seventh grade. I know what it's like to try to work one of those things," he said, pointing to her sewing machine. He smiled at the memory. "If it wasn't for Caroline Caulder, I would have flunked that class."

"She did your homework for you?" she guessed.

He nodded. "We had to make this pillow. She sewed all the edges. I did help her stuff it, though."

"I bet you did," she said with a sly grin. "Can you stay for a while?"

Her question made his heart sing. "As a matter of fact, I can. Kevin's asleep and Sara's watching TV." He sat down on the love seat, hoping she'd sit next to him.

"Need something to drink?" she asked.

He shook his head and patted the seat next to him. "All I need is you." When she sat down beside him he pulled her close and kissed her. "I've missed you."

"I've missed you, too," she said, kissing him back with equal fervor.

"I have something to tell you."

"If it's about the kids, I think I already know."

"Leonie told you?"

She nodded. "She said they're staying until the end of June."

"It's not going to be easy—I know next to nothing about kids—but we'll make it work. I owe it to Doug and Patsy. I know if the situation had been reversed, Doug would have done the same thing for me."

"I don't know what else to say except I'm sorry."

He shrugged. "Stuff happens and life doesn't always go as planned," he stated philosophically. "I just hope I can do right by them. Sara's really having a hard time."

"She's scared and lonely and terribly sad."

"And she was counting on only having to spend a few days here. I know it was a big disappointment for her to hear her aunt wasn't going to be able to take them until July."

"What about Kevin? Was he upset with the news, too?"

He shook his head. "Not at all. Just the opposite, actually."

"He's become quite attached to you already, hasn't he?"

"You've noticed?"

She smiled. "It's rather obvious."

"It's probably because I'm a guy."

"You make him feel safe in a world in which he's lost his only sense of security."

"He's like a shadow. He doesn't like to let me out of his sight for even a minute. I'm hoping that once he starts school he'll lose some of that insecurity."

"School might be good for both of them," Dena commented.

He leaned his head back and closed his eyes. "I still can't believe this has happened."

She gently traced his forehead with her fingertips. "I wish I could erase all the stress I see in your face.

"You do, just by being here."

She placed a butterfly kiss on his lips, and it was sweet temptation. When she slipped two fingers inside his shirt to undo the buttons, his eyes opened.

"Do you need to get back to the kids?" she asked as her fingers caressed his chest, reminding him of a need he'd been trying to ignore.

"No, but we need to talk."

She stilled her fingers.

"We need to decide if we should continue on with the way things have been," he told her, holding her gaze.

"Is there a reason why we shouldn't?"

"Only the obvious one. The kids."

"I don't want things to change…unless you do?"

"You're okay with our original arrangement?"

She nodded. "Aren't you?"

He smiled in relief. "Yeah, I am. It's just that I know it's going to be difficult to make time for us while I'm guardian to Kevin and Sara."

"We knew when we started seeing each other that time was going to be at a premium," she said, her hands sliding down his chest until they reached his waist. When they fumbled with his belt buckle, he inhaled sharply.

"That's why we need to make the most of whatever time we have," he said, slipping his hands under the tank top. His fingers found naked flesh. She wasn't wearing a bra. Seeing the look on his face at the discovery, she smiled.

"That's right. We have to take advantage of every opportunity."

He pulled the tank top over her head and stared at her beauty. "I've been dreaming about this ever since I left on the final road trip."

"No more dreaming," she said, her eyes darkening with desire as she undid his belt buckle.

The ringing of the phone stilled her hands. She grimaced in frustration, then went to answer it. Quinn knew by the look on her face that it was for him.

"It's Sara," she said, confirming his suspicions as she handed him the phone.

"Hi, Sara, what's up?" he asked, trying not to sigh at the sight of Dena covering her naked breasts.

"You'd better come back up here."

"Why? What's wrong?"

"Kevin threw up in your bed."

Quinn knew at that moment that he'd seen his last glimpse of naked female flesh for a while.

DENA KNEW Quinn was frustrated. She was frustrated, too. Neither one was used to having to work their schedules around kids. Both agreed they would do whatever was necessary to make sure they did spend time together.

That's why Dena didn't want to turn down any of Quinn's invitations to go out with him and the children. During the following week, she went with them to the pizza parlor, the movies and the shopping mall, hoping her presence would help Quinn in some way.

She doubted that it did. Although Kevin warmed to her, Sara treated her with the same insolence she showed Quinn, which Dena tried not to take personally. It was hard not to feel uncomfortable, however, when the girl made it so obvious that she resented Dena's presence.

When Dena eventually mentioned her concerns to Quinn, he told her that, in his opinion, the girl was simply working through her grief. Dena didn't want to be the one upon whom she worked it through, and she told him she thought it was better if she didn't go along on the next outing.

The next evening Quinn showed up on her doorstep. She invited him in, but he declined.

"If I come in I'm not going to want to leave," he told her, his eyes full of desire.

"I know. That's why I asked you," she said with a tempting grin.

He shoved her into her apartment and kissed her until she thought her knees would buckle. Then he sighed. "I can't stand not seeing you. I have a plan."

She folded her arms across her chest. "Go on. I'm listening."

"Being the kids are new to this area, I thought I'd give them a Minnesota experience. Do you know what next weekend is?"

"I've been working so hard I don't even know what today is," she quipped.

"It's the fishing opener." His eyes lit up at the thought. "When we were kids my mom and dad always took us camping on that weekend. We'd go to this campsite where they rent boats and there's this little bait shop…" He went on, expounding on the wonders of the Pinecone Campground.

When he finally stopped, Dena said, "You want me to go camping?" She did her best not to show him just how unappealing it sounded.

Apparently she did a good job because he continued. "It'll be fun. I've got a tent and all the equipment. And I've already checked with reservations. We can get a campsite at Pinecone. We'll take the kids fishing, play some games, sit around the campfire and eat s'mores. What do you think? Will you come with us?"

He was so enthusiastic, she had a hard time telling him what she really thought of the idea. When he reached for her hands and said, "I know this is a far cry from Mexico, but at least we can be together," she found it hard to voice any objection. And then there was that look of promise in those blue eyes.

"I've only been camping once when I was about nine, but I was a Girl Scout," she confessed.

"I'll teach you what you don't know. I've already seen what a quick learner you are," he said with a grin that reminded her of other things he'd taught her.

A weekend with him in the woods would be wonderful. The problem was the kids would be there, too. From the way Sara had been treating her, she knew it could get uncomfortable for both of them.

"I'd like to go, but I'm not sure it's a good idea. Sara's made it clear that she—"

He silenced her by placing his finger on her lips. "Sara's getting better slowly. Just say you'll come. Please."

She felt her resistance cave in. "Let me check my calendar." She glanced at her desk and sighed. "I promised my brother I'd watch his kids that weekend. I'm sorry."

His face fell momentarily, then he said, "Bring the kids along."

"I can't do that!" She already felt inept when it came to taking care of kids when they were in a safe environment like a home. She'd never manage in the wilderness.

"Why not? It'll be fun."

"It'll be a lot of work," she corrected him.

"Camping is camping whether there are two or seven. The more there are, the easier it is to play games."

Dena thought she had to be crazy to even contemplate the idea, but she did want to be with Quinn. And at least Jeremy, Bethany and Luke liked her. It would be nice to have friendly faces around to counteract Sara's hostility.

"I'd have to okay it with my brother and his wife," she found herself saying.

"Call and ask them."

She glanced at her watch. It wasn't *that* late. Lisa thought it was a terrific idea for Jeremy and Bethany to go on the camping trip, but had reservations regarding three-year-old Luke.

Just when Dena thought it wasn't going to work out, her sister-in-law offered to ask her best friend to take Luke for the weekend. Thanks to three-way calling, the arrangements were completed in a matter of minutes.

When Dena hung up the phone, Quinn asked anxiously, "We're set?"

She nodded. "You do realize that my nephew could very well become another Kevin, not leaving your side the entire weekend? He's one of your biggest fans."

Quinn smiled. "Do I take it that means you're bringing your niece and nephew?"

She nodded. "I hope this isn't going to be a big mistake."

He kissed her quickly. "No way. This is going to be great. You'll see."

After he'd gone up the stairs, Dena stood in the doorway pondering what she'd just agreed to do. A weekend in a tent in the woods with four kids. What kind of power did Quinn have over her, anyway? She didn't think she should search very hard for that answer. It was better not to know.

CHAPTER NINE

THEY LEFT for the campground as soon as school was out the following Friday. Quinn was as excited as the kids as he loaded the camping gear into the back of his SUV. He'd made a list of everything they'd need, checking it carefully as everyone piled their stuff inside the vehicle.

They hit the freeway, joining the procession of cars, campers and pickups leaving the city and heading north for the weekend. The two girls sat in the very last seat, the two boys in the middle and Quinn and Dena in the front.

Bethany and Kevin didn't have a problem getting acquainted, but Dena could see by the way Sara looked at Jeremy that there was no way she was going to consider him a new friend. That was why Dena suggested the two girls sit together. Jeremy didn't object, for it meant he was closer to Quinn.

Although Dena knew that Quinn was good with kids, taking a three-hour drive with them showed her just how much patience he had. Wisely, he'd brought movies to play on the vehicle's DVD entertainment system in the ceiling over the passenger area. Except for Sara, who looked totally bored with the entire experience, the kids were content.

The sun was close to setting when they arrived at the campground. Quinn worked quickly to unload the tent from the carrier on top of the SUV, and in a surprisingly short time had their weekend abode in place.

"Well? What do you think?" He looked at Dena for her opinion.

"It's...." She searched for the right word, wondering what he expected her to say about the tent. She didn't think he wanted to hear that it was a little smaller than she expected, which was exactly what she thought. "It's perfect!" she said with an enthusiasm she wasn't feeling. "Two rooms, windows...poles." She smiled lamely.

Her sole camping experience had been in a trailer home that had beds, a small refrigerator, a stove and even a bathroom. This tent was nothing but a large square with a canvas wall down the center, a zippered entrance and an awning.

Sara had a similar reaction to the sight of the tent. She screwed up her face and said, "We all sleep together?"

"It's camping," Quinn said amiably. "Grab your sleeping bags and claim your spots."

It didn't take long for the other three to scramble to get their sleeping bags and spread them in the tent.

"Maybe the girls should be in one room and the boys in the other," Dena suggested as Sara rolled her eyes when Bethany spread her bag next to the boys.

"Okay!" the eight-year-old girl said, dragging her sleeping bag to the opposite side of the tent. "Can I sleep next to you?" she asked her aunt.

"Everybody's going to be touching everyone else," Sara pointed out with a look on her face that conveyed exactly how unattractive the thought was.

For the next few minutes they rearranged the bags

several times before everyone was finally content with the layout—everyone, that is, except Sara. By the time everything had been unloaded, it was dark.

"All right, listen up," Quinn told them. "We have two lanterns. One stays in the tent, the other is for you to use if you need to make a trip to the bathroom. I really don't want any of you going alone. Ask me or Dena to go with you."

"I don't need anyone to go to the bathroom with me," Sara stated defiantly, a look of haughtiness on her face.

"You'll have privacy once you get there," Quinn assured her.

"Can we make a campfire?" Jeremy asked.

"You bet. We're going to have s'mores. We've got chocolate, marshmallows and graham crackers."

Three of the four children voiced their approval, helping Quinn pick up the dead branches near the campsite to build the fire. Only Sara refused to join in, slumping down onto the picnic table bench to watch the others.

Whether it was the lure of chocolate or the fact that her brother repeatedly told her how good the s'mores were, Dena wasn't sure, but before long, Sara reached for a stick and a marshmallow. It gave Dena hope that tomorrow would go more smoothly.

It didn't.

They awoke to the sound of Sara screaming and shaking her sleeping bag up and down. "There's a creepy bug in here!"

It was Jeremy who scrambled around the canvas wall to slap at the invader with his shoe. "It's only a spider," he said when he'd thumped it a good one.

Sara turned to Quinn and said in an accusing tone,

"I thought you said there wouldn't be any bugs in here."

"There aren't. Spiders are arachnids, not insects," Jeremy told her, which didn't do much to console her.

"They're still creepy," she said on a shiver, straightening her sleeping bag.

"He probably crawled in through the opening. The zipper wasn't shut all the way," Quinn said as he unzipped the door and pushed aside the flaps.

Sara wasted no time following him outside, mumbling, "I'm not staying in there. At least out here I can see what's crawling around."

Dena heard him say, "Looks like a perfect morning. Sun's shining, lake's calm." He tied back the entrance flap so that those inside could see out.

"Are we going fishing?" Kevin asked, crawling out of his bag.

"We sure are. The question is, do we want to go before or after breakfast?" Quinn asked.

The consensus was that it would be better to eat first, fish later.

"I'm not doing anything until I shower." Sara's voice carried on the still morning air.

Dena understood the sentiment. Having slept in her clothes in a tent made her wish she could hop in a hot shower about now, too. She scrambled outside and told Sara as much.

"You know where it's at," Quinn said, nodding toward the hill behind them where the building with the public showers was located. "I'm going to set up the fishing rods."

"I'm not going fishing," Sara stated in her usual **defiant** tone.

Dena knew the young girl couldn't stay behind by herself, and said, "Maybe I won't go, either."

Quinn looked as if he wanted to protest, but he simply shrugged. "Okay. I'll take Jeremy, Kevin and Bethany." He leaned into the tent and said, "You three want to go out on the pontoon and catch some fish, don't you?"

Their enthusiastic responses told Dena that she'd be left alone with Sara. A challenge probably far greater than trying to bait a hook or take off a fish.

Actually, everything at the campsite turned out to be a challenge. Dena had no experience cooking for six people, let alone trying to do it on a two-burner camp stove. Cleanup was an equally difficult challenge, having to heat the water before dishes could be done and using a small plastic container for a sink. Quinn took everything in stride, relishing the obstacles the outdoors presented. It didn't seem to bother him when the children complained, either.

Not so Dena. She liked peace and quiet and harmony. With four kids there was constant commotion. It didn't help that Sara was so obviously unhappy. No matter what anyone said or did, she seemed determined not to have a good time.

Dena was at a loss. She had no idea how to help a kid who'd just lost her parents in a terrible accident. It was obvious from Sara's behavior that she wasn't looking for help from Dena. If anything, she seemed to resent her presence, bristling whenever Dena tried to talk to her.

Quinn didn't miss the tension between the two of them, pulling Dena aside to ask, "Are you sure you don't want to come fishing? I'll tell Sara she has to come."

She put a hand on his arm. "No. If you do that, she's going to resent me."

He put his hands on his waist. "It seems to me she's resenting just about everything anyway. Do you really think it'll matter?"

She chewed on her lower lip. "Probably not, but I just feel so bad for her. She's hurting."

"I realize that, but the pain isn't going to go away by her being difficult. She can bring her CD player and her headset and just sit on the pontoon. She doesn't have to fish," he told her.

Dena wondered if he wasn't right. "Maybe it is better to do everything as a group."

A few hours later, however, Dena wasn't so sure. Although Sara was no longer sullen, she was still very quiet. She sat off to one side of the pontoon, her headset on as she listened to CDs. She was polite to everyone, but Dena could see that she was unhappy.

That was the pattern for the rest of the day. In every activity, Sara was a reluctant participant. The other three kids couldn't get enough of Quinn's attention, yet when it came to Sara, the kinder Quinn was toward her, the more prickly she became. To Dena's amazement, he didn't give up, but kept encouraging her and giving her every opportunity to have fun.

He showed all of the kids the same amount of attention. Dena had expected that Jeremy would be impressed by him. He was, after all, a hockey player. But even Bethany was charmed. Dena thought Quinn was a bit like the Pied Piper. Instead of a flute he used his athletic ability to lead the kids on all sorts of fun escapades. They fished, they tossed a Frisbee, they hiked, they played catch, and by the time they had roasted hot dogs for dinner, they were all yawning.

Dena offered to do the cleanup and told the kids to go into the tent and get ready for bed. Quinn was soon at her side.

"They're bushed," he said, nodding toward the tent.

"They should be. You kept them busy."

He smiled. "Yeah. I didn't do too badly, did I?"

She shook her head. "You have a lot of patience with all of them." In a lower voice she added, "Even Sara."

He sighed and stepped closer to her so he could lower his voice, too. "I think I saw a hint of a smile when we were watching those baby ducks trail after their mother."

Dena sighed. "I wish there was something I could do."

"Have you tried talking to her one-on-one?"

She nodded. "It didn't do much good." Dena didn't want to tell him that Sara behaved as most women did around her—as if she needed to be on her guard. If Quinn was hoping the two of them would bond female to female, he was in for disappointment. "I think she's determined not to have any fun."

"She'll come around in time," he said with confidence. "I predict that by tomorrow night she'll have a smile on her face just like the rest of them."

But Sara looked pretty much the same, slumped in the back seat of the SUV on the ride back to the city, as she'd looked on Friday afternoon when they left. Unhappy.

Dena didn't think it was possible that she could have complained more on Sunday than she had on

Saturday, but she was certain that if she'd kept score, she would have had more marks on the second day of their camping trip. But then, it had been a difficult day for all of them. The warm spring weather had been pushed away by a cold rain that had them finally admitting defeat, packing up the tent and heading home.

Dena was as relieved as Sara that their camping experience was over. The weekend hadn't gone as smoothly as she'd hoped it would, either. She'd made a mess of the cooking, struggled with the camping chores and was marginal at best when it came to the sporting activities.

She was quiet on the trip home, and Quinn didn't seem to mind. As the windshield wipers swished back and forth across the glass to clear away the drizzling rain, she wondered what thoughts were going through his mind.

She found out later that evening when he showed up at her door with a bottle of wine and two glasses.

"Got time for a nightcap?"

She should have said no. It was late and she had to work the next day. She pulled him by the elbow into her apartment. "I have time for you."

He smiled. "That's what I like to hear."

She pushed him toward the love seat. "Sit and I'll get us a corkscrew."

"No need," he said, setting the glasses down on the trunk that doubled as a coffee table. He pulled a corkscrew from his pocket and wiggled it in midair. "I came prepared to celebrate."

"What's the occasion?" she asked.

He worked the cork loose and said, "We survived the weekend."

She smiled. "Just barely."

"It was difficult, wasn't it?" he said, pouring the wine into the glasses.

She nodded in agreement. "We probably shouldn't have brought my niece and nephew. Taking care of two kids is enough work without adding two more."

"I'm not talking about the work of taking care of the kids, Dena." He handed her a glass. "Camping with kids is fun."

"You didn't think it was difficult?"

"No, what was difficult was sleeping in the same tent as you and not being able to touch you."

The look on his face sent a shiver through her. She lifted her glass to his and said, "Here's to more romantic settings than a tent."

He clicked his glass against hers and took a sip. "Four kids kept me awake—not because they were a lot of trouble but because they were in between you and me in that damn tent."

"They're not here now." And Dena wanted to make the most of their privacy. She placed her hand on his thigh, then slowly moved it up his leg.

It was all he needed. Before she could utter another word, the wineglasses were on the table, their clothes were on the floor and they were behind the silver screen separating her sitting room from her bedroom.

It was the first time they had made love since Quinn had come home with the children. For the past couple of weeks she'd wondered if things would ever be the same between them, but once his hands began their intimate exploration, she knew that nothing had changed. Magic happened when she was in his arms.

There was no use pretending he wasn't someone special in her life. When she was with him, she felt as if everything was right in her universe, and she told him with every movement of her body.

When their passion was spent, she lay cradled in his arms.

"I didn't come down here for this," he said on a satisfied sigh.

She raised herself up on one elbow and said with a sexy smile, "Yes, you did, and I'm glad. I've missed you."

He kissed her tenderly. "I've missed you, too."

"I wasn't sure if we could get back what we had before…" She didn't finish her thought, not wanting to mention the tragedy that had changed their lives. She rubbed her hand across his chest.

A sparkle lit his blue eyes. "I was hoping you'd say that it was better than what we had before."

She grinned. "Of course it was. I thought that went without saying. But I mean this. Being here together…it's as if nothing's changed."

"But things have changed," he said on a sigh. "And I have two kids upstairs." He placed a hand along her cheek. "As much as I hate to say this, I should be getting back up there."

"I wish you didn't have to."

"Me, too." She nodded in understanding and he pushed aside the covers to swing his legs over the side of the bed. "Of course, there is always tomorrow night."

"I thought you said you had to take Sara to some program at her school tomorrow," she said, slipping her robe over her naked body.

"I do. You could come along," he suggested, reaching for his pants.

She shook her head. "She doesn't need me tagging along."

He looked as if he wanted to protest, but simply reached for his shirt and pulled it on. They went over their schedules, trying to figure out when they could squeeze in some time together during the upcoming week.

As they slowly made their way to the door, he said, "I'm glad you came along on the camping trip. You were great, by the way."

"Yeah, great at making a mess of pancakes on a camp stove."

"It was your first time. You weren't supposed to know the tricks of the trade," he told her.

She chuckled sarcastically. "It's okay. You won't hurt my feelings if you speak the truth. Let's face it. I won't ever be asked to give demonstrations at the camping show."

"Maybe not, but you were a good sport about the whole thing."

"I didn't have much choice, unless I wanted to look like a total idiot in front of my niece and nephew."

He kissed her again. "You could never look like an idiot."

"I sure feel like one sometimes when I'm around kids. I guess it shouldn't come as any great surprise. I mean, I haven't exactly been around them much."

He put a finger under her chin and tilted her head up until her eyes were looking into his. "You really don't feel comfortable around them, do you?"

"Not the way you do. It's like I don't speak their language."

"We can change that. Just hang out with me and

you'll be talking kid-speak in no time at all,'' he said on a lighthearted note, but Dena knew he was suggesting something more serious.

She should have reminded him that she wasn't interested in getting that kind of experience at this time in her life—she was focusing on her career.

She wrapped her arms around his waist and cuddled closer to him. ''By the end of next month it won't matter. We'll go back to being just the two of us. It's more fun that way, don't you think?'' she asked, sliding her hand into his waist in a tempting manner.

''Much more fun.'' He reached for her roving hands and brought them to his lips. ''I've got to go. I'll call you tomorrow.'' He kissed her one last time, then left.

Dena crawled back into the bed that still held traces of his scent. She pulled the pillow close to her face and inhaled the lingering fragrance, wishing she could turn back the clock so they were once more two carefree adults who enjoyed each other's company.

Only they weren't carefree. At least he wasn't for another six weeks. She'd have to be patient—as difficult as it would be.

''HI, AUNT DENA.''

Dena didn't expect to find her nephew on the steps of 14 Valentine Place when she got home from work on Monday. He wasn't alone. There was another slightly smaller boy with glasses sitting next to him.

''Jeremy, what are you doing here?''

''I came to visit you. Aren't you happy to see me?''

She gave him a quick hug. ''It's always nice to see

you. I'm just surprised, that's all. How did you get here?''

''We rode our bikes.''

She looked questioningly from him to the boy beside him.

''This is my friend Zach,'' he said, introducing his friend.

The boy mumbled a hello shifting from foot to foot.

Dena smiled politely, then unlocked the door. ''Have you boys had dinner?''

''Yeah. It's past seven o'clock.''

Dena glanced at her watch. ''You're right. Are you supposed to be out this late on a school night?''

He chuckled. ''Seven o'clock isn't late.''

A glance around the neighborhood confirmed those words as several kids played in the yard next door. ''Does your mom know you're here?'' she asked.

''Mom knows I was coming over here. She doesn't care. I told her I was going on a bike ride.''

Dena wasn't convinced and suggested he come inside and call her. She pushed the door open and motioned for him to enter. ''Want something to drink?''

''I am kinda thirsty,'' he said, and followed her inside. Zach trailed behind him.

Instead of taking them up the stairs to the second floor, Dena led them into the kitchen, which to her relief was empty. ''How about a juice box?'' she asked when he'd finished his phone call home.

''Sure,'' both boys answered.

Dena grabbed a bottle of iced tea for herself and joined them at the table. ''So you two were just out riding around on your bikes and decided to pay me a visit?''

Jeremy nodded. "I thought it would be cool for Zach to see where you live."

Dena suspected that it wasn't her home that had aroused their curiosity, but the fact that she lived in the same building as Quinn Sterling.

Her suspicions were confirmed when her nephew asked, "Does Quinn eat dinner down here in this kitchen?"

"Sometimes," she answered, then changed the subject, asking the two boys about school and whether or not they'd made any plans for the summer. They answered her questions, but it was obvious by the way their heads kept turning toward the doorway that they had hoped to see Quinn.

"I told Zach all about our camping trip," Jeremy boasted proudly. "We had fun, didn't we?"

"Yes, we did," she agreed.

"Quinn Sterling is cool, isn't he?"

"Very," she agreed.

"Is he your boyfriend?"

"He's a friend, yes."

"Is that his red Ferrari out back?" Zach wanted to know.

Dena hadn't seen the cars out back because she'd taken the bus that day and had come up the front walk. She got up and went over to the window. Sure enough, next to the garage was a red Ferrari. She'd never noticed it before and wondered if it could possibly be Quinn's.

"Well?"

"I don't know whose car that is," she said, letting the curtain fall back into place.

Jeremy looked at her as if he didn't believe her.

"You rode in Quinn's car," she reminded him. "It's a silver SUV."

"Yeah, a Lincoln Navigator. That's what I told Zach, but he thought a hockey player would have a Ferrari, too. I heard some professional athletes have like five cars."

"Maybe he has a friend visiting him who drives a Ferrari," she stated simply, then headed back to the table.

"There might be another hockey player upstairs?" Jeremy asked, the possibility causing both boys' eyes to widen.

If Dena had any doubt that her nephew had come to visit Quinn, it was now erased. Footsteps on the stairs told her he was about to get his wish. Seconds later, Kevin came galloping into the kitchen.

"Hi, Jeremy. Guess what? I get to go get an ice-cream cone!" the seven-year-old said as he slid onto the chair next to Dena's nephew.

"Who's taking you?" Jeremy asked.

"Quinn." Seconds later the hockey player strolled into the kitchen, looking more attractive than Dena imagined possible. He wore a pair of jeans and a T-shirt that outlined the firm muscles in his arms and chest. Dena's heart thumped as he smiled at her.

"Hi! What's up?"

Before she could answer, Jeremy was off his chair and dragging his friend Zach over to meet him. Once again Dena saw how easy it was for Quinn to entertain the boys. He didn't look the least bit annoyed by their never-ending stream of questions, answering each one patiently.

"Is that your Ferrari out back?" was one of the questions Jeremy asked.

"No, it belongs to a friend of mine. He needed to borrow my SUV so we swapped cars for a day."

"Cool! I've never seen a Ferrari with a back seat. I bet it's really neat to ride in!" Jeremy's eyes were wide.

"It's pretty cool," Quinn said with an amused grin.

Finally Kevin spoke up. "Hey—we're supposed to be going to get ice cream," he reminded Quinn, tugging on his arm.

"You boys want to come along?" Quinn asked. "I think there just might be room in the back for two more."

Dena interrupted their jubilation. "What about Sara? Isn't she going?" she asked as the four of them headed for the door.

It was Kevin who answered. "She's being bull-headed."

Zach said, "She doesn't want to ride in a Ferrari?" The rolling of his eyes revealed how dumb he thought that was.

Dena looked at Quinn, who gave her a helpless shrug. "I think she's doing homework. I'll bring her back something," he assured her.

Dena nodded, then watched as the boys rushed outside, marveling at the change that had come over Kevin since he'd come to stay with Quinn. In a very short time Quinn had gone from being an acquaintance of his father to someone he trusted and looked to for guidance.

Dena walked over to the window and saw the boys run ahead to gape at the Ferrari in awe. Again she was aware of how easy it was for Quinn to be around children. He let each of them take a turn sitting in the driver's seat, before getting behind the wheel and driving away.

While they were gone Dena made herself a chef's salad for dinner and sat down with a magazine. As she was eating, Sara came downstairs. She looked surprised to see Dena and nearly turned around and exited as quickly as she'd entered, but Dena stopped her.

"Come on in, Sara."

"I don't want to interrupt your dinner," she said politely.

"You're not interrupting." She patted the table. "Come sit down. I want to ask you something."

Sara hesitated before taking the chair next to her. Dena shoved the magazine in her direction. "Which of these two ads do you like better? This—" she pointed to a cartoon featuring a woman's body separated from her feet "—or this?" She flipped the page to an ad featuring no people, only shoes.

"I like the second one better," she answered.

She flipped several pages and said, "What do you think of this one?"

"It's too bright. It almost hurts by eyes," she said of the psychedelic patterns in the ad for a retail store.

Dena smiled. "I'm glad you said that, too, because my boss has been trying to get me to put more geometric patterns into my work, and I think for some people they're okay, but there are a lot of us who find them hard on the eyes."

She nodded. "Is that what you do at work? Draw ads?"

"Sometimes, but mainly I work on packages." She took a sip of her iced tea, then asked, "Do you have art class in school?"

"Yes, but I hate it."

Dena nodded in understanding. "Lots of people feel that way. Art is one of those things that seems to come naturally to some people and for others...well, it's just a big source of frustration. That's how I feel about sports."

"You don't like sports?"

"No, do you?"

She nodded. "I'm on the girls' soccer team...or I was until I had to come here."

Dena could see the unhappiness in her face and longed to reach out and touch her. She wanted to comfort her, to give her a reassuring hug and let her know that in time everything would work out. She wanted to tell her that she'd play soccer again and that she'd make new friends when she went to live with her aunt. But Sara sat so ramrod straight with that "don't touch me" look on her face that Dena did nothing.

The sound of the door opening had both of them looking up. Within seconds, Quinn and the boys came bounding into the kitchen. He carried two ice-cream sundaes in paper cups with plastic covers over the top.

He set one down in front of Sara, the other in front of Dena. "Sweets for the sweet," he announced.

Dena beamed a smile of gratitude. "Ooh... chocolate. My favorite. Thank you."

Sara simply looked at hers with disdain while the boys paid no attention, gushing on about how cool it was to ride in the Ferrari. As usual, Kevin treated Quinn as if he'd known him all of his life. Even Zach and Jeremy looked more comfortable around him than Sara did. Dena's heart ached for the girl.

She didn't understand why Sara hadn't softened toward him. He was trying so hard to be good to her. Dena looked at him and thought, *how could anyone not love him?*

It was at that moment she realized that was exactly what had happened to her. She'd fallen in love with him.

It was a sobering realization. When she'd started seeing him it was with the intention that he would be a passing fancy in her life. Her romantic relationships never lasted more than ninety days. There'd been no reason to think that Quinn, a professional athlete, would even make it that long. She'd thought she could keep her heart from getting involved, that they could have a relationship that allowed both of them the freedom they wanted.

Only now she hardly felt free. He'd made no promises, no commitments, and she'd agreed to do the same, yet she now felt almost trapped by her feelings. It was exactly what she hadn't wanted to happen. And it was frightening. She needed some time alone to think about this. And she needed some distance from Quinn.

"I hate to break up the party, but I think it's time Jeremy and Zach headed home," she announced, interrupting the conversation the boys were having with Quinn.

The two older boys groaned.

Quinn glanced at the kitchen clock. "Dena's right. It's a school night."

Reluctantly the boys said good-night. Quinn sent Kevin and Sara upstairs, telling them he'd be right up. Dena wanted to escape with the kids but knew Quinn had deliberately stayed behind to talk to her.

"How did you get Sara out of her room?" he asked when they were alone.

She shrugged. "I didn't do anything. She came down on her own and I asked her to sit and talk to me."

"Thanks. She's still having a rough time of it. I think it helps to have a woman to talk to." He brushed the back of his fingers across her cheek.

"I really didn't do anything," she insisted, trying to ignore the sensations his touch created.

"Yes, you did. You were you." He bent then and kissed her. "You're a unique woman, Dena Bailey. The kids and I are lucky to have you." Then he was gone.

Dena stood in the kitchen thinking about his words long after he had left. He hadn't simply said, "I'm lucky to have you." He'd said, "The kids and I are lucky to have you."

He'd sounded like a parent.

Tonight he'd looked very little like the Quinn she'd started dating two months ago. He looked more like a family man. And that scared her just about as much as her feelings did.

CHAPTER TEN

"IS THIS LIKE old times or what?" Shane asked as he lifted a beer bottle in salute to the other three guys sitting in his family room. He'd invited Quinn, his brother Garret and Dave Duggan, an old high school friend, over to watch the Stanley Cup playoffs on TV.

"How many hockey games do you suppose we watched at your mom's when we were kids?" Dave asked.

"Probably more than she cares to remember." Quinn hoisted his bottle in acknowledgment, then took a long drink.

"With five men in the house she had no choice but to accept there was always going to be some sporting event on TV and someone was going to watch it," Garret added.

"This was a great idea, Shane, getting us together to watch the game. It's just too bad Quinn isn't playing." Dave used his beer bottle to point at the television.

"He should have been. Minnesota can skate with these guys. A couple more goals in critical games and we would have been there," Shane boasted. "Sometimes you need the breaks to go your way."

"Guess it wasn't meant to be this year," Quinn stated philosophically.

"Is it a big letdown when the hockey season ends every year?" Dave wanted to know.

Quinn shrugged. "You're always disappointed when your team doesn't make the playoffs, but you're also tired. The consolation prize is that you get time off."

"Considering everything that's happened in the past few weeks, it's probably a good thing your season ended when it did," Garret noted.

"That's true. I don't know what I would have done with Sara and Kevin if I was on the road right now," Quinn said.

"It's not much longer until they go to live with their aunt, is it?" Shane asked.

He rubbed the back of his neck. "Naw. It's a good thing they've had school to keep them occupied. I don't know very much about being a parent."

"According to Mom, you make a great temporary dad," Garret said.

"I hope so."

"Hope nothing. You do." Shane punched him playfully on the arm. "Take it from a real dad. I think Doug and Patsy were right in making you their legal guardian."

"It's a big responsibility for any man," Garret said.

"I've had help from my mom and my sisters," Quinn acknowledged.

"Aren't you forgetting one other particular female?" Shane asked with a sly smile.

"What's this? You've got yourself a woman, Quinn?" Dave asked.

"He sure does, thanks to our dear, sweet mom," Shane teased.

"Oh, please," Dave cried out in mock agony.

"Tell me it isn't true. The mighty Quinn doesn't need a romance coach to find love?"

"Ha, ha, ha," Quinn drawled sarcastically. "No, I didn't hire anyone to coach me in romance. I can find my own women."

"Especially when they live right below you," Shane quipped.

"You're seeing one of mom's tenants?" A look of apprehension crossed Garret's face.

"Relax, little brother, it's not Krystal," Shane reassured him.

Garret's smile of relief was a wide one. "So Dena Bailey's caught your eye. I'm surprised I haven't heard about that before now."

"Yeah, I am, too, considering the amount of time you spend at Mom's," Shane stated.

"Guess that means your mother is discreet," Dave pointed out.

"She has to be, in her business," Garret said, then turned to Quinn. "So how serious are you about Dena?"

Dave held up a hand. "Whoa! Hold it right there. The 's' word doesn't exist when it comes to Quinn's love life. He's a professional hockey player, for crying out loud."

"Living the *vida loca* and loving every minute of it, eh, Quinn?" Garret said with admiration.

Quinn took the good-natured teasing with a grin. "Hey—I've just been doing what Garret is doing...putting my love life on hold until I have the time it takes to dedicate to a relationship."

Garret grinned and held up his hand for a high-five. "Duty first, women second."

"Maybe for you, but you don't have a bevy of

good-looking babes following you around like you're some kind of celebrity," Dave added.

Quinn raised his eyebrows. "A bevy of babes?"

"That conjures up quite an image, doesn't it?" Garret said with a grin.

"So just what is going on with you and Dena?" It was Shane who wouldn't let him avoid answering the question about his love life.

Lately Quinn had found he was asking himself that very question. He wasn't sure what was happening. However, he wasn't about to admit to his friends that he was uncertain about his feelings. And even more uncertain about Dena's.

"Hey, the game's going to start. Turn up the sound," Quinn ordered, shifting their attention away from his personal life and to the hockey game. It was much easier to talk about hockey than about Dena.

If it hadn't been for the fact that she'd seemed a little distant the last few times they'd been together, he would have said more about his relationship with her. But despite her assertions that the only reason she'd been a bit preoccupied lately was because of pressure at work, he couldn't help but wonder if she wasn't giving him a sign that things were cooling down between them.

When they'd started dating she'd told him that she'd never dated a guy longer than ninety days. He hadn't thought much about it at the time, but now as that three-month mark drew closer, he was wondering if he wasn't about to suffer the fate of the other men she'd dated.

He hoped not. He didn't want to think about breaking up with her and seeing other women. She'd gotten under his skin but good.

At first he thought it was because she presented a challenge to him. She hadn't wanted to date him, and that, combined with her attitude toward his occupation, was enough to put any red-blooded man in the pursuit mode. Then they'd had that incredible physical attraction that had been impossible to ignore. Not even the presence of two kids had been able to dampen the desire between them.

Now he knew it was much more than physical. He just liked being with her. She was a good listener, she had a great sense of humor, she was smart—

"That was a horrible call, don't you think, Quinn?"

His attention was drawn back to the game and to reminiscing with his three friends over talk of hockey. They ate pizza and drank beer, cheered when a goal was scored and booed when they disagreed with the penalty calls.

"So what do you think? Is Minnesota going to be in the finals next year?" Dave asked during one of the commercial breaks.

"They've got a good shot at it if everyone stays healthy," Quinn told him.

"If they are, you can bet we'll be sitting there at the Excel Center cheering you on," Shane told him with a pat on the back.

Dave lifted his beer. "Here's to next season."

Quinn clinked his bottle with theirs, but he wasn't sure there would be another season for him. Ever since Doug and Patsy's deaths, he'd been doing a lot of thinking. Mainly about Doug.

His life may have been cut short, but he'd lived it with a purpose. He was a generous man who had worked hard, opening his restaurant on holidays for free meals to those who had no place to go. He'd taken a different path than Quinn, living a life full of meaning and leaving behind a legacy that would never be forgotten.

After the funeral was over and Doug had been eulogized, Quinn had sat in the church alone, contemplating what would be said about him if he were to die that very day. That he could keep the best of them from scoring? That he never made an All-Star game, but he was a star player?

Becoming a professional hockey player had been his goal for as long as he could remember. He'd fallen in love with the game the first time his dad had laced up a pair of skates on his feet and put a stick in his hand. A day hadn't gone by when he hadn't thought about playing. Yet now as he sat watching the Stanley Cup playoffs and hearing his friends extol his skills, he wondered if he'd even be playing hockey next season.

At thirty-one he wasn't exactly over the hill, but he wasn't one of the young and upcoming stars anymore, either. *Retirement* was a word most players avoided saying, yet it had been echoing in his head the past few weeks. He hadn't voiced any of his thoughts aloud, hoping that if he didn't speak them they would disappear.

Only they hadn't. Now he found himself thinking more and more about the future and what it would bring. A few weeks ago he thought he'd be returning to the Cougars in the fall. Now he wasn't so sure.

Listening to Shane, Garret and Dave speculate on his role in the Cougars' next season made him feel a bit deceptive, so he said, "I might not be a Cougar much longer."

"They wouldn't trade you after the season you had!" Dave stated with indignation.

"Dave's right. They brought you here because they needed a good defenseman," Shane seconded. "Besides, the fans love you."

They proceeded to rattle off statistics and talk about specific plays he'd made during the past season. Their voices were filled with such obvious pride he didn't have the heart to tell them it wasn't a trade that might make him turn in his jersey, but retirement.

Dave clapped him on the shoulder. "It's really good to have you back, Quinn. The future's looking damn good for Minnesota hockey."

"And for you," Garret added, cocking his beer bottle in his direction.

Quinn wished he could feel as confident.

DENA ARRIVED HOME one evening to find Quinn outside washing his SUV. Kevin was helping him, but Sara was nowhere in sight.

"Hi, stranger. I haven't seen you much lately," he said when she'd climbed out of her car.

"I've been putting in really long hours at work," she told him, wishing her heart still didn't race every time she saw him. He wore a pair of cutoff jeans and a faded blue T-shirt.

He let his sponge drop into the bucket of sudsy water at his feet and came closer to her. In a low voice meant only for her ears, he said, "Are you sure that's all it is?"

"What else would it be?" she asked, knowing perfectly well that she'd been avoiding him. She'd had to—she'd fallen into the trap of thinking about him more than about her work, and that was just crazy.

Her career was number one in her life. It was the one constant she could count on.

"I've called and left you messages." His eyes pinned hers.

"I know." She rubbed a hand across the back of her neck where the muscles were tight from stress. "It's been really crazy at work."

"You're talking to someone who's had a whole season of craziness," he said with an understanding smile. Blue eyes scrutinized her. "You look tired."

"I'm working on an important project," she told him.

"And spending too many hours in front of the computer. That's why you're tense. It's hard on the neck muscles," he said, concern darkening his eyes.

The sound of a screen door slamming had Quinn looking past her to the house. "Where are you going?" he called out.

Dena turned and saw that Sara had come out of the house. "Over to Katie's," she called back. "You said I could go over there to do my homework."

"Okay, but be back by nine."

Sara gave him a defiant look but didn't protest.

When Quinn gave Dena his attention again, she said, "You sound an awful lot like a father."

He chuckled. "Yeah. By the time I have kids of my own I'll be an old hand at this."

Kids of his own. Months ago they'd both agreed that children were possibilities of the future, not probabilities. Now she wondered if he wasn't regarding them as the latter.

Before either of them had said another word, Leonie came running out of the house looking as if she'd burst with excitement.

"I have news!" she called out.

"It must be good. Your smile could light up the whole city," Quinn said to her.

"Oh, it is good!" she said, bubbling over with happiness. "I just talked to Maddie and Dylan on the phone. They told me I'm going to be a grandma for the second time."

Quinn gave Leonie a hug. "So there's going to be another Donovan for you to spoil. Congratulations. That Dylan didn't waste any time, did he?" he said with a grin.

"I suspect Maddie had something to do with it, don't you?" she said with a wink.

Dena knew she had to say something. "That's wonderful news, Leonie. I'm very happy for you."

"It *is* wonderful, isn't it," she said, a note of wonder in her voice. "Maybe this time I'll finally get a little girl."

"Hey, boys are nice, too," Quinn teased. "They wash your cars for you," he said, nodding toward Kevin, who was hard at work scrubbing the tires on the SUV.

"So what do you think of Maddie and Dylan's news?" Quinn asked when Leonie had gone back inside.

"I think it's nice," Dena answered. "Maddie will make a good mother."

"If Dylan's anything at all like Shane, he'll make a good dad, too," he noted.

Dena shifted from one foot to the other, uncomfortable with the direction the conversation had taken. She worried that Quinn would ask her again how she felt about children.

"I'd better go inside," she said, glancing toward the house.

He lifted a hand to her cheek and tenderly pushed back an errant curl that had escaped from the leather slide holding the rest of her hair at the back of her neck. "Yeah. You look done in. I was going to ask you if you wanted to go out tonight, but I can see you're exhausted."

She nodded. "I am tired."

"Before you go, I want to ask you something."

"Sure," she said with a shrug.

"I asked one of my sisters if she'd take Sara and Kevin on Saturday night." He glanced back over his shoulder and saw that Kevin was squirting the car with the hose. "Hey—watch where you're spraying that thing. Leonie doesn't need her car washed, too," he told him.

As Quinn bent to show Kevin how to hold the hose, she again thought how easy it had been for him to slip into the role of father. With his usual patience, he explained to the seven-year-old the right and wrong way to rinse off the car.

When he was done, he turned back to Dena. "Sorry about that. Where were we?"

"You said your sister was taking the kids on Saturday?" she reminded him.

He grinned. "Ah, yes. How could I forget? A friend of mine has this lake cabin near Brainerd. He gave me the keys and told me to feel free to use the place anytime this month because he's going to be in Europe. What do you think? Feel like running off to a deserted island with me?"

When he looked at her with that tender smile on

his face, he could get her to do just about anything. "How deserted is it?" she asked.

"It's going to be nothing like the camping weekend," he was quick to point out. "No cooking outdoors, no hauling water to do the dishes, no hiking to the showers." Then he leaned close and said in a low voice. "No kids sleeping between us."

"Sounds like my kind of getaway," she said on a sigh.

"I know it's mine." His gaze flicked to Kevin and back. "There's only one way onto the island, and that's by boat. There are lots of pine trees, a beautiful beach where we can watch the sun set."

The picture he painted was a tempting one, yet she hesitated. She'd decided to see less of him, not put herself in a position where she'd only fall more deeply in love. "I'd like to say yes, but..."

He reached for her hand. "Will you come if I say I'll let you bring a laptop?"

"I don't have a laptop."

"Then I'll buy you one."

Her eyes widened. "I can't let you buy me a laptop."

"Then say you'll come with me without one, because one way or another, I'm getting you to that island cabin," he warned her with a devilish glint in his eye.

When he brought her hand to his lips and placed a kiss in the palm, she knew she wasn't going to turn him down.

"All right. I'd love to go with you."

IT WAS A TWENTY-FOUR HOUR fantasy for Dena. Their time at the cabin couldn't have been more romantic.

There was no talk of children, no worrying about what the rest of the world was doing while they pretended to be the only two people on the planet.

The only exploring they did was of each other's minds and bodies. They drank wine in front of a fire, swam naked in the moonlight and slept until the sun was already high in the sky. Being with Quinn made Dena think that once the children were gone from their lives, everything would once more be as it was before that last hockey game of the season.

"You're smiling," he observed as they drove back to the city.

She sat with head back, her eyes shut. "Hmm. I'm languishing in contentment."

He reached across and took her hand in his. "I'll take that as a compliment."

"You should." She sighed. "I don't think I've ever enjoyed twenty-four hours more."

He brought her knuckles to his lips. "I feel the same way. I mean, I knew when I planned this thing it was going to be great, but it went way beyond my wildest expectations."

She giggled. "Makes me want to buy an island."

"I have the place for the rest of the month," he reminded her.

"Ah, don't tempt me."

"We'll go next weekend."

"No can do. I have work."

He groaned. "You work too much."

"Don't you?"

He didn't answer immediately, and she realized that he was changing. At one time he never would have chastised her for working on a weekend. He was changing, and it made her nervous.

"You're not going to work the weekend after the next one, are you?"

"Is there a reason why I shouldn't?"

"You mean besides being with me?" he asked with a grin. "Yeah, it's Father's Day. You don't talk about your dad very much."

"There's not much to talk about. He lives in Iowa. Works at a bank." She didn't add that the reason she seldom went home was because he'd always made her feel as if she'd never lived up to his expectations. "I don't know much about your father, either," she pointed out, wanting to take the focus off of her dad.

"He's a good guy. He's a pipe fitter. I think you're going to like him."

Which meant he intended for her to meet him soon.

"If you come with me when I pick up the kids, we can stop in and say hello to him and my mom. My sister just lives a couple of blocks away."

Again she felt as if he was pushing her to do something she wasn't quite ready to do. "I would, but I really need to do some work this evening." When he groaned again, she added, "This isn't the off-season for me."

"Guess that means I can't get you to take a couple of days off during the week and sneak away with me then, either?"

"No, and I'm surprised you're not working. I thought you said you had training during the off-season."

"Not this year," he told her.

"Because of the kids," she deduced.

"No, because of me." As they approached a wayside rest sign, he said, "I could use something cold to drink. What about you?"

"If you want to stop it's okay with me."

He pulled off the highway and into the small parking area. It was a small rest stop compared to the ones found on the interstate. No building housing travelers' information, no vending machines with snacks and soft drinks. There were several picnic tables, all of them in the shade and all of them empty.

"Guess we'll have to settle for a cold drink of water," he said, eyeing the stone fountain.

"That's fine." She looked around as he took a drink. "It's quiet here. You wouldn't know the highway's right on the other side of those trees."

He nodded. "Not a bad place if you want to stop for a picnic lunch while on your journey." He turned his head. "There must be running water somewhere. I can hear it."

"Maybe there's a creek," she said, nodding toward the copse of trees.

"Want to find out?" he asked.

"Sure."

He led her by the hand along a narrow dirt path, pushing aside overhanging branches so that they wouldn't brush against her. They hadn't gone far when they saw the brook. A footbridge stretched across it at the point where the water fell over a small damn of rocks.

Dena ran up onto the wooden bridge. "Isn't this quaint? I bet people don't even realize this is here." She took off her sandals and dangled her feet over the side so they could splash in the water.

"You look at home," Quinn said as he stood staring at her.

"This feels good. Come join me," she urged him, patting the wooden planks beside her.

He did as she requested, dipping his toes into the rippling water. "I feel like a kid."

"That's the way you're supposed to feel," she told him, her feet splashing about in the creek. "Sometimes you have to think like a kid to experience the simple pleasures in life."

He smiled at her then and said, "You're my kind of woman, Dena Bailey."

"I'm glad to hear that," she answered.

"Am I your kind of man?" he asked, his face now serious.

"You need to ask that after what happened at the cottage?" That brought the smile back to his face.

She leaned back until she was lying down staring up at the canopy of leaves filtering the June sun. "I wish I had my sketch pad right now. I love the way the sunlight plays through the leaves."

He stretched out beside her, staring up at the sky.

"See what I mean? Isn't that just the most incredible pattern?" she asked him, her finger pointing overhead.

He agreed, then said, "So you do love the outdoors as much as I do."

"Almost as much," she added.

They remained there on their backs, looking up at the sky while their feet dangled in the creek. They didn't talk because they didn't need to. They were simply enjoying the moment. The silence, however, was broken by giggling. Both Dena and Quinn pushed themselves up on their elbows to see that another couple had found their idyllic spot.

They stood, arms entwined, looking a bit embarrassed that they'd interrupted Dena and Quinn.

"We're sorry," the girl said, clinging to her boyfriend as if he were a lifeline. "We didn't mean to intrude."

"It's all right," Dena said, sitting upright. "We have to go soon anyway."

As she and Quinn pulled their feet from the creek and reached for their shoes, the young man said, "Are you...do you play for the Cougars?" He had asked hesitantly, as if suddenly embarrassed to have brought up the fact that he'd recognized Quinn.

Dena was the one who said proudly, "Yes, he does. He's Quinn Sterling."

The young man stumbled in his haste to get across the footbridge to shake Quinn's hand. Dena watched as he reached into his pocket, pulled out a receipt from a gas station and asked for an autograph. Quinn obliged him, talking with the young couple for a short while.

As he led Dena back to the car, he said, "I'm sorry about that."

"Don't be sorry. I thought it was sweet the way he fussed over you."

"Sweet?" He made a face.

"Well, maybe not sweet, but I did enjoy it. I was the one who confirmed his suspicions that you were a Cougar."

"Yeah, and I have to admit I'm a bit surprised. When we first met you didn't even want to date me because I was a professional hockey player," he reminded her.

"I know, but I've gotten used to it. In fact, there are times I think it's rather cool to be seen with a Minnesota Cougar." She gave him a quick kiss.

"How about being seen with a former Minnesota Cougar? Would that be just as cool?"

"You're not going to be traded again, are you?" She stopped dead in her tracks, her heart missing a beat at the thought.

He stopped, too. "No, I haven't been traded."

She exhaled a long sigh. "Thank goodness. There are a lot of people in Minnesota who will be as happy as I am to hear that." She started walking again and he joined in step with her.

"I doubt there will be any more trades in my future."

"Management's wised up, then?"

"No, I did."

She chuckled. "I'm not following you."

"It's kind of difficult to trade someone who's retired."

Again she stopped. "Retired?"

"I've been thinking it might be time for me to let the younger guys get some of the spotlight."

"You're only thirty-one!"

He smiled. "I'm one of the older guys on my team."

"And one of the best."

"I've always believed an athlete should go out at the top of his game."

She stared at him in disbelief. "But you love hockey."

"And I always will, but I'm losing some of the passion I need to be a player in the NHL. I'm tired of being on the road, of missing out on family events, of missing out on relationships. It's a grueling schedule. Most people only see the glory of being a professional athlete, but it's not an easy life. You've seen what it's done to my body."

She had seen what injuries had done to him, still, she countered, "But you're so good!"

"It's not enough to be good."

"Just a few weeks ago you told me that as long as you could play the game, you'd be out there on the ice, playing your heart out," she reminded him.

"But that's just it. I'm not sure my heart is in it anymore."

She gave him another puzzled look. "You're serious about this, aren't you?"

"Yes, and you haven't answered my question. Would it be just as cool to date a former Cougar?"

"I'm not with you because you're a hockey player. You ought to know that by now." She started to walk again, annoyed that he'd even think she was that shallow.

He reached for her hand. "I do know that. Look, I'm sorry. I don't want us to be snapping at each other over my job or yours."

"Work is important to both of us," she reminded him.

"Yes, and that's why I wanted you to know I've been thinking about changing careers."

She still couldn't believe it. They'd reached the SUV and stood next to the passenger door. She'd assumed that he was going to be the kind of athlete who had trouble calling it quits.

"You told me hockey is your life."

He opened the door for her to get into the SUV. "It *was* my life. I've found other more important things I need to put first."

Dena wanted to ask him what, but she wasn't sure she was ready to hear the answer.

"I can see by your face that I caught you by surprise,'' he said a few minutes later when they were back on the road.

"Yes, you did."

"Tell me what you're thinking."

"That it must take a lot of courage to walk away from a professional career in hockey."

"It does, but I feel good about it. As to how my family's going to react…" He shrugged. "I'm worried my dad will be disappointed."

"Fathers can have pretty high expectations of their children," she commented.

"Especially hockey dads. He's been at every single home game I've ever played in except for one—that was when he had his appendix out and he was in the hospital."

"When are you going to tell him?"

"Tonight."

So he'd told her before he'd even told his family.

"Will you come with me?" he asked her for the second time.

"I can't." The words were out before she could even think about it. "I told you I have work to do."

"Can't you forget about work for one night?" he said on a note of frustration.

"No, I can't," she spat back.

Silence stretched between them. They'd had their first fight. Things definitely had changed. He had disregarded the first rule of their agreement. Work would always come first.

She leaned her head back and closed her eyes. Her relationship with Quinn was supposed to be one day at a time, yet he was now talking about the future. And she had a terrible fear that the future Quinn saw was not the same one she had in her vision.

CHAPTER ELEVEN

As DENA PASSED the kitchen on her way to the laundry room, she noticed Quinn sitting at the table with books and papers spread out before him, a perplexed look on his face.

"Heavy stuff?" she called out from the doorway.

He looked up and smiled. "It's a course schedule for the university. You're right. I love hockey too much to leave it completely, so I'm going to go back, finish my degree and coach high school kids."

"They'll be some mighty lucky kids."

"You think so?"

She nodded.

He leaned back in his chair and eyed her appreciatively. "Got time for a beer?"

She noticed the Rolling Rock on the table, then glanced at the clock. "No, but I'll have one anyway...if you have a spare," she said with a grin.

He went over to the refrigerator. "Need a glass?"

"Nope," she said, taking the bottle from him and easing onto a chair. "I'm surprised you are down here."

"Two reasons," he said, sitting back down at the table. "One is that Sara sleeps on the roll-away in my apartment..."

When he paused, she finished for him, "And the other is that Kevin's asleep in your bedroom."

"No, the other is I was hoping I'd run into you. I know you do your laundry on Wednesdays."

She took a sip of the beer, then said, "You could have just come to my room."

"If I had, then this—" he pointed to the registration materials "—wouldn't get done."

She met his smile with one of her own. "There is that possibility."

"Possibility nothing," he said, then pushed his chair back and patted his knee. "Come here."

"What for?" she asked, knowing perfectly well what he had in mind.

"I want to show you something," he answered.

Setting the bottle on the table next to his, she slid onto his lap, wrapping her arms around his neck. "Okay, what is it?" she asked, staring into his baby-blue eyes.

"This," he said, just before his mouth captured hers in a kiss that had her hands spreading across the hard play of muscles on his back.

"I keep thinking it should be getting better, but it's only getting worse," he said as he lifted his mouth, his forehead resting against hers.

"What is getting worse?" she asked softly.

"This ache I feel inside for you. The more I see you, the more I want you." He nuzzled her neck, trailing hot kisses across her flesh.

"We shouldn't be doing this in the kitchen. Anyone could walk in," she said as he fondled her breast.

He gave her one last kiss, then released her. "You're right. You'd better get back on your own chair or I'm not going to be able to keep from touching you."

They both sighed as she got up from his lap and

took the chair across from him. She waved her hand over the college catalogs. "So I guess this means that you've been to see someone at the university?"

He nodded. "I can start fall quarter."

"That's great!"

"Then you approve?"

"Of course."

"Good, because I'm doing this for us."

That sent a prickle of anxiety through her. "Quinn, your decision to retire from hockey…"

"What about it?"

"You didn't consider me when making it, did you?"

He chuckled. "Of course I considered you." He clasped her hand. "I wouldn't make such a huge decision about my future without thinking of us."

There were those two words again. *Future* and *us*. Lately he'd been using them in the same sentence, as if he assumed that their futures were entwined. She wasn't sure just when it was that he'd started looking at their futures as being one and the same. One day they'd been in a relationship with no strings attached, the next she'd discovered that he was regarding them as a single entity.

He had expectations of her. The thought caused her anxiety.

It must have shown on her face, for he said, "Look. You don't need to worry that I quit hockey because you weren't exactly thrilled with the idea of your boyfriend being a jock."

She sighed. "That's good, because I told you I liked Quinn the Cougar."

"I know you did. I'm not unhappy being a hockey player."

"But you still think it's time to retire."

"Yeah, I do. I told you. I want to go out while I'm at the top of my game. I've been doing a lot of thinking lately."

"Because of Doug and Patsy's deaths?"

He nodded. "You know that Doug and I were best friends in college. We were a lot alike. When I look back at how he lived his life and then I look at mine... He was a good man, Dena."

"So are you," she said sincerely.

"He did good things with his life."

"So do you, Quinn. You're a role model for thousands of kids."

"That's why I'm quitting. I've been a role model on the ice. Now it's time to be one off the ice."

"You already are. What about Quinn's Kids?"

"It's a great program, but I can do more. It's time for me to move on, to find new ways to inspire kids."

She stared at him, amazed by his resolute attitude. "You really have been doing a lot of thinking about this, haven't you?"

"It's a big step for me—leaving professional hockey—but it's also an inevitable one. Sooner or later, every athlete has to retire. Once I realized that I have other goals to achieve, the decision didn't seem that tough."

"You mean like finishing college."

He nodded. "Yup. And having a family. I don't want to be one of those fathers who has to say, 'Mind your mother,' to his kid over the phone because he's in another city halfway across the country."

He had been making plans for his future. Although he hadn't included her in those decisions, after everything that had happened between them the past few months, she knew that he meant for her to play an important role in his life.

His next words confirmed her suspicions. "I'm going to be there for my wife and family," he told her, looking her squarely in the eyes, as if making her a promise.

She suddenly felt short of breath and warm, as if there wasn't enough air in the room. If he thought she wanted to hear those words, he was wrong, and she owed it to him to tell him that. But when she opened her mouth to speak, she discovered nothing would come out.

Fortunately, he didn't expect her to say anything. He smiled rather sheepishly and said, "It's not what most people would expect the bad boy of hockey to be saying, is it?"

She took a deep breath. "It's not what I expected you to say," she admitted. "We both agreed from the start that there would be no talk of promises and commitment, Quinn."

He grinned. "I know what we both said, and we both know what happened. I fell in love with you, Dena. Certainly I've said it often enough."

Yes, he had said it often, but never in this context. "You've said it, but I didn't know you meant it in that way. I mean, all guys say it when they're...well, you know..." She looked down at her hands.

He stood and moved closer, draping one arm around the back of her chair, setting his other arm on the table so that she was imprisoned. "They weren't just words said in the heat of passion."

He pinned her with his eyes. "We're not in bed now, Dena, and I'm going to tell you again. I love you. I didn't plan on it happening this way. I don't even know how or when it happened. All I know is I love you, and when I think about my future, I see you in it.''

"Oh my God, that is so romantic!" Krystal drawled from the doorway. "Oh, you guys, I am so sorry for interrupting, but that is the sweetest, most beautiful thing...I could cry." She raised a hand to her mouth, then flapped it in the air. "Forget I walked in on you. But you should know, Leonie just got home, too." Then as quickly as she'd appeared, she disappeared.

Quinn grinned and slipped back onto his chair. "You did try to warn me that we were in a public place."

Dena's heart pounded in her chest, and not because of Quinn's nearness. She felt as if the room was closing in on her. "Quinn, I—"

"Shh." He cocked his head toward the door and she saw the reason for his shushing her. "Leonie! You're out late," he said as their landlady came into the kitchen.

"I was visiting with some friends and we always have so much fun we hate to see the evening come to an end." She looked around. "What happened to Krystal? I thought she was going to have a cup of tea with me."

"Ah, she went upstairs, I believe," Dena said, getting to her feet. "And I need to get my laundry out of the dryer." She turned then to Quinn. "We'll talk tomorrow, okay?"

He offered to come with her, but she insisted he stay and finish working on his schedule. Then, as fast as her legs would carry her, she hurried out of the kitchen and down the hall to the laundry room, hoping Quinn wouldn't come after her.

He didn't. When she passed by the kitchen on the way back to her room, he sat at the table talking with Leonie. Dena gave a quick wave of her fingertips as she walked by, then scurried up the stairs.

She was relieved that Krystal was nowhere in sight when she reached her apartment. After everything Quinn had said to her, she needed time alone to think. She should have been deliriously happy. He'd declared his love for her; he wanted them to have a future together. It should have felt right to her.

But it felt all wrong because it was wrong. He needed a woman who understood kids. A woman who would make a good mother to his children. A woman who could stay with a man for more than ninety days.

She glanced at the calendar. They'd been seeing each other three months. Panic rose in her throat.

This time it wasn't her fault. Right from the beginning she and Quinn had agreed they would not have a serious relationship, yet he was now talking about love and their future together. She needed to talk to him…and she would. Soon.

THE NEXT MORNING Dena skipped breakfast, not wanting to see either Quinn or Krystal in the kitchen. On her way to work, she picked up a bagel and orange juice, which she ate at her desk. She was grateful to have a project that needed her immediate attention, because it made the day pass quickly. It also kept her from thinking about Quinn.

She knew she needed to speak to him. Shortly after she arrived home, there was a knock at her door.

Thinking it might be Quinn, she took a deep breath and opened it. Standing outside was Krystal.

"Do you have any white thread I could borrow?" she asked.

Dena wasn't sure the hairdresser even knew what to do with a needle and thread, but she didn't question her request. "Sure. Come on in and I'll get it for you."

Krystal stepped inside, closing the door behind her. "I have to sew on a button."

Dena pulled a spool of thread from her sewing basket and handed it to her. "Do you need a needle?"

"Yes, please," she said on a hiccup.

It was then that Dena realized she'd been crying. "Are you all right?"

She could see Krystal was trying to keep a stiff upper lip. "I'm fine."

Dena looked at the puffy red face. "You don't look fine. This isn't about some guy, is it?"

"Roy called, but let's not talk about him," she said quickly. "I want to come over and apologize for walking in on your romantic moment last night."

Dena shrugged. "Don't worry about it. It wasn't what you think."

"Yeah, right. A gorgeous guy like Quinn tells you he loves you and it's no big deal? You don't need to downplay your happiness just because my love life's in the toilet."

Dena groaned in sympathy. "You're not still eating your heart out over Roy, are you? What happened to the Krystal who's always saying there are too many fish in the sea to worry about the one that got away?"

Krystal sank down onto the love seat and rested

her head against the back. "She's thinking she should give up fishing."

Dena placed her fingers on Krystal's forehead. "Are you running a temp? You sound delirious to me. You are the juggling queen, or have you forgotten?"

Krystal shoved her hand away and sat forward. "I shouldn't have come over here. I should have known you wouldn't understand."

They were words that cut at Dena's core. It had always been that way. She'd always had problems getting close enough to women to become their confidante.

"I'm sorry," she apologized to her neighbor.

"For what? Having a guy who loves you?" She got up and started for the door, but Dena stopped her.

"Wait. Don't go, Krystal. Please."

She turned around and looked at Dena, her eyes misty. "Look, if you're going to tell me how pretty I am and that there are lots of other guys out there and someday I'll find my Quinn, too, I don't think I'm up for it." Her voice broke and Dena felt awful.

"I wasn't going to say that." This was her opportunity to try to reach out to her, woman to woman. She liked Krystal and she wanted to confide in her, but something held her back. It was the same thing that had held her back all of her life. Uncertainty.

Yet she wanted to make Krystal feel better, so she said, "I was hoping you could give me some advice."

"If it's about men, I'm probably not the best person to be asking right now," she told her.

"Maybe it's not so much advice I need, but rather someone to listen." Dena took a deep breath and said, "It's about Quinn."

"You can't possibly be insecure about his feelings for you, not after that declaration last night."

"I'm not. That's not what worries me...well, actually I guess it is."

Krystal frowned. "Wait a minute. Back up here. He says he loves you, so you're worried but you're not worried?"

Dena went to the love seat and sat down, resting her elbows on her knees. Krystal followed and sat down beside her.

"You don't think he was just saying those things and didn't really mean them, do you? Because, Dena, I've known a lot of men in my lifetime, and I can almost always tell the sincere ones from the phonies. He was sincere."

"I know. That's what worries me."

She gasped. "You don't want him to be in love with you? Dena, he's Quinn Sterling, one of the hottest guys to put on a pair of skates. My God, he's smart, sweet and a dozen other adjectives."

"I know who he is, Krystal, and it's not the love part that has me worried."

"Well, I should hope not. Good grief, girl, there are literally thousands of women who would kill to be in your shoes!"

"You're not making this any easier," Dena said under her breath, with a lift of her brows.

Krystal patted her hand. "Okay, I'm sorry. Tell me why a declaration that should have you walking on air has you looking as if you've been given a life sentence."

"You've got that right. I have been given a life sentence. Krystal, Quinn's planned my future for me."

"And that's bad?"

"It is when you're not ready for it."

"How can you be not ready?" she practically screeched, then quickly apologized when she saw the look on Dena's face. "Oh, sorry. I wasn't going to do that, was I. Look, if that's all that's worrying you—that everything happened too fast—my grandfather married my grandmother six days after he met her, and they just celebrated their sixtieth wedding anniversary," she stated proudly.

"Yes, but I'm not sure that this is that kind of love."

"You don't know until you give yourself a chance to find out."

"I don't think I can," Dena told her.

Krystal threw up her hands in exasperation. "You make it sound as if he's asking you to jump out of plane without a parachute or something. This could be a once in a lifetime thing. Can't you see that?" Before Dena could answer, Krystal jumped to her feet and headed for the door. "I'm probably not the best person to be having this discussion with right now. I'd better go."

It was another blow to Dena's already bruised ego. One that she should have expected. She didn't think like other women. That's why she'd had so few female friends.

She wished now that she hadn't said a word to the stylist. She'd tried to reach out to her and had failed. Instead of feeling better for sharing confidences, she felt worse.

She paced the floor, tried to work at her PC, paced the floor some more and finally picked up the phone.

She needed to get this situation straightened out with Quinn or she was going to go crazy.

"Hi, it's me. Could you come down here. I need to talk to you," she told him when he answered.

"Want to come up? We're having pizza and there's plenty for one more."

"No. Thanks. Just come whenever you can," she told him, then glanced at the clock, wondering how long it would be before he showed up.

He must not have finished eating, because he was at her door almost immediately. He smiled at her, the wonderful, charming smile that could still make her heart miss a beat.

"I'm so glad you called. You must have sensed I needed to see you." He pulled her into his arms and held her close. He didn't kiss her, but simply held her, as if drawing sustenance from her. When he released her he said, "There. I feel better already."

"Why did you feel bad?" she asked.

"I had this big blowup with Sara." He raked a hand over his hair. "Usually I'm able to stay calm when I talk to the kids, but she pushed all the right buttons today and I blew up big time. I really made a mess of things."

"I can't believe it was that bad," she told him.

He sighed. "It was bad enough. I just don't know how to reach her. I thought that with time it would get easier...you know, after she grieved for a while she'd soften a bit toward me, but it's like she hates my guts, Dena, and I don't understand why."

Sympathy swamped her. She knew how hard he'd tried to make Sara feel at home, to give her the space she needed. "It's been a big adjustment for her."

"I know that." Again he raked his hand over his

head. "Now that school's out she's been begging me to let her go back to South Carolina for a visit."

"She just hasn't made friends as easily as Kevin, has she?" Dena observed.

"No, the move's been tough on her."

"Is there someone in South Carolina she could stay with for a couple of weeks? Maybe you could talk to the family of one of her friends...see if it would be possible for her to spend some time with them."

"You don't think it would make it that much more difficult to have to leave her friends and go live with her aunt?"

"Maybe, but she's not happy here, is she?"

He rubbed a hand across his chin. "No, she's not. I'm just not sure if I'm comfortable with her being so far away. I am responsible for her."

"You could go along. Take Kevin and make a vacation out of it."

"And be away from you?" The look on his face told her what he thought of that idea.

It was the perfect opportunity to bring up the subject of their relationship. "It might be good for us to have some time apart."

"Good to be away from you? Not funny, Dena," he drawled. "Please, don't try to make a joke out of this."

"I'm not. I'm serious."

That brought his head around with a jerk.

She turned away from him, unable to look him in the eye. "I wanted to tell you this last night, but Leonie came home and..." She took a deep breath before continuing. "When we started dating we agreed that our relationship wouldn't be serious, that there'd be no talk of the future."

"But things have changed between us," he said quietly.

"They've changed for you." She still didn't look at him.

There was dead silence except for the faint ticking of her clock. Then he spoke. "Are you saying you're not in love with me?"

She couldn't lie to him. "No. I'm just not ready for..." She struggled to steady her nerves.

"For what? Commitment?" he asked soberly.

"We agreed there would be no demands, no promises," she said weakly.

He just stood staring at her. She glanced at his face, and her stomach balled into a knot. She wanted to kiss away the pain she saw there, but she knew she couldn't let herself do it.

He walked toward the door and opened it, pausing to say, "My mistake." Then he left.

A chill crossed her body. The door closed behind him, creating a sound that was as hollow as the feeling in her stomach.

DURING THE NEXT HOUR she looked at the clock repeatedly, wondering how she was ever going to get through the next few weeks if she couldn't even get through an hour without thinking about Quinn. She was about to slip on her shoes and go for a walk when there was an urgent knock at her door.

Automatically her heart moved into her throat as she wondered if it could be Quinn. When she opened the door and saw him standing there, she felt a rush of desire so strong it frightened her. He looked terrible, his face white, his eyes weary.

"I didn't expect to see you," she said to him.

"I need your help. Sara's gone."

"What do you mean gone?"

"I took Kevin for a bike ride. She stayed here to do her homework. When we got back, she was gone."

"Maybe she went to a friend's house."

He shook his head. "She left this note."

Dena read the message scribbled on the piece of lined notebook paper. In it she had written that she was going back to where she belonged. "You think she's going to try to find a way to get to South Carolina?"

He nodded. "I need to find her. Will you help me?"

"Of course. Let me grab my keys," she said, turning back into her room to reach for her purse. "Did she have any money?"

He nodded. "Do you know what happens to runaway girls?"

She could see the fear in his eyes. She put a hand on his arm and said, "She's going to be all right, Quinn. She's not a runaway. She just wants to go see her friends and familiar places."

"She's got to be either at the bus depot or the train station. She can't get on a plane without an ID. We'll need to check both places."

She nodded. "We'll get Krystal to help us. What about notifying the police?"

"I've already called. I've got a friend in the department. Right now our best bet is to find her before anything happens."

Dena agreed.

CHAPTER TWELVE

WHILE QUINN WENT to the bus depot, Krystal headed to the train station and Dena got in her car to search the neighborhood streets, hoping that the twelve-year-old was on foot and hadn't climbed into a car with a total stranger. After combing several blocks, she was beginning to think it was a hopeless cause. Then she saw her.

Her backpack was slung over her shoulder as she walked, her dark hair flying in the breeze. Dena wanted to honk her horn to get her attention, but she worried that if she did, the girl would flee. She drove up ahead to the next block, parked her car and called Quinn on his cell phone.

"It's me. I found her," she said as soon as he answered.

"Thank God," he said on a long sigh. "Where are you? I'll come get her."

"Why don't you let me bring her home," she suggested.

"Is she there? Let me speak to her."

"She's coming up the block but she hasn't seen me yet. Look, I gotta go. Call Krystal and tell her we found her. I'll meet you back at the house."

"Are you sure you can get her to go back with you?"

"If I can't, I'll call you." Then she clicked off,

waiting for Sara to come closer. She watched her
progress in the rearview mirror, and as soon as Sara
was even with her front fender, she hopped out.

"Sara!" she called.

The girl turned. For a brief moment she looked
paralyzed with fear, then she began to slowly walk
backward. She looked around, as if trying to judge
which direction she should run.

"Sara, please don't run away," Dena begged.

"I'm not running away. I'm going home," she told
her, still moving backward slowly.

Dena walked toward her. "You mean South Carolina?"

"I don't belong here and I don't want to stay with
Quinn."

"But your dad made Quinn your guardian. He
wanted you to be with him," she argued.

"I think it was a mistake. I should be in South
Carolina. When it rains in June there it's a warm rain.
It's cold here...a lot."

"I know. And I think you should go back to South
Carolina this summer, too. I even told Quinn that."

She looked at her suspiciously. "You did?"

Dena nodded. "Just tonight. I told him you probably have friends you could stay with in South Carolina. You do, don't you?"

She nodded. "But Quinn would never let me go.
He's the one who made me stay here when all I
wanted was to go home."

"He had to keep you here with him. He's your
legal guardian now," she said for the second time.

"He's acting like he's my father, and he's not.
He'll never be my father."

It had started to rain and a cool wind had arisen.

Dena had an umbrella in her car, but she worried that if she tried to get it, Sara would run. "Why don't you come sit with me in the car and we'll talk. If we stay out here we're going to get wet."

"No, I'm going to leave. You can't stop me," she warned, although Dena noticed she had stopped moving her feet.

"I'll tell you what. If you'll give me fifteen minutes in the car, I promise I won't try to stop you. I just want to talk to you."

She eyed her suspiciously. "You won't drive me back to Leonie's?"

"Not unless you want me to," she answered, hoping she wasn't making a promise she couldn't keep.

Thunder cracked and the rain became heavier. "Sara, I'm getting really wet," Dena called out, a plea in her voice.

"All right," she finally conceded and pulled her backpack from her shoulder so she could climb into the car.

Once inside, Dena started the engine and Sara's hand flew to the door handle.

"I'm not going anywhere, Sara! I just want to get us a little heat so we'll dry off. See?" She raised her hands. "I'll keep my hands off the wheel."

Sara watched her closely, mistrust in her eyes. "You're not going to talk me into staying."

Dena knew it was going to be an uphill battle to say something to convince her. There was only one thing she thought that may have some impact on her actions. "I wanted to tell you something not many people know," she began.

"Does Quinn know?"

She shook her head. "It's something I don't like to talk about because it's painful."

"Then why do you want to tell me?"

"Because I think it might help you."

She wrapped her arms across her chest. "I don't need any help. I'll be fine if I go back to South Carolina."

Dena didn't argue the point, but said, "I know what it's like to lose your mother, Sara. When I was thirteen I lost mine."

Her eyes narrowed. "She died?"

"No, she just decided one day that she didn't want to be my mother and she left." Dena had to swallow to get rid of the lump that memory still produced. "She moved far away, leaving me and brother in the care of my father, and I never heard from her again."

"Why would she do that?"

"I don't know," she answered honestly, because to this day she didn't understand how a mother could turn her back on her own children. Dena had heard all the suppositions people had made—that she was in love with another man, that she'd run off to pursue the stage career she'd always wanted, that she'd become tangled up in drugs. All had been unsubstantiated rumors.

"What did you do?"

"I went looking for her."

"You did? Where did you go?"

"She used to always talk about this friend she had when she was young, a woman named Trudy. She lived in Des Moines—that was about an hour away from where I lived. My mother told me she and Trudy had always said that someday they'd travel around the world. I thought maybe that's what she was planning to do, so I got on a bus and went to Des Moines.''

"Did you find her?''

"No. I did find Trudy, though. She called my dad and he came and picked me up.''

"Did you get into trouble?''

Dena grimaced at the memory. "Oh, yeah. He sent me away to boarding school after that.'' She shuddered at how clear that day was in her mind.

"And you haven't seen your mom since?''

"No. So you see, Sara, I know how bad the pain is when you lose someone you love,'' Dena said softly. "At the time you think you'll never stop hurting, that you'll never get over missing them.''

Sara looked down at her hands, which she had clasped in her lap. "I won't,'' she said in a choked whisper.

Dena reached across the seat and put her hand on her shoulder. "Probably not, but the pain will hurt a little bit less as time goes by. You need to believe me when I say that. And you also need to let the people who care about you help you get through this painful time in your life.''

"I know,'' she said in a voice choked with emotion. "That's why I want to go back to South Carolina.''

"I know you have friends there who care about you,'' she said in understanding.

"Then will you help me get back home?'' She looked at her with a hopeful look in her eyes.

She sighed. "I can't put you on a bus without talking to someone in South Carolina. How about if you come back with me to 14 Valentine Place tonight, and tomorrow we'll sit down and plan out a safe trip for you."

When Sara didn't respond, Dena said, "Sara, if you're worried about what Quinn will say, you don't need to be. I'm certain he'll take you to South Carolina this summer. I'm just surprised he didn't mention that we discussed it when he got back from my place."

She looked down at her hands. "He did say he wanted to talk to me after he took Kevin on his bike ride, but he seemed so crabby I thought he was going to tell me something bad."

Guilt surged through Dena at the thought that she was responsible for his mood. "Then he *was* planning to tell you." The windshield wipers beat in a steady tempo as the rain poured down. "You don't really want to start your journey on a night like this, do you?"

"No," she said weakly.

"Then I can take you home?"

"14 Valentine Place isn't my home," she said. "I don't even have a real bed."

"I tell you what. How about if you sleep at my place tonight? You can have my bed."

"Where will you sleep?"

"On my sofa. It pulls out into a bed. And I have a screen that separates my bedroom from the rest of my apartment so you'll have privacy. No little brother will walk in on you in the morning."

"You really want me to?"

Dena squeezed her shoulder. "It would make me feel better if you'd come home with me, Sara. Will you?"

She didn't answer immediately, then said in a near whisper, "All right."

They were two words that sent relief rushing through Dena. "Okay. To my place then," she said, and put the car in gear.

BECAUSE QUINN HAD BEEN at the bus depot in downtown Minneapolis, Dena was able to get back home and have Sara settled in her bed before he arrived. When he showed up at her door, he looked exhausted.

"Where is she?" he asked as soon as Dena opened the door.

She put her fingers to her lips indicating they should be quiet. "She's asleep," she whispered, nodding toward the screen. "Why don't you just leave her here for tonight? I don't mind."

"Are you sure?"

"It's no problem. Really. Where's Kevin?"

"He fell asleep in Jason's room downstairs, so Leonie said I should leave him with her."

She nodded in understanding.

"Do you mind if I just check on her?" he asked, looking past her shoulder.

She opened the door wider and gestured for him to come in. He crossed the room and poked his head around the room divider. When he turned back to Dena, there were fewer lines on his face.

"Where did you find her?" he asked.

She motioned for him to follow her outside to the landing. Then she gently pulled the door shut behind them.

"Over on Snelling. She told me she was on her way to South Carolina, but I don't think she had made a plan to get there," Dena told him.

"Thank God you found her," he said, closing his eyes. "When I thought of all the horrible things that could happen to her..." He shuddered and Dena placed a hand on his arm.

"It didn't happen. She's safe."

He sighed. "I'm supposed to be protecting her, not chasing her away."

"Don't be too hard on yourself. You have to remember that she's suffered a terrible loss. She's homesick and wants to see her friends. I told her you would take her to South Carolina."

He nodded. "If we need to stay there until her aunt takes over, then that's what we'll have to do. I don't want to risk anything happening to her during these last two weeks of my guardianship."

"I think that's a good idea," Dena agreed.

"Thank you for what you did this evening," he said to her, gazing at her in that way she'd always found so compelling.

"I was glad to help out."

"I don't know what you said to her, but whatever it was, it got her back here."

"We can talk tomorrow. I'll see you at breakfast?" she asked, putting a hand on her doorknob to indicate she was going to go back inside.

"Yeah. Tomorrow at breakfast," he concurred, then headed up the stairs.

She watched him walk away, wishing she could call him back. She wanted desperately to take him in her arms and kiss away the worry lines on his face, but she knew she couldn't. Not after what had happened between them earlier that night. Instead of comforting each other, they were alone. Tears trickled down her cheeks as she stepped back inside.

DENA MOVED QUIETLY as she made the love seat into a bed, tucking the linens beneath the mattress and spreading a quilt over the top. All she needed was a pillow and she'd be ready to climb under the covers. As she craned her neck around the room divider, she saw that Sara was only using one of the two on her bed, which meant Dena could take the other.

As she did, however, a small wooden jewelry box went tumbling to the floor. As Dena picked it up, the top flopped open and its contents spilled onto the carpet.

Scattered on the floor were a locket, two rings, several old coins, a charm bracelet, a rabbit's foot, a photograph and a small stack of air mail letters tied together with a piece of pink ribbon. The photo was a family picture of Sara, Kevin and their parents. Dena felt a tug on her heart as she stared at the smiling faces. She put the photo back into the wooden box, then reached for the other items. When she picked up the stack of letters, she saw that the top one was addressed to a Patsy Martin at a University of Minnesota address. The postmark was dated thirteen years ago.

Dena knew that Sara's mother's name was Patsy and assumed Martin had been her birth name. She wondered why Sara would be carrying around a letter addressed to her mother. She looked at the return address and saw that it was from a Carolyn Martin. She thumbed through the stack and saw they all were from her.

Dena figured she was either Patsy's sister or her mother. Dena returned them to the carved box and set it on her dresser top, thinking that tomorrow she'd asked Sara about the letters. If there was another relative on Patsy's side, Quinn needed to know.

DENA WAS AT HER PC when Sara awoke the following morning. "Good morning," she said as the sleepy-eyed girl staggered toward her.

"I had a box under the pillow," the twelve-year-old said, concern furrowing her brow, one arm pointing toward the bed.

"I know. It fell to the floor when I had to borrow the pillow last night, so I put in on my dresser."

Dena noticed Sara wasted no time in getting it or in opening it. Out of the corner of her eye Dena could see her checking its contents. Then she put the box into her backpack and zipped it shut.

Dena got up and walked over to the bed, sitting down next to her. "Sara, when the box landed on the floor the contents fell out."

A look of panic crossed her face. "You didn't read the letters, did you?"

"No. I wouldn't do that. They weren't addressed to me," Dena said in a soft voice. "Were they your mother's letters?"

She nodded, biting down on her upper lip. "They're from my grandma. And they're personal."

"I understand. You should treasure them. I don't have any of my mother's correspondence."

"My mom didn't write them. My grandma did. Before I was born. I never knew her because she and my grandpa were killed in a riot in a third world country. They were missionaries trying to help people. My dad said they were in the wrong place at the wrong time."

"Unfortunately that happens. At least you know they were trying to do good things."

Sara nodded.

"And you have a little piece of your grandmother in that box. It was thoughtful of your mother to save those letters for you."

She lowered her eyes. "She didn't know I had them."

Dena frowned. "She didn't give them to you?"

She shook her head, again biting down on her upper lip. "I found them after she and my dad left for the convention. I needed pictures for a family tree project we were doing at school." She paused, then stared out the window. "She had this locked drawer in her desk where she kept important stuff."

"And you opened it when she was gone?"

She nodded. "I knew the key was under the ivy she keeps in the corner of her bedroom. I saw her put it there one time when she didn't know I was watching her. I tried to call her in Florida to see if it was okay if I looked in that drawer for pictures, but she wasn't in her hotel room."

There was such a sadness on her face, Dena put her arm around her. "Sara, I'm sure if she had taken your call she would have told you it was okay to open the drawer. You shouldn't feel guilty about this."

The dark head drooped and she said in a broken voice, "But I shouldn't have looked at her private things. Now everything's all messed up."

"What's messed up?" Dena asked gently.

"I can't tell you." Her voice broke and she began to cry.

"Oh, Sara, it can't be that bad. Do you want to tell me about it?"

The girl shook her head.

"Are you sure?"

"I c-can't," she said on a hiccup. "Because it's a secret. No one else knows."

Dena couldn't imagine what could be in the letters that could cause this child so much distress. It could have been any number of things that had caused a mother to write letters to her daughter while she was away at college. Some of them could seem pretty serious to a twelve-year-old, especially one who looked up at her mother as a role model.

"Sometimes when secrets are shared, they're a little easier to bear. It might help to tell me, Sara."

"I can't," she said on a pained note. "I just wish I'd never found those stupid letters."

Dena gently stroked her back in a comforting manner. "Are you sure you don't want to tell me what's in them?"

"If I do, then you'll know that..."

"I'll know what?"

Just when she thought she wasn't going to be able to talk Sara into telling her what was in the letters, the girl said in a whisper, "My mom did a bad thing."

Dena pulled her into her arms and rested her chin on her head, closing her eyes briefly before saying, "You know what? Mine did, too, and I'm okay. And you're going to be fine, too. You've got to trust me on this, Sara."

"I don't know why she did what she did."

"Me, neither," Dena said softly, thinking of her own mother, not Sara's.

"My grandma was mad at her for it."

"So was mine," she said, remembering how upset

her own grandmother had been when she'd heard the news that Dena's mother had left. Dena didn't think that anything Patsy had done could compare to the sins of her mother.

"I wish I'd never found those letters," she repeated.

Dena wished Patsy hadn't saved them. They were, after all, written while Patsy was single and in college, a time in her life when she obviously hadn't made the best choices. This little girl didn't need to be reminded of that. Maybe if she had discovered them when she was a college student herself, she could have looked at them with a different perspective, but being so young and so vulnerable because of her mother's death, they were only causing her pain.

"You know what I think you should do with those letters?"

"What?"

"Throw them away."

"Really?"

"They're only making you unhappy, right?"

"Well, yeah, but…"

"If other people see them, will any good come out of it?"

She shook her head.

"I'll tell you what. You think about it. Right now you need to get dressed so you can get some breakfast, and I need to get to work."

"Did I make you late?"

"Yes, but that's okay. I often work past quitting time, so being a little late one morning won't matter," she said truthfully, slipping her feet into a pair of Doc Martens.

"You wear really cool socks," Sara commented.

Dena pulled up a pant leg to reveal more of the crossword puzzles on her socks. "You like these?" When the girl nodded she said, "I have a whole drawer full of different ones. You can help yourself to a pair if you like."

"You'll let me?"

Dena nodded and showed her which drawer contained the socks. Sara rummaged around, pulling out a black pair with pink lips on them. "These are cool. Were they a Valentine's Day gift?"

"No." They were from Quinn. He'd come back from one of his road trips with them and showered her with kisses so that she wouldn't be wearing more on her ankles than her mouth. They were special, and she was relieved when Sara put them back and settled on a pair with handbags all over them.

BECAUSE DENA WAS THREE HOURS late getting to work, she stayed three hours past quitting time. "You're too damn conscientious," one of her co-workers said as he waved goodbye.

She was. She simply couldn't leave that evening when everyone was walking out the door.

On the way home she stopped at the local Chinese restaurant and got one order of Kung Pau chicken to go. Instead of eating in the kitchen, she decided to take it upstairs to her room. When she arrived at the second-floor landing, Quinn was there.

"Hi. What are you doing here?" she asked as she fumbled with her keys.

He took the keys from her and opened her door. "Waiting for you." He gestured for her to go in ahead of him.

"I haven't eaten dinner yet," she said, wary of the look in his eyes. He was upset and she wasn't sure she wanted to hear why.

"I'll just take a couple of minutes," he told her, closing the door behind him. "I need to talk to you about Sara."

"Aren't you going to sit down?" she asked when he remained standing.

He didn't answer, but paced back and forth. She'd never seen him in such a state.

"Are you saying today didn't go any better than yesterday?" she asked, setting the bag of Chinese food on the coffee table.

"Better? No, we haven't reached the better part yet," he said on a bitter chuckle.

Dena became more worried. "What went wrong?"

"You mean besides her starting a fire in my bathroom trash can?"

"What!" Dena's mouth dropped open.

He reached into his pocket and pulled out a partially charred stack of letters. Dena recognized them as the very same pile of letters that had been in Sara's wooden jewelry box.

"She tried to burn these in my trash can in the bathroom. She said you told her to get rid of them." There was accusation in his eyes.

"I didn't say to burn them!"

"But you did say to get rid of them, didn't you?"

"Yes. They're letters from her grandmother to her mother that were written during Patsy's college days, and they contained stuff that Sara found very disturbing."

"With good reason. They are disturbing." He

glared at her. "You didn't see any reason she should show these letters to me?"

"No. Sara was upset enough to find out that her mother had done something bad in college. She didn't need anyone to see them."

"Something bad?" He stared at her in disbelief. "Is that what you think Patsy did?" He shook his head. "I don't believe this. You're too much. I don't know why I bothered to even come down here." He started for the door.

"Quinn, wait!" She tugged on his arm. "I don't know what's in those letters, because I didn't read them."

He stopped then and turned to face her. "And Sara didn't tell you what was in them?"

"No! She didn't want me to know. I assumed they contained details of her mother's embarrassing moments in college. We all have them."

He chuckled but it was not a humorous sound. "They contained more than that."

"You read them?"

He nodded soberly, then tossed the loose letters onto the table next to her Chinese food. He dropped down onto the love seat and rested his elbows on his knees, his hands holding his head. "I've read them and reread them and I still can't believe what they say."

He lifted his head from his hands and glanced up at her. "I'm Sara's father, Dena. When Doug married Patsy, she was pregnant with my child, not his."

Suddenly she understood the reason Sara was so upset with the secret she'd uncovered. It also explained Sara's attitude toward Quinn. "That's what's in the letters?"

He nodded. "Patsy's mother thought I had a right to know. Obviously, Patsy didn't agree."

"And Doug? Did he know?"

He shrugged. "Who knows? I'd like to believe that if he had known, he would have told me."

"He did make you Sara's godfather and the children's legal guardian."

"Because we were best friends in college. The three of us. We all met our freshman year." Again he laughed, but there was no humor in the sound. "What kind of friendship is that? She had one guy's kid and married his best friend."

The kind that left Dena speechless. Finally she found her voice and asked quietly, "You never suspected?"

"No. Why would I? Patsy and I fooled around a bit when we were in college…hell, she fooled around with a lot of guys in college. That was just Patsy. It drove Doug nuts. He'd loved her since the day he met her, but he didn't tell her until they were juniors. Once she found out, he was the only man for her, and she made that perfectly clear to everyone. They ran off and got married six weeks later."

"Because she was pregnant."

"They didn't say she was at the time. It wasn't until later that he announced she was going to have a baby. I never paid any attention to due dates or any of that. When Sara was born she was a tiny thing, and Doug said she'd come early." He shrugged. "There was no reason for me to suspect anything."

"And if you had?"

"I would have done something. What, I don't know, but something." He shook his head in regret. "It would have been a mess because Doug was crazy

about Patsy and she was crazy about him. He would
have done anything for her. He even quit the hockey
team so he could spend more time with her during
her pregnancy.'' He rubbed his eyes. ''I just can't
believe they never told me.''

Dena didn't understand it, either, but she knew
Quinn needed to try to make sense of their deception.
''You're not certain that Doug even knew the truth,
but if he did, they probably thought they were doing
what was best for Sara.''

''Is that what you think?''

''Why else would they keep such a secret? You
said Doug was a good man. He had to have thought
he was doing the right thing,'' she contended.

His chuckle was full of self-deprecation. ''Or else
he knew what kind of lifestyle I had and wanted to
protect Patsy's child from it.''

She sighed. ''You don't know that. Patsy and Doug
aren't here to defend their actions, are they? Maybe
it's better not to drive yourself crazy with questions
you might not ever be able to answer.'' From the look
on his face, she hadn't convinced him.

''I feel so cheated.'' He stared straight ahead as he
spoke. ''I missed out on twelve years of my daughter's life. Twelve years, Dena. That's almost her entire childhood.''

Dena didn't know what to say. There were no
words that would make him feel any less bewildered,
any less angry. So she said nothing, but stood over
him as he stared into blank space, trying to make
sense out of what he'd learned.

Finally he said, ''I'm sorry I came barging in like
that. I thought you knew what was in the letters.''

''It's all right,'' she said, wrapping her arms around

her chest so she wouldn't be tempted to put them around him. "What will you do now?"

"This changes everything. I'll need to talk to the attorney in South Carolina. I'm not sending Kevin and Sara to live with Doug's sister. I can't."

She nodded in understanding.

"It's actually been something I've been considering for a while. The only reason I hesitated was because Sara was so unhappy here."

"How do you think she'll react to that news?"

He shrugged. "At this point I'm not sure of anything. All I know is that I'm going to do everything I can to try to build a father-daughter relationship between us."

"Have you told her this?"

"Yeah, but I don't think she wanted to hear it just yet."

Dena's heart wrenched with sympathy for the girl and for Quinn. "It's going to take time for her to get used to the idea."

"I know. I can hardly believe it myself. I can imagine how difficult it must be for her. It had to be a terrible shock to find those letters, and then before she had a chance to confront her mother about them, Patsy was killed in a plane crash." He grimaced at the thought.

"It certainly explains why Sara's been so hostile toward you," Dena pointed out.

"I'm sure she's feeling confused and angry. So am I." He looked at her with torment in his eyes.

Dena dropped down beside him and put her arms around him in a gesture that was purely one of comfort. "I'm sorry, Quinn. I wish there was something I could say or do to help."

He shook his head. "It's just going to take more time for all of us to adjust. Even Kevin."

"I think Kevin and Sara are lucky to have you. And I also think that Doug and Patsy knew what they were doing when they made you the kids' legal guardian."

He sighed. "I'm sure they never expected that I'd have to fulfill the obligation. Hell, I never thought I would. In the blink of an eye I became a single parent."

He searched her face, looking for what she wasn't sure, but she knew he didn't find it. He simply got up and said, "I'd better get back upstairs and check on the kids." He picked up the scorched letters from the coffee table.

As she walked him to the door, he said, "By the way, I don't know what you did with Sara last night, but you made quite an impression." He clasped her hand. "Thank you for being so kind to her."

"You don't need to thank me. I remember what it was like to be twelve going on thirteen."

"Well, whatever you said to her, it helped. She asked me if you could come with us to South Carolina."

"Then you are planning a trip back?"

"Yes. I need to see the lawyer and get this paternity issue straightened out. I think it'll be good for the kids to go back to what is so familiar to them." He paused at the door, then said again, "Sara asked if you could come along."

Dena felt as if a hand reached out and squeezed her heart. "I can't leave my work."

"What about coming just for a weekend?"

She wanted to tell him yes, but something held her back. ''I can't.''

The tiny sparkle of hope that had been in his eyes disappeared. ''That's too bad. Sara wanted you to be there.'' Without another word, he dropped her hand and left.

CHAPTER THIRTEEN

"THANKS FOR HAVING ME over for dinner," Dena told her sister-in-law as they sat in two Adirondack chairs on the porch watching Ryan play basketball with Bethany and Jeremy. "Dinner was excellent."

"Why, thank you. I'm glad you could make it. It's too bad your dad couldn't come up for the weekend as planned," Lisa said.

"Yes, well, you know my dad and emergencies at the office," Dena said without any bitterness. She was simply stating the truth.

"We've invited him often and always something comes up and he can't make it. We should probably load up the kids and drive down there."

Dena put a hand on her arm. "Don't feel guilty that you haven't. He hasn't changed, Lisa. He still would rather be working than spending time with family." Again there was no sourness in her tone.

"Well, I'm glad we convinced you to get away from your work for at least one day. We don't get to see enough of you," she said with a gentle pat on her arm. "Is that because of work or because of Quinn?" she asked with a sly grin.

Dena focused her attention on the glass of iced tea in her hand, tracing a pattern with her thumb on the condensation. "Work. Unfortunately, in that respect

I am my father's daughter. I've been putting in a lot of hours.''

"How are things going between you and Quinn? I thought maybe you'd bring him to dinner today. Jeremy and Bethany talked about him for weeks after that camping trip you took. Ryan and I would like to get to know him better, too.''

She looked down at the glass in her hand. There was no point in pretending that she and Quinn were still seeing each other. "That's probably not going to happen, Lisa.''

"You're not together?''

She swallowed the lump in her throat. "No.''

"Oh, Dena, I'm sorry. I thought you looked a little uncomfortable every time Jeremy mentioned his name.''

"It's that obvious?''

"Well, maybe not to the men in this family. You want to talk about it?''

Dena shook her head. "Not really. It's just not working.''

Lisa reached across to give her hand a squeeze. "I'm really sorry. We like Quinn.''

"So do I,'' she confessed. "But things are rather complicated right now.''

"You mean because of the kids?''

"Yes.'' She didn't elaborate, not wanting to reveal how Quinn's situation had changed in the past few days.

"That's to be expected. Neither one of you was expecting to be acting like parents at this stage in your relationship.''

Dena didn't correct her. "It's a foreign world to me, that's for sure.''

"It is for all adults at one time or another. The only difference is that most parents get some time to prepare for the arrival of a child. See your brother out there?" She motioned toward the driveway where Ryan played basketball. "*That* is a work in progress. He didn't know diddly about raising kids when Jeremy was born."

"We didn't exactly have great role models, Lisa," Dena pointed out.

"Is that what worries you? That you'll make the same mistakes your parents did?"

"No. I know I'm nothing at all like my mother," she said quietly. They were words she said often enough to herself, hoping that in time she would believe them.

"I think someday you'll make a wonderful mother, Dena," Lisa said sincerely.

She sighed. "I just don't know."

Jeremy interrupted their conversation, calling out from the driveway. "Hey—Dad says we need two more players."

"What do you think?" Lisa asked Dena.

"I think my brother knows better than to even ask. Me playing basketball is not a pretty sight."

Lisa smiled. "Come on. You can't be any worse than I am."

Dena knew she probably was, but at least it would put an end to their conversation about her relationship with Quinn. "All right. But be warned. It could get ugly."

THE FOLLOWING WEEK WENT BY slowly for Dena, mainly because Quinn and the children were gone. He hadn't told her exactly when he was leaving, and if it hadn't been for Krystal, Dena wouldn't have known they'd gone. But the hairdresser, who didn't work Monday mornings, had seen him loading up the suitcases and had talked to him then. She filled Dena in that evening when she came into the kitchen.

"He doesn't know how long he'll be gone," Krystal stated, then eyed Dena curiously. "How come I'm telling you this when he's your boyfriend?"

She knew the younger woman was waiting for her to confirm what she already suspected—that they'd broken up. She didn't see any point in denying it.

"We're not seeing each other anymore," she confessed.

"Oh, please. Tell me you didn't break up with him!" There was a pained expression on Krystal's face. When Dena didn't deny it, she said, "Omigosh, you did. Dena, do you realize what a catch he is?"

Dena was in no mood to be given any sort of advice on her love life. She slammed the teakettle down on the stove. "Krystal, men are not *catches*. They aren't fish in the sea we reel in if we wear the right color clothes or say the things they want to hear. Not everyone thinks that love is a game nor does everyone want to talk about romance as if there's nothing else of importance in the world!" She stopped abruptly when she realized the effect her words were having on her housemate.

Krystal's face was white, her eyes moist with unshed tears. "Well, excuse me for trying to be a friend. I wish you hadn't waited this long to tell me what a pest I've been." With a quiet dignity that made Dena feel like a jerk, she turned and left the room.

"Krystal, wait! I'm sorry," Dena tried to say, but

the words never came out of her mouth. They were stuck in her heart.

She sat down at the table and dropped her head in her hands, wondering why relationships with other women were so difficult for her to maintain. It was how Leonie found her, slumped at the table.

"Are you all right, Dena?" the gentle voice called out.

She lifted her head and nodded, then immediately shook her head. "No, I'm not."

Leonie sat down beside her and took her hand in hers. "Is there anything I can do?"

She bit on her upper lip and again shook her head. "But thank you for offering."

Leonie looked at the half-empty plate of macaroni and cheese that Krystal had been eating. "Is that yours?"

"It's Krystal's. I said some things I shouldn't have said to her, Leonie. I'm sorry."

"Maybe you should be saying that to her instead of me," Leonie said, her eyes full of compassion.

Dena sighed. "I will when she returns. She left...and I'm not sure when she's coming back."

The water Dena had been heating whistled in the kettle. "Was that Krystal's, too?"

"No, I was heating it for me. You can use it if you like."

"You're not having any?" Leonie said, getting to her feet.

Dena shook her head. "I think I'll just go upstairs."

"Oh, please. Stay and visit with me. I'll make the tea."

Dena didn't protest, and watched as her landlady

moved about the kitchen. When she sat back down, she had two of her finest china cups.

"I usually just use a mug," Dena said as she set one of the cups in front of her.

"I know. Me, too, but whenever I need an extra pick-me-up, I like to sip from fine china. It makes me feel a little special. You know what I mean?"

Dena took a sip of the tea and said, "You're right. It does make a difference."

"Tell me how your day went at work," Leonie urged her.

"Actually, it was good. I was assigned to a new project. An important one."

"That must mean they like your work."

Dena nodded. "It's nice to know they think highly of me. Of course, with the job comes more stress."

They shared stories about their experiences in the workplace. No mention was made of the words she'd had with Krystal.

Finally Dena said, "How come you haven't asked me what it was that Krystal and I argued about?"

"I figured that if it had something to do with you two sharing the second floor, you'd tell me." Leonie took a sip of her tea, then looked at Dena over her cup and said, "Of course, that doesn't mean I won't listen if you feel you need to talk."

"No. There's really nothing to talk about." She pushed the hair back from her face. "I've been under a lot of stress lately and I think I overreacted to something Krystal said."

"If that's all it was, then a simple apology will probably make it right," Leonie said in an optimistic tone.

Dena nodded, not wanting to admit to her landlady

that it would take more than an apology to fix what had gone wrong in her relationship with Krystal. It had always been that way. With the exception of Maddie, every time Dena thought she was getting close to having a true friendship with a woman, something happened.

If she were honest she'd admit that it happened with her men friends, too. Maybe she was just destined not to be close to anyone, ever.

Dena put her cup back in the saucer. "Thank you for being so understanding." She glanced at Krystal's half-eaten plate of food. "I just wish I'd kept quiet. I guess if I hadn't had such a difficult day I would have."

"Stress makes all of us say things we wished we hadn't," Leonie said sympathetically.

"I don't know, Leonie. I seem to be doing that an awful lot lately. Maybe I should be living alone. I've never been very good in group situations."

"But you fit in here just fine."

"Do I? I just drove Krystal out of the house, and Quinn doesn't even want to talk to me." She hadn't meant to bring up his name, but it had slipped out. "I'm sorry, Leonie. I shouldn't have said that."

"I know you and Quinn are having problems," Leonie said.

"He told you?"

"You can stop looking so panicky. Quinn doesn't talk to me about his love life." She chuckled. "He would never do that. It was Sara who told me the two of you had broken up."

Dena's shoulders slumped again. "I didn't realize she knew what was going on."

"Children can be very perceptive when it comes to adult emotions," Leonie said in a knowing tone.

When Dena didn't say anything, she continued. "You know I keep my two hats on separate hooks. When I'm your landlady, I'm not a romance coach. That doesn't mean I can't be here as your friend, Dena. If you need someone to listen, I'm here...whether you want to talk about love or simply about life."

Dena wanted to confide in her, but years of keeping everything bottled up inside refused to allow her to take that risk. "Thank you, Leonie. I appreciate that, but I don't think talking is going to help."

Leonie patted her hand. "If the time comes and you think it might help, I'm here for you."

Dena gave her a grateful smile as she got up from the table. She was just about to leave when Krystal returned. The hello she tossed out was a general one to no one in particular.

She walked over to the table and picked up the remains of her dinner, then carried it to the garbage. "It's hot out there today," she said as she scraped the leftover food into the trash.

Leonie stood. "Yes, it is, which is why I should water my flowers. If you two will excuse me."

Dena knew her landlady had left so that she could be alone with Krystal. Only her neighbor clearly did not want to be in the same room with her. Krystal would have hurried out of the kitchen right behind Leonie if Dena hadn't stopped her.

"I'm sorry, Krystal, about what happened earlier. I shouldn't have said what I said." Dena knew it sounded lame, but she wasn't sure what else to say. Apologies were never easy.

The redhead stopped at the door, then turned. "It's all right," she said, although, judging by her body language, it was anything but all right.

"No, it's not. I don't think you're a pest. You're a very sweet and considerate neighbor, and I feel badly because I hurt you. And I didn't want to do that. If you had stayed I would have told you that right away, but you left."

"Because I knew I was going all emotional," she said candidly. "I find that if I go for a walk and think about things, I'm much calmer when it comes to discussing them."

"That makes sense."

"Yeah, well, I've been taking a lot of walks lately. I don't know what's wrong with me. I keep having these emotional outbursts."

"I was the one who blew up, Krystal."

"Maybe we both weren't our usual good-natured selves," she said with a half grin.

"Maybe. I'm not feeling very good about what happened between me and Quinn, and it's probably better if we just don't talk about it." It was the best she could do. She hoped Krystal would accept her attempt at making amends.

"Then we won't talk about it."

"Friends?"

Krystal smiled. "Friends."

QUINN WAS GONE almost two weeks. Dena knew she should have been grateful he was out of town, because it meant she didn't have to worry about running into him in the kitchen or the parking lot or even on the stairs. Only she found instead of being relieved, she was lonely. She missed him and found herself wondering what was happening in South Carolina. What decisions had he made concerning Sara and Kevin? Were he and Sara coming to terms with their recently discovered relationship?

They came home on the last Saturday in June. Dena had her windows open and heard their voices outside. Immediately her heartbeat increased. She thought about going downstairs to see them, but she didn't. She sat at her PC, trying to work, when all she could think about was Quinn.

A short while later she heard footsteps coming up the stairs, then a knock on her door. She opened it and there stood Quinn and the two kids.

"You're back!" She feigned surprise.

"We have something for you," Sara said. She elbowed Kevin, who extended a white box to her.

"What's this?" she asked.

"Saltwater taffy. We got a box for Krystal and Leonie, too," Kevin answered.

"Why, thank you. That's very sweet of you," she said, trying to focus her attention on the kids while her eyes longed to stare at Quinn.

"And I have this," Sara said, producing a small paper bag.

Dena opened the sack and pulled out a pair of socks that had a beach scene on them. There was blue water, an umbrella, a chair and a pail on the sand. Dena smiled. "Thank you. They're perfect."

"That's the beach where we always go," she told her when Dena read the words stitched across the toe.

"They wanted to bring back souvenirs," Quinn explained, and Dena finally met his eyes. What she saw there made her want to melt in his arms. He was so handsome and she'd missed him so much.

Kevin tugged on Quinn's shirt. "I have to go to the bathroom."

"In a minute," Quinn told him. "Let me talk to Dena first."

"But I gotta go real bad," Kevin said.

"He can use mine," Dena told him, nodding across the hallway.

"Kevin, go use Dena's bathroom," Quinn told him.

The seven-year-old looked at Quinn with an appeal in his eyes. "I don't know where it is."

Sara pointed to the door between Dena and Krystal's apartments. "It's right there. Just walk in."

"Will you come with me?" Kevin asked his sister.

"I'm not taking a boy into the bathroom," Sara protested. "Quit being a baby."

"I'm not a baby," he shouted back.

Quinn looked at Dena and said, "I'll be right back," then grabbed Kevin and took him into the bathroom across the hallway.

"So do you like the socks?" Sara asked.

"Yes, I do. And I'll wear them tomorrow. I have just the outfit for them. Want to come inside?"

She nodded eagerly and followed Dena into her apartment. They left the door open so Quinn and Kevin could come back in without knocking.

"Did you have a good trip?" she asked Sara.

She shrugged. "It was okay."

Dena wanted to ask her how her relationship with Quinn was going, but didn't want to risk him walking in at any moment and hearing her answer. Instead, she asked, "Did you see your friends?"

"A few. Some were gone on summer vacation."

They were talking about the different places she'd

been when Quinn and Kevin reappeared. The face that only minutes ago had looked rested and interested in seeing her now was tense.

"Sara, would you take Kevin upstairs? I need to talk to Dena for a few minutes."

The twelve-year-old looked as if she wanted to protest, but simply shrugged and pulled her brother by the hand, calling out goodbye to Dena as she left. As soon as they were alone, Quinn shut the door and faced Dena like an interrogation officer.

"How are you feeling?" he asked brusquely.

"I'm fine, thank you."

"Fine? Didn't you say before I left that you hadn't been feeling well...that you'd been tired and tense?"

Of course she had. She'd been losing sleep over him. "Yeah, but I feel fine. I think I was run-down."

"And you're feeling your usual self again."

She nodded.

He stood there staring at her, as if he didn't believe her. Maybe he wanted her to say that she'd made herself sick because she was so crazy in love with him. It wouldn't have been far from the truth. He had turned her whole world upside down.

"So there's nothing you want to tell me?"

"Quinn, what are you getting at? If you want to ask me something, why don't you just come out and say it?"

"Because I was hoping you'd tell me without me having to bring it up."

"Tell you what?" she asked on a note of frustration.

"About this." He put his hand in his pocket and pulled out a box. On it were written the words, "early pregnancy test." It had been opened.

"Were you going to tell me about this?" he asked, waving it under her nose.

"Where did you find that?"

"In your bathroom. When I took Kevin in I found it on the vanity."

She looked at it briefly. "It's not mine."

"You sure?"

"Of course I'm sure. That's not my private bath, in case you've forgotten," she said, crossing her arms over her chest. "Other people use it."

Mainly Krystal, which meant there was a good chance that Dena's housemate was pregnant. It would explain why Krystal had been so emotional recently.

"Then you're not pregnant?" he demanded.

"No."

Relief chased away the lines on his face.

"You know we took precautions," she said.

"Yes, well so did Patsy and I."

"You shouldn't jump to conclusions."

His shoulders drooped. "No, I guess not. I'm sorry. I saw that box staring up at me, and with everything's that's happened, I thought…" He paused, then said, "I don't know what I thought." He moved toward the door.

When he had his hand on the knob he turned to her and asked, "If it had been yours, would you have told me?"

"Probably," she answered honestly.

It caused him to shake his head. "What is this 'probably' stuff? You either would have or you wouldn't have. Which is it?"

"Why does that it matter? I'm not pregnant."

"It matters because I need to know you wouldn't do what Patsy did."

"I wouldn't," she stated with conviction. "But it's a hypothetical question because I'm not pregnant."

"And don't ever foresee yourself becoming pregnant, either. Isn't that what you told me? Kids weren't in your career plan?" His eyes flashed with anger.

"Do you think this would be a good time for either one of us to become parents, Quinn?" she asked.

"I just did, Dena. They're upstairs. And you know what, it's a good feeling being a parent. That's something I'm not sure you even want to try to understand." There was anger in his voice. He pulled open the door and left without another word.

DENA KNEW she should have stopped him from leaving. She should have told him he was wrong. She wanted to understand exactly what he was going through with the kids. Yet she couldn't.

Because she was afraid. If she dared to hope that she could have a happy family life with him, she would put herself in a position that she'd vowed never to be in again. A happy family was an illusion. All one had to do was look around. Broken families had become the norm. Parents divorced and children suffered. She'd lived that life, and she'd decided long ago that she'd never be the one responsible for putting another person into that risk category.

Long after Quinn was gone, she sat in her room thinking about her relationship with him. It had been far too intense. She'd almost convinced herself that he was her soul mate—that such a thing actually existed.

A knock on her door had her wondering if Quinn had come back. She hesitated answering, not sure she wanted to confront him a second time.

"Dena, are you home?" Krystal's voice called out.

She got up from the bed and opened the door. The hairdresser looked pale and tired.

"I have to ask you something," she said as she came into the room.

"Sure. Have a seat."

Krystal didn't sit down, however. "I left something in the bathroom and now it's gone."

Dena retrieved the early home pregnancy test kit from her desk. "Is this what you're looking for?"

"Yeah, it is. Thanks," she said, snatching it from her. "You shouldn't take stuff out of the bathroom that doesn't belong to you."

"I didn't. Quinn did."

She gulped. "He knows, too?"

"No one knows anything. Someone left a pregnancy test kit in our bathroom. Other people use that bathroom."

She eyed her steadily. "I don't suppose there's any point in me trying to tell you that a friend of mine came over and took the test, then left?"

"If that's what you say happened, I'll believe you." She held her gaze, her eyes assuring her that she had her trust.

Krystal sighed and sat down on Dena's desk chair. "I wish I could say this belongs to a friend," she said, waving the box in midair. "I never thought I'd be in this situation."

Dena could have pointed out that she didn't think many single women did, but remained silent. Krystal needed her to listen, not comment.

"I know people think that I'm having sex with all the guys I date, but the truth is I've had sex only once in the past six months. Once! And look what happened!'' she cried out in frustration.

"This may be a really dumb question, but did you use birth control?"

"Yes! So let this be a lesson to you." She hung her head in her hands. "Oh, God, I can just hear my mother saying, 'Abstinence is the only one-hundred-percent method of birth control.'"

"Well, it's not the method you used, so I guess there's no point in thinking about it now, is there?" Dena stated practically. "Do you know what you're going to do?"

"No." The answer came quickly and with a plea for help. "I can't get past the shock that I'm pregnant."

"Could it be an error?" Dena asked, wanting to give Krystal hope. "I mean, aren't there situations where you could get a false positive?"

She shook her head. "I haven't been to a doctor, but I went on the Internet to see what the symptoms for early pregnancy are, and I have almost all of them." She groaned. "I'm afraid that, ready or not, I'm going to have a baby."

"What about the father? Have you told him?"

"Oh, good grief, no! I can't...not yet. I want to see my gynecologist first before I even think about telling him. And, of course, I need to get my emotions under control."

"Does anyone else know?"

"Just my friend, Shannon. And you and Quinn. You don't think he'll say anything to Leonie, will he?"

"No, why would he? He has enough on his mind

with the kids. I really don't think he's even given this a second thought.''

"I hope not. It's going to be really hard to have to tell Leonie."

"She'll be her usual sweet, understanding self," Dena stated with confidence.

"I'm not so sure about that," Krystal said pensively. "I'd better get back to my room. My tummy's not feeling right." She got up to leave.

"Krystal, if there's anything I can do to help you, please let me know."

She nodded gratefully. "I will, but I doubt there's anything anyone can do."

CHAPTER FOURTEEN

WHEN DENA HAD STARTED seeing Quinn, she hadn't given much thought as to what it would be like when their relationship ended and they still were neighbors. Partly because in the other places she'd lived, she'd always managed to stay detached from the tenants in her building. The other reason was that she'd been swept off her feet and had ignored logic when it came to being with Quinn.

Living at 14 Valentine Place, however, wasn't the same as living in a large apartment complex where no one knew much about anyone else except for the names and numbers on their mailboxes. Krystal had witnessed Quinn's declaration of love, and Sara had told Leonie that she and Quinn were no longer seeing each other.

That's why Dena started avoiding the kitchen, not wanting to talk to either of them about the breakup. Although she'd run into Krystal in the hallway and she'd been friendly, Dena noticed a coolness about her that hadn't been there previously. She wasn't sure if it was because of her pregnancy or if it was because she thought Dena had been a total idiot when it came to Quinn.

Whatever her reasons, Dena found the possibility of running into Leonie or Krystal an uncomfortable one. Soon she started feeling like a prisoner in her own apartment. It didn't help that July brought warmer weather, and Quinn, Sara and Kevin were outdoors more often. It wasn't unusual for them to be in the yard when she came home from work. That's why Dena often didn't return home until after dark, although even that didn't guarantee they'd be inside. One night she'd found the three of them sitting on the back porch steps watching for fireflies.

When Lisa called to invite her for dinner one evening, she gladly accepted the invitation. She hadn't realized just how trapped she was feeling until she drove up to the house and saw her brother and his kids in the backyard. Ryan was at the grill on the wooden patio, and Bethany sat with Luke in the sandbox. As soon as Dena climbed out of the car, Jeremy came flying out of the house.

"Hey, Aunt Dena, it's not true, is it? Quinn's not really going to quit, is he?" His eyes begged her to tell him it wasn't so.

"What makes you think he is?" she asked, wondering if Quinn had already made the official announcement.

"Because everyone's talking about it. One of the reporters said he heard it from a reliable source."

She didn't want to lie to her nephew, yet she didn't feel she should be talking about Quinn's professional life, either. "That source wasn't me," she told him.

"Then you don't think he is going to retire?"

Ryan closed the lid on the grill with a clang. "Jeremy, you shouldn't even be asking your aunt that question. That's taking advantage of her relationship with Quinn." He turned to Dena and said, "Hi, sis. Welcome to the Bailey bunch."

Because the windows were open, Lisa had heard

Jeremy's questions and stuck her head out the back door. "Jeremy, I could use your help in here."

Dena quickly spoke up. "I'll help you."

"No, you won't. You'll take a chair and visit with your brother. You're a guest. Besides, it's Jeremy's week for kitchen chores," Lisa said, beckoning her son to come.

Dena would have protested, but her brother stood, shaking his head and waving a giant pair of tongs back and forth. "You don't want to upset the chores rotation or I'll never hear the end of it." He grinned, then asked, "So is Quinn going to retire?"

She grimaced. "Can we not talk about him?"

"Oh, it's like that, is it?" His brows lifted knowingly. "Want a margarita? I made a pitcher of them for dinner. I thought they'd go good with this Santa Fe chicken I'm cooking."

"I'll wait. Thanks." She sank down onto one of the padded patio chairs and sighed.

"Rough day at work?"

"They're all rough."

"I thought Lisa said you'd worked on a project that won some advertising award."

"Yeah, I did."

He chuckled. "You don't sound very excited about it."

She shook her head. "I am...or at least I was. I thought my idea was a stroke of genius. Unfortunately, designers don't get the credit for their brilliant moments. The art director does."

"Well, that sucks."

She shrugged. "It's just the way it is."

"Certainly the fact that you did the work will help

when it comes time to getting that promotion you want.''

''At one time I thought it would, but now I'm not so sure. Unfortunately that sound you hear when you step off the elevator and walk into the agency isn't the air-conditioning unit but all the sucking up that's going on.'' She leaned her head back and closed her eyes. ''You know I've never been very good at sucking up.''

''Me, neither. Guess we didn't take after Dad as much as he hoped we would, did we?''

She didn't respond, but simply sat there in the shade, content to relax. She willed her mind to go blank, not to think about work or Quinn. She focused on the smell of the chicken grilling and thought about how nice it was to be a guest at someone's dinner table. She'd been spending far too many nights alone with a sandwich.

Then Ryan said, ''Speaking of Dad...he called today with some interesting news.'' That brought her head up with a jerk. ''He's planning to move to Arizona.''

''Dad in Arizona?'' It seemed almost too preposterous to be true. ''What happened? Did the bank open a branch there?''

Ryan shook his head. ''No, he says he's retiring.''

''I don't believe it.'' She stared at him, then narrowed her eyes. ''He's not sick, is he?''

''No, he's getting married.''

''Married?'' That brought her to her feet. ''No way! He doesn't even date. He told me he doesn't have time for a personal life.''

''I know. He's told me the same thing a hundred times, but there definitely is a fiancée in the picture.''

"Well, someone should warn that poor woman. The marriage will never last. He's never home." She couldn't keep the bitterness from her voice.

"Didn't you hear me? I said he's giving up his job for her."

"Then he must be sick. Maybe he has cancer...or Parkinson's disease or something. There's got to be another reason. You know Dad. He would never just quit his job."

"It could be that he finally figured out that it's not the most important thing in his life," Ryan suggested. "Maybe he's lonely."

She lifted one brow. "Yeah, right."

He didn't respond to her sarcasm, but simply said, "You should call him."

She nodded. "Yeah, I will."

"I mean it, Dena. I know the two of you haven't been getting along very well lately, but maybe this is a good time for you to go visit him."

"I'll call, but I'm not going to Iowa. I don't have the time," she told him.

He eyed her critically. "You're a lot more like him than you want to admit."

"Maybe that's why we don't get along," she said with a weak smile.

He shook his head. "That is what I don't understand. You were always the apple of his eye," he said wistfully. "He loved to brag about your good grades in school and all your achievements. When you landed that marketing job straight out of college he practically burst with pride."

"Yes, and then when I left marketing to do graphic design he nearly exploded with anger," she reminded him.

"Is that why you're not close to him anymore?"

"Ryan, I was never close to him. He may have shown up at the awards programs at school and talked about my accomplishments with all of his friends at the bank, but he never spent any time with me. You probably didn't realize that because you left as soon as you graduated from high school and moved here."

"Things were a bit strained between me and Dad for a while. I didn't live up to his expectations of me," he admitted.

"Well, join the club," she stated soberly. "I'm done trying to please him."

"Are you?"

"Yes."

He shot her a dubious look, which only annoyed her. What did he think? That she still needed her father's approval? Certainly her behavior the past few years had proven she didn't.

"How's that chicken coming?" Lisa called out through the window.

Ryan lifted the grill cover. "Give me about ten more minutes," he called back to her, using the giant tongs to turn the pieces. To Dena he said, "Dad's a good guy."

She folded her arms across her chest. "And when did you develop such fond feelings for him? If I recall, you moved here to get away from him."

He used the tongs to point at Bethany and Luke, who played in the sandbox. "They're the reason. Becoming a parent helped me to understand him. Someday you'll see what I'm talking about."

"When I become a parent, you mean."

He nodded. "It's amazing how it can put your re-

lationship with your own parents into perspective.
You'll see.''

"If I ever have children," she added.

"You will. Just because Quinn isn't the right guy
for you, doesn't mean you won't meet someone who
is." He gave her a reassuring pat on the arm.

Dena wondered what he'd say if she told him that
the reason Quinn wasn't the right guy was because
he already had children. What would his opinion be
of her if she said she wasn't ready to be a mother,
that she wasn't even ready to think of making a commitment to another person?

Would he understand or would he think that she
was like their mother—self-centered and cold. It was
a risk she couldn't take. She couldn't bear for Ryan
to look at her as if she were defective because she
wasn't good enough to be a mother.

So she didn't tell him the real reason she and Quinn
had gone their separate ways. Neither Lisa nor Ryan
asked about him again that evening. They knew she
didn't want to talk about her feelings for Quinn.

She was a private person. She always had been and
she didn't think it was ever going to change, which
only made her wonder if she would ever have what
Lisa and Ryan had together. They had a family, they
had each other, and they were happy.

"Yes, but you have your work," she told herself
as she drove home that night. And as she climbed
into bed, the last thing she saw was Quinn's bobblehead doll staring at her. Yes, she had her work.

THE FOLLOWING EVENING when Dena arrived home
from work she saw the Apartment For Rent sign up
on the front lawn. Someone was moving. The ques-

tion was, who? She had a sinking feeling in her stomach that she already knew the answer.

As she walked around to the side entrance she saw her landlady on her knees next to the flower garden. "Leonie, why is there a For Rent sign on the front lawn?" she asked after they'd exchanged greetings.

Her landlady pulled a clump of weeds from the soil and tossed them onto the small pile at her side. "Quinn bought a house over in Highland Park. He's moving out at the end of the week."

"So soon?" The words were out before she could stop them.

"He was lucky. The house was vacant and he can move right in."

"I see," Dena said absently, feeling as though someone had just taken the wind out of her sails, which was ridiculous. For weeks she'd been tiptoeing around the house doing everything she could to avoid the man, and now that she was no longer going to have to worry about bumping into him in the hallway, she felt a bit lost.

"It's a lovely place," Leonie told her. "Lots of room for the kids to play, a park nearby, and the school bus stops right around the corner. Perfect for a man with a family." She sat back on her heels and wiped her brow. "I hate to see Quinn go, but it's time he moved on."

Dena wondered if the words were meant for her, as well. "Moving on can be difficult."

"Yes, it can." She pulled off her gardening gloves and got to her feet. "Do you like to garden, Dena?"

"I haven't really ever had an opportunity to have one," she answered.

"You should try it sometime. I find it very therapeutic. When I've had a stressful day I come out here. I think of the weeds as my problems. With every jerk of my hand I get rid of one." She pointed to the small pile at her feet. "See what I mean? My worries are all down there."

Dena glanced at the patch of daisies and day lilies stretching alongside the house. "I'd need a bigger garden than that."

"You have a lot of problems, do you?"

Dena sighed. "If only pulling a few weeds could get rid of them."

"Do you want to talk about them? I have my landlady hat on if you need an ear," Leonie offered.

Dena mentally debated whether or not to accept her offer. Maybe it would be a good idea to talk to someone like Leonie, someone who truly did understand romance. On the other hand, she knew that Leonie treated Quinn like a son. Could she be objective when it came to their relationship?

When she didn't answer right away, Leonie asked, "Or maybe you would rather I wear my romance coach hat?"

Dena wasn't sure what it was, but something about the way Leonie looked at her had her blurting out, "I'm in love with Quinn."

Leonie smiled in understanding. "I figured as much. So what's the problem?"

"It's complicated."

"Love usually is."

Again Dena had the urge to confide in her, but found it extremely difficult to admit to her landlady what she didn't want anyone else to know. "Sara's probably told you what happened."

"Actually, she hasn't."

"What about Quinn?"

She shook her head. "He hasn't, either. Do you want to tell me?"

She dropped down onto the picnic table bench. "I don't know where to begin."

Leonie sat down beside her. "Well, one thing I know is that Quinn loves you."

"He told you that?"

"Not with words, no, but every time he says your name there's a light in his eye I've never seen before." She placed a hand on her arm. "That isn't why you broke up, is it? Because you thought he didn't love you?"

She shook her head. "No, I know he loves me."

"And you love him, so what's the problem?"

Dena looked away, out at the children playing ball across the street. "It was just the wrong time for us."

"Because of Sara and Kevin?"

There was no censure in Leonie's eyes, simply compassion.

"They're only part of the problem. I'm not the kind of woman Quinn needs right now."

"He seems to think you are," she said gently.

"Did he tell you that?"

"He didn't need to. I told you. It's in his voice when he says your name, it's in his eyes when he sees you."

"So why can't I believe it?"

"Because you could be right about the timing. Maybe you're not ready for a man like Quinn."

Dena could have told her she was right but chose to remain silent.

"Are you a cautious person by nature, Dena?"

She shrugged. "I'm not reckless."

"Do you dip one toe in the water before going swimming to see how cold it is, or do you just dive right in?"

"I dip a toe. Why?"

"I'm just curious. That's all." She brushed the flecks of grass from her knees and stood. "Come with me into my office. I want to give you something."

Dena did as she requested, following her landlady into the house, down the hallway to her office. Once there, Leonie went straight to her desk and sat down. She pulled a notepad from her drawer and wrote some numbers on it. Then she folded it in half and gave it to Dena.

"This is Quinn's new address. Hang on to it…just in case the timing changes," she said, her eyes full of encouragement.

Dena slipped the paper into her pocket, not wanting to look interested in what was written on it. She'd already revealed much more of herself than she'd intended. But as soon as she was on the stairs going up to the second floor, she pulled it out.

It wasn't the house number and street, however, that held her attention. It was the quote imprinted at the bottom of the notepaper. It was by the philosopher Bertrand Russell. "Of all forms of caution, caution in love is perhaps the most fatal to true happiness."

FOR FOUR DAYS Dena wondered if she'd see Quinn before he moved. By Friday night she had resigned herself to the fact that he wasn't going to come see her before he left. She had the feeling that he had been avoiding her, just as she'd been avoiding him.

From Krystal she'd learned that Quinn had hired movers who would be at 14 Valentine Place early

Saturday morning. Dena didn't want to be around to witness his departure and arranged to work on Saturday.

As luck would have it, she saw the moving van pull away from the curb just as she stepped off the bus on her way home. She used the side entrance and went straight to her apartment. She didn't miss, however, that the silver SUV still sat parked near Leonie's garage.

She wondered if he'd stop and say goodbye to her. There was no reason he should, not after the way she'd treated him. That didn't stop her heart from racing when there was a knock on her door.

She opened it to find Sara standing in the hall. "Sara, hi. I thought maybe you'd already gone."

"I came by earlier but you weren't here," the young girl said. "I wanted to say goodbye and to tell you that I'm really glad you stopped me from getting on the bus that night I wanted to run away to South Carolina."

Dena stared at her, thinking how much she looked like Quinn. They had the same blue eyes, the same dark hair. She hoped that in time they developed the kind of father-daughter relationship they both deserved.

"Thank you for saying that. I know how hard these past few months have been for you." She stepped aside and motioned toward the apartment. "Do you have time to come in for a soda?"

She nodded. "I think it'll be okay, because Quinn's talking to Leonie."

At the mention of Quinn's name, Dena felt a pain in the area of her heart. "I've got root beer and lem-

onade and bottled water,'' she told Sara as she held
open the door on her tiny refrigerator.

''I'll take root beer, please.''

Dena handed her a can and gestured for her to sit
on the love seat. ''I hear your new house is pretty
cool.''

She popped the top of the can and took a sip. ''I
get my own room. Quinn says I can change the color
if I want. It's an ugly blue right now.''

''And Kevin likes the house, too?''

She nodded. ''He's got his own room, too. Plus
there's two extra bedrooms, so if I want my friends
to come stay, they can.'' She took another sip of her
root beer. ''I still miss my old house, though.''

''I'm sure you do. You've had to deal with a lot
of changes these past few months, Sara. When you
thanked me for talking you out of leaving for South
Carolina…does that mean you're starting to like living here in Minnesota?''

''I like summer and I'm sorta getting used to having Quinn be my father.''

''Sorta?'' she gently prodded.

''It's hard to think of anyone but Doug Grant being
my dad,'' she said with a touch of both sadness and
innocence that tugged at Dena's heart.

Dena dropped down beside her on the love seat.
''It's going to take time, Sara, to get used to the idea
of having another father in your life. No matter what
anyone else says, Doug will always be your father,
too. He loved you and you loved him, which is why
it was so painful for you to lose him.''

''Quinn told me that he and my dad were best
friends in college and that they looked out for one
another. He said that even if nobody had ever found

my mom's letters, he would have adopted me and Kevin.''

Dena didn't doubt that it was true. She'd seen how attached he'd become to the children before the news of Sara's parentage had surfaced. ''He's a nice man, Sara. You're lucky to have him. I know it was a shock finding out the way you did that he was your father, but you have to remember that it was the same kind of shock for him. He had no idea that he had a daughter.''

''It's all my mom's fault,'' she said quietly. ''She told a lie, and I don't understand why. Didn't she think I had a right to know the truth?''

Dena didn't know what to say to comfort her. ''You're angry at her, aren't you?''

She nodded miserably. ''I don't want to be. Quinn says that everyone makes mistakes and that my mom did what she thought was best for me.''

Dena knew it couldn't be easy for Quinn himself to come to terms with Patsy's deception, yet he was doing his best to see that Sara didn't blame her. She felt a surge of admiration for him.

''Quinn says we both need to remember the good things about her. He's going to help me try to get over being mad at her because he doesn't want me to grow up and still be angry at my mom when I'm old. Anger isn't good for a person. It keeps you from being happy.''

Emotion blocked Dena's throat, and she had to swallow before she could speak. ''Quinn's a very smart man.''

Sara took another sip of her root beer, then said, ''Well, one good thing about all of this is that I now have a grandma and grandpa.''

"You've met them?"

"They're really nice. I never knew my other grand-parents because they died when I was a baby," she explained. She looked at her watch. "I'd better go. I promised Quinn I'd only stay fifteen minutes."

And those fifteen minutes were up and she would soon be walking out of Dena's life for good. Just as Quinn would be. She could barely stand to think about it.

Sara set the root beer can down on the coffee table as she stood. She reached in her pocket and pulled out a slip of paper. "I wrote our address down in case you want to come visit us. Quinn said you could even though you and he—" she pulled a face "—well, you know."

Dena nodded. "I'd like that," she told the girl, knowing perfectly well that the way things were between her and Quinn, it would be unlikely she'd stop by the house.

"So I guess I'll say goodbye then," Sara said as she stood next to the door.

Dena felt tears welling in her eyes. She gave Sara a hug, trying to keep her voice level as she said, "I'm going to miss seeing you around here."

"I'll miss you, too," she said in return. "It's too bad you and Quinn can't be together."

Dena bit down on her lip and simply nodded. When she'd swallowed back the emotion, she asked, "Do you know why we aren't?"

"He said that right now it's important that we learn how to be a family—just the three of us." She looked up at her with such uncertainty in her eyes that Dena's heart ached.

"And he's right. You are a family—a brand-new

family, and it'll be good for you to get to know each other without anyone else around.''

She didn't look convinced. Dena suspected that Sara was as confused as she was. "I have to go."

Dena opened the door for her and watched her walk away, feeling as if she took a piece of her heart. She wanted to go with her downstairs to the kitchen, to see Quinn one last time, but she didn't. She simply watched from her window as the SUV moved away from the curb.

As the sun set and the room grew dim, she lay on the bed, staring at the bobblehead doll. Quinn was gone from her life. So was Sara. As she thought about her conversation with Sara, she remembered her saying that she didn't want to grow up and still be angry at her mother.

Which meant she didn't want to grow up and be like Dena. She pulled open the drawer on her night-stand and dug beneath the small stack of papers until she found the photo she kept hidden there. It was a picture of her mother holding her when she was a baby. Like every mother, she had love in her eyes as she gazed at her daughter.

For what seemed like the millionth time, Dena wondered where that love had gone. How could she have turned her back on her children? It didn't make any sense, but then she realized that what Sara's mother had done hadn't made any sense, either. Both women had deceived their daughters. Dena's mother had abandoned her when she had needed her most. Sara's mother had kept her biological father from her. Dena felt a rush of anger toward both women.

Then she heard Sara's words. "Anger isn't good

for a person. It keeps you from being happy.'' Dena knew they were really Quinn's words.

She began to cry, thinking of what might have been if she hadn't let her own bitterness toward her mother keep her from being happy. Because she knew now it was the anger she still carried for her mother that had prevented her from thinking of a future with Quinn. Why hadn't she realized that sooner? Now it was too late. He was gone from her life. He'd told Sara it was better for the three of them if she wasn't in their lives.

Unable to stop herself, she went up to the third floor, needing to be in a place where he'd been. To her relief, the door wasn't locked. She stepped inside, stunned by its emptiness. Gone was the baseball mitt chair, the leather sofa and the entertainment center. She pushed opened the bedroom door and felt a pain in her chest. The bed where they'd shared their passions might not have ever been there.

She'd hoped that his scent would have lingered in the air, but the only smell was that of disinfectant and soap. As she passed the closet she saw hangers but no clothes. Unable to bear the emptiness, she was about to leave when she noticed something in the back. She slid the door all the way open and discovered his summer jacket.

She reached for the sleeve and brought it to her face, hoping that it would have a trace of his scent on it. She wasn't disappointed. It smelled like the campground where they'd taken the kids on the fishing opener weekend.

She closed her eyes and inhaled its freshness. It tickled her nostrils and tormented her heart. Fresh tears fell as she pulled the jacket from the hanger and slid her arms into the sleeves, relishing the feel of having something that belonged to him around her neck. She waltzed around the empty rooms, remembering what it was like to be with him, and ending up in the bathroom, where she gazed into the mirror so she could see how she looked in his jacket.

"Isn't this how we first met—in a men's washroom?"

She turned and saw him standing in the doorway.

"What are you doing here?" he asked.

"I wanted to see how I look in this," she said, gesturing to the jacket.

"You're crying."

She swiped at the tears on her face with the back of her hands. "I...I didn't get to say goodbye."

She wished he would come and take her in his arms, but he stood in the doorway staring at her. "I'm here now."

She swallowed with difficulty. "Didn't you want to say goodbye to me?"

"No. Saying goodbye is something I never want to say to you, Dena. You ought to know that." His voice was tender and sweet, like it had always been after they'd made love.

"Is that why you didn't come to see me? You never even told me you were moving...you didn't call, you didn't stop in."

He stood with his hands in his pockets. "And if I had, what would you have told me? That you wanted more space, that you weren't ready for the kind of commitment I wanted?"

She looked down at the floor, knowing he was right. She sniffled, then said, "I don't know. All I know now is that I'm miserable, and now it's too late.''

''Too late for what, Dena?''

''For us.'' She couldn't stop the rush of tears. ''Sara told me about the three of you being a family and that it's better if I'm not in the picture.''

Then he moved closer to her. ''I only said that to try to cheer her up because she was hoping you were going to be in the picture. But me? I never thought that living without you would make anything better.''

She looked at him through her tear-filled eyes and saw the same sincerity that had attracted her to him in the first place. He was the man she loved, the man she'd caught and released. How could she have been so dumb?

''Dena, you're the one who didn't want to make plans for the future.'' He tugged on his ear. ''I have to admit, it was a first for me. I never expected to fall in love with a woman who wanted nothing but sex from me.''

''That's not true. I wanted more, Quinn. It was just that I was afraid.''

He lifted her chin with his finger. ''Afraid of what? A future with me?''

''Yes,'' she answered honestly. ''I didn't understand why I could never get past my ninety-day mark with men. I thought it was because I hadn't met the right guy, but then I met you and the same thing happened.''

''You said your career was more important than anything else in your life,'' he reminded her. ''I understand those feelings, because at one time they were true for me, too.''

''And it's what I wanted to believe. When I was

growing up, to work hard was the only way to get my father's attention, but even work was a convenient excuse to avoid dealing with the real issue.''

"And what is the real issue, Dena?"

"My fear of being hurt again. My mother left when I was thirteen. She didn't die like Sara's, she simply chose not to be a part of my life.''

"I know. Sara told me."

"And you didn't tell me you knew?"

"You're such a private person, Dena. I wanted you to talk to me, to share your hurts and disappointments, but you always pulled back whenever I tried to get too close to the real you.''

She knew she had. It had been a self-defense mechanism. "Sara told me what you said to her...about her letting go of her anger toward her mother.''

"It's something we have to work on. Both of us do.''

"I'd like to work on it with you, if you'd let me.''

He gave her his answer by taking her in his arms and kissing her. "Are you sure about this?" he asked when their lips finally came apart.

"Yes. I know it's going to be a challenge.''

"Me or the kids?" he asked with his crooked grin.

"Both, but you ought to know that if there's one thing I love, it's a challenge.''

And she'd spend the rest of her life proving it to him.

Corruption, power and commitment...

TAKING THE HEAT

brenda novak

A gritty story in which single mom and prison guard Gabrielle Hadley becomes involved with prison inmate Randall Tucker. When Randall escapes, she follows him— and soon the guard becomes the prisoner's captive... and more.

"Talented, versatile Brenda Novak dishes up a new treat with every page!"

—*USA TODAY* bestselling author Merline Lovelace

Available wherever books are sold in February 2003.

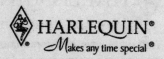

HARLEQUIN®

Makes any time special®

Visit us at www.eHarlequin.com

PHTTH

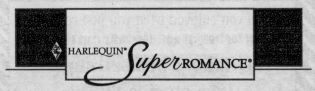

HARLEQUIN® *Super* ROMANCE®

Koomera Crossing

**Welcome to Koomera Crossing,
a town hidden deep in the Australian Outback.
Let renowned romance novelist Margaret Way take
you there. Let her introduce you to the people of
Koomera Crossing. Let her tell you their secrets....**

In **Sarah's Baby** meet Dr. Sarah Dempsey and
Kyall McQueen. And then there's the town's
matriarch, Ruth McQueen, who played a role
in Sarah's disappearance from her grandson
Kyall's life—and who now dreads Sarah's
return to Koomera Crossing.

Sarah's Baby is available in February
wherever Harlequin books are sold.
And watch for the next Koomera Crossing story,
coming from Harlequin Romance in October.

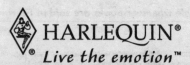

HARLEQUIN®
Live the emotion™

Visit us at www.eHarlequin.com

HARLEQUIN SUPERROMANCE®

HSRSBK

If you enjoyed what you just read,
then we've got an offer you can't resist!

Take 2 bestselling
love stories FREE!

Plus get a FREE surprise gift!

Clip this page and mail it to Harlequin Reader Service®

IN U.S.A.	IN CANADA
3010 Walden Ave.	P.O. Box 609
P.O. Box 1867	Fort Erie, Ontario
Buffalo, N.Y. 14240-1867	L2A 5X3

YES! Please send me 2 free Harlequin Superromance® novels and my free surprise gift. After receiving them, if I don't wish to receive anymore, I can return the shipping statement marked cancel. If I don't cancel, I will receive 6 brand-new novels every month, before they're available in stores. In the U.S.A., bill me at the bargain price of $4.47 plus 25¢ shipping and handling per book and applicable sales tax, if any*. In Canada, bill me at the bargain price of $4.99 plus 25¢ shipping and handling per book and applicable taxes**. That's the complete price, and a savings of at least 10% off the cover prices—what a great deal! I understand that accepting the 2 free books and gift places me under no obligation ever to buy any books. I can always return a shipment and cancel at any time. Even if I never buy another book from Harlequin, the 2 free books and gift are mine to keep forever.

135 HDN DNT3
336 HDN DNT4

Name	(PLEASE PRINT)	
Address	Apt.#	
City	State/Prov.	Zip/Postal Code

* Terms and prices subject to change without notice. Sales tax applicable in N.Y.
** Canadian residents will be charged applicable provincial taxes and GST.
   All orders subject to approval. Offer limited to one per household and not valid to
   current Harlequin Superromance® subscribers.
   ® is a registered trademark of Harlequin Enterprises Limited.

SUP02   ©1998 Harlequin Enterprises Limited

eHARLEQUIN.com

For great romance books at great prices,
shop www.eHarlequin.com today!

GREAT BOOKS:
- **Extensive selection** of today's hottest
  books, including **current** releases,
  backlist titles and new **upcoming** books.
- **Favorite authors:** Nora Roberts,
  Debbie Macomber and more!

GREAT DEALS:
- **Save every day:** enjoy great savings
  and special online promotions.
- *Exclusive* **online offers:** FREE books,
  bargain outlet savings, special deals.

EASY SHOPPING:
- Easy, secure, **24-hour shopping** from the
  comfort of your own home.
- **Excerpts, reader recommendations**
  and our **Romance Legend** will help
  you choose!
- **Convenient shipping and
  payment methods.**

Shop online
at www.eHarlequin.com today!

INTBB2

HARLEQUIN® *Romance®*

**is thrilled to present
a brand-new miniseries
that dares to be different...**

TANGO

*FRESH AND FLIRTY...
IT TAKES TWO TO TANGO*

Exuberant, exciting...emotionally exhilarating!

These cutting-edge, highly contemporary stories
capture how women in the 21st century *really*
feel about meeting Mr. Right!

Don't miss:

February:
CITY GIRL IN TRAINING
by RITA® Award-winning
author Liz Fielding (#3735)

April:
HER MARRIAGE SECRET
by fresh new Australian
talent Darcy Maguire (#3745)

*And watch for more
TANGO books to come!*

HARLEQUIN®
Makes any time special®

Visit us at www.eHarlequin.com   HRTANFEB03

The world's bestselling romance series.

HARLEQUIN®
Presents~

Seduction and Passion Guaranteed!

Secret Passions

A spellbinding series by
Miranda Lee

Desire changes everything!

Women are always throwing themselves at Justin McCarthy—
picturing themselves spending his millions and cuddling up to
his perfect physique! So Rachel is Justin's idea of the perfect P.A.—
plain, prim and without a predatory bone in her body. Until a
makeover unleashes her beauty and unexpected emotion....

AT HER BOSS'S BIDDING
Harlequin Presents, #2301
On-sale February 2003

Pick up a Harlequin Presents® novel and you will enter
a world of spine-tingling passion and provocative,
tantalizing romance!

Available wherever Harlequin books are sold.

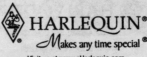

HARLEQUIN®
Makes any time special ®

Visit us at www.eHarlequin.com

HPSPM

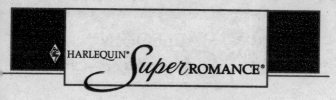

HARLEQUIN *Super*ROMANCE®

*presents a compelling family drama—
an exciting new trilogy
by popular author Debra Salonen*

THOSE SULLIVAN SISTERS

**Jenny, Andrea and Kristin Sullivan are much more
than sisters—*they're triplets!* Growing up as one of
a threesome meant life was never lonely...or dull.**

**Now they're adults—with separate lives, loves,
dreams and secrets. But underneath everything that
keeps them apart is the bond that holds them together.**

MY HUSBAND, MY BABIES
(Jenny's story)
available December 2002

WITHOUT A PAST
(Andi's story)
available January 2003

THE COMEBACK GIRL
(Kristin's story)
available February 2003

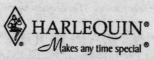

HARLEQUIN®

Makes any time special ®

Visit us at www.eHarlequin.com

HSRTSS

HARLEQUIN® *Super*ROMANCE®

Two brothers—
and the women they love.

Nate Hawkins. He returns to Colorado to attend his father's unexpected second wedding—and runs into Laurel Pierce. A woman he fell in love with ten years before. A woman who was his best friend's wife. A woman who's now pregnant with another man's child....

***Another Man's Wife,*
coming in February 2003**

Rick Hawkins. He comes home for the same reason his brother did. Then he meets Audra Jerrett, a woman he didn't expect to like. After all, she's the first cousin of his father's new wife. But she's just suffered a devastating trauma—the kind of trauma Rick understands.

***Home to Copper Mountain,*
coming in May 2003**

Two of Rebecca Winters's trademark larger-than-life heroes.
Two of her passionate and emotional romances.
Enjoy them both!

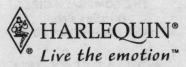

HARLEQUIN®
Live the emotion™

Visit us at www.eHarlequin.com

HARLEQUIN SUPERROMANCE®

HSRAMW